THE ROGUE'S FATE

THE RAVEN CHRONICLES: BOOK 1

MISSY DE GRAFF

STONE PHOENIX PRESS

Edited by Zero Alchemy
Cover design by Paradise Cover Design

Second Edition
ISBN 978-1-7370270-2-7
ASIN B0BT4VDKSH

May the brightness of a full moon always shine through your darkest hour...

CHAPTER 1

LUCINDA

LEANING against a large boulder nestled between two tall oak trees, I wipe my clammy palms on my jeans and watch the sunrise through the trees—it could be my last.

A rogue wolf entering pack territory is asking for a death sentence. Packs don't like us, and we're not supposed to like them. We separate ourselves from packs because we need to be free and independent.

At least, that's what I keep telling myself.

A chill races up my back as I stand in the tree line of the State Forest. A cool breeze blows, and dead leaves rustle at my feet. I take a deep breath to slow my rapid heartbeat, and fresh pine swirls around me.

The members of this pack will pick up the scent of an intruder soon. Until then, I calm my racing mind and wait.

I want to live, but the man tracking me has other plans. Hopefully, the Alpha of this territory will give me a chance to explain my situation.

All I need to do is find Mia; I hope she's still here. She'll help me figure out what to do. I only have a couple of days to find her, because that's all I can afford. Anything longer than that, and it wouldn't be fair to this pack.

My presence could cost them their lives, and I've seen enough bloodshed for one lifetime.

The musk of someone approaching tickles my nose, and I flinch. With any luck, the patrol member is in human form and not wolf form. The other half of my soul—my wolf—is already on edge. Keeping her in check is exhausting. A human is usually less threatening.

Usually being the operative word there. Because there was one man...the man I once loved: Felix. He was terrifying in any form, man *or* wolf. I fell for him before he revealed his true nature, but now I would rather die than be bound to him for eternity. Because there isn't anything in this world worth living for if my fate lies with that monster.

The patrol wolf approaches from below my position. He snarls in my direction and paces back and forth, twitching his rusty-brown tail with enough force to kick up a breeze.

Shit. Today's not my day.

I force my inner wolf to submit to the patrol's assumed dominance and kneel on the pine needles that litter the hard ground. "Please, this is a matter of life and death. May I cross through your territory?"

After a moment, a man steps out from the shadows of a walnut tree and strokes the wolf's back. He stares at me. "What's your name?"

My shoulders fall. *What name do I give him? I have so many.*

"Raven," I whisper. It's not a total lie. Raven is my family name. Lucinda is my given name, but I only share that with people I trust, and trust is earned.

The hairs on my forearms stand tall as the high-pitched croak of a raven echoes through the woods. I glance over my shoulder. The narrow two-lane road below me is clear, but my heart skips a beat when the black wings of a bat soar in and out of the tree line high in the sky.

"Expecting someone?" the man asks.

"No."

"Then why do you keep looking over your shoulder?"

I bite my lip. "Please, sir, I need to cross through your territory."

"Why don't you go around?"

"That would take too much time."

"We don't take in strays, especially not ones bringing trouble."

"I can't go back that way."

Not unless I want to find myself in chains and facing a future of nothing but doom.

He crosses his arms across his broad chest.

"May I speak with your Alpha?" I ask.

His jaw muscles clench, and his nostrils flare. The wolf circles around me and growls.

Finally, the man says, "Follow me, Miss Raven."

Glancing over my shoulder one last time, that damn bat still circles overhead. It's the same bat that's been following me around for years, I recognize him by the small white V marking on his chest.

After a moment of hesitation, I step forward to follow the man, hopefully not to my death.

I wish my predicament hadn't come to this. I hate asking for help. My late father would be ashamed to know I've disgraced our family name by coming to this pack. And I wish I were here under different circumstances: as a diplomat, a friend, or anything other than a shameful rogue.

When I step from the protection of the forest, I draw in a long breath to relax my racing nerves.

We walk, single file, along the white line of the two-lane road. My wolf within me stays alert, searching for signs of danger and an escape route in case I need it. The rusty-brown wolf keeps pace alongside us but is careful to stay in the protection of the forest.

Silence lingers between us for several miles until we reach the outskirts of a small, quaint town. This must be Floyd. My father always complained the Blood Moone pack claimed to live rurally, but compared to us, they don't.

Though, I'd say the Dark Raven pack was more primitive than rural.

I blink back tears at the thought of my old pack. *I can't show weakness here.*

My escort leads me through the crowded streets, and people step out of their shops to stare. A group of men loiter in front of the country store and growl as I near. The man leading me nods to the men as we pass. The light breeze carries whispers from another group standing idle on the street corner.

"Filthy rogue—"

"Disgusting piece of scum."

"Why is she still alive?"

I dig my nails into the soft flesh of my palm, but I restrain my wolf and keep walking. As we weave through the humans and dodge the wolves, my nose twitches when I catch a scent that is all too familiar.

Mia. My heart bursts with renewed hope, and I smile.

But then another scent tickles my senses. The familiar scent stirs memories of my childhood best friend, Dylan Sparrow. The memories, both sweet and painful, still haunt me to this day.

Damn him. Why is he here? He makes everything complicated.

Thinking of our unique relationship and troubled past, a smile plays at the edges of my lips, and I blink back tears. My wolf and human side are in disagreement.

My wolf is drawn to him, but my human heart can't forgive his shortcomings.

Relief washes over my soul knowing he's still alive, and anger steams from the depths of my soul that I may have to see him again. I grab my head to combat a dizzy spell that threatens to knock me off balance.

I grit my teeth and hope I don't cross paths with him today. *That won't end well for anyone.*

I glance to the sky.

Lunchtime. As if on cue, my stomach churns. *I wish I ate breakfast—my wolf gets uneasy on an empty stomach.*

I startle at movement in the tree line near us. Peering into the thick woods, several more wolves have joined the rusty-brown wolf from earlier.

Great, an entourage. Or worse: a killing party.

As we near what I assume to be the Pack House, an intoxicating aroma swirls in my nostrils, one composed of scents familiar and foreign. Both are woodsy and masculine, but Dylan's scent is sweeter. Notes of cumin and freshly cut grass drift through the air, stirring up the most painful memories.

But the new scent fills my nose with its spicy undertones and something else. I suspect bergamot. Inhaling again, the woodsy, citrusy notes make my stomach twist.

I climb the steps of the porch and clench my fists.

Please don't let Dylan be inside.

CHAPTER 2

CAIDEN

"Alpha," a distant whisper echoes in my mind.

I close my eyes and dip my head under the warm water of the shower as I search through the pack mindlink, looking for the one reaching out to me. When I find the individual, I tune in the thread and strengthen the connection.

The patrol wolf's deep voice rumbles more clearly now. "I found a female rogue trespassing during my patrol this morning."

Over the past few months, we've been experiencing an increase in rogue wolves attacking our pack members. But lately, to make matters worse, they've escalated to an all-time high, and now the innocent humans in my territory are targets.

Unacceptable.

"Where?" I growl.

"Concealed in the forest, waiting."

"For what?"

"She asked to speak with you. She wants to cross through the territory."

"Why?"

"She won't say. Only that it's a matter of life and death."

"Possibly hers, if I don't like what she has to say." I run my fingers through my wet hair as I decide what to do. "You know what? Fuck it. I'll send someone to escort her here. This better be as important as she says."

I hurry to finish my shower. One of the downsides of the mindlink when you're an Alpha is you never get privacy unless you close the link. Of course, closing the mindlink comes with criticism from everyone.

I send Dylan, my Beta and second-in-command, a message through the mindlink. "Sammy is escorting a rogue here. Be on guard for anything unusual."

"Do you want me to handle it?" he asks.

"If by handle, you mean kill, then no."

"We shouldn't be taking risks—"

"I'll decide what we should and shouldn't do," I snap. And then even my tone. "I will hear her out first. *Then* you can kill her."

———

I rummage through my drawers, tossing out shirts that are either torn or dirty.

The uncontrollable rage has to stop.

A low growl vibrates my throat as I throw another ripped T-shirt across the room.

I need better control of the damnation that is my wolf raging inside me.

My pulse quickens, and I fight against my wolf for control. After grabbing a pair of jeans, I head downstairs in search of a clean shirt and ice to calm the fury of the cursed beast begging to be released.

A whiff of a stale stench lingers in the air. *Sabrina.* An involuntary snarl escapes my lips as I jump over the banister and head down the hall to my office, unseen. Exaggerated laughter spreads through the house, and my nostrils flare.

I've known Sabrina since we were kids, and she's continuously failed to respect my role as Alpha, always forcing me to take her down a notch. While that's enough to keep the respect of everyone else in the pack, we both know that she's gotten under my skin.

Something an Alpha should never let happen.

She's a manipulative and cunning creature, hiding within a beautiful body, and as narcissistic as they come.

Calm down. I can't meet the rogue like this, or else it won't matter what she says.

I glance at the clock. No time for a cool down run. Instead, I focus on the old leather speed bag hanging in the corner of my office. It's been years since I used it, and right now, a sparring session will be perfect.

I punch the bag. The quick movement of the jab feels good.

Sabrina is all about power. She wants to be the Alpha's mate, Luna of the pack.

Jab, jab.

Call me traditional or old school, but I still believe in the stories of Fated Mates.

These days, many of our kind don't find their Fated Mate, so they accept the bond with another. But the bond with your Fated Mate is rumored to be surreal—something you shouldn't ignore or take for granted. If that bond breaks, your entire existence shatters. One cannot live without the other—or so the Pack Elders say.

From personal experience, I disagree on a certain level. However, the concept of Fated Mates sounds nice enough that I'm not about to give that up for scum like Sabrina.

Jab, jab.

I witnessed firsthand what happens when a bond breaks; sometimes death is the easier choice. Still better than her, though.

Jab, jab.

Now Sabrina's dug her sharp claws into my Beta, Dylan. I should be thankful she has her sights off me, but I have a sick feeling she's just using him. The question is, for what?

An intoxicating smell of mint and honey drifts in the air, and a surge of power ripples through the room. Stepping outside my office, Dylan's voice echoes down the hallway as I walk.

"Hey Lux," he says to our guest, the rogue.

Her body turns rigid, and her pupils dilate and grow black before she closes them. Her chest rises with the intake of a deep breath. It seems this rogue and Dylan are prior acquaintances. And it's obvious she wasn't expecting to find him here.

Upon opening her eyes, her nose twitches, and a slight crease forms on her forehead.

I lean against the doorway. Our eyes meet for a second before she looks away. Something about her triggers a familiarity deep inside my soul.

Sammy points to the girl. "Alpha Caiden, this is the rogue who asked to speak with you."

She turns her head in my direction, but her gaze stays transfixed on Dylan and Sabrina entangled in each other's arms.

I send a small push of power surging through the room. *I want her attention.*

Her shoulders tremble, and I smirk when she diverts her gaze to the ground.

The sound of soft moans and lip-smacking causes me to grunt. Dylan and Sabrina are putting on a show for the unwanted guest. Sabrina's dark hair slips over her shoulder as she nibbles a path from Dylan's ear to his neck. My lips turn up into a silent snarl.

I send Sabrina and Dylan a warning through the mindlink. "Enough!"

Sabrina slides off Dylan's lap and curls up next to him, cutting her gaze toward our visitor.

The rogue's jaw clenches. "I'll be going now. I'm done here."

Dylan grins. "Oh, come on, Lux. You just got here."

Her shoulders relax as my scent floods the room. She continues her deep breathing but continues to glare at Dylan. It's only a matter of time before she loses control.

Laughing, Dylan pulls Sabrina back on his lap. "You may have learned to control your temper, but you're not fooling anyone. I can smell...*her*. Your wolf wants out. You can't lock her up forever."

"Why would anyone want to?" Sabrina giggles, then crushes her lips against his. A moan escapes the couple, and a low growl erupts from the rogue.

The rogue's hands clench open and close.

An old trick to staying in control.

Dylan moans as Sabrina caresses his body. "Come on, Lux. Learn to live a little. There's plenty of me to go around."

Sabrina swats at him when he says this.

At the same time, I send another command through the mindlink. "I said, *enough!*"

Dylan startles but remains calm, and Sabrina pouts as she adjusts herself on the couch.

In the newfound silence, Sammy speaks through the mindlink. "I don't think the rogue is an assassin or a spy, but I can't figure her out."

Dylan smirks before giving his own mindlink reply.

"She's neither. I can vouch for her. She's a pain in the ass, but means us no harm."

I nod and continue to observe her tense posture.

Her eyes narrow, and she leans forward on the balls of her feet.

My wolf senses power radiating off her slender frame; tendrils reach out for me, and my own power surges forward.

Whoa. Intense.

As she turns to leave, I walk with a long stride across the room to block her path. "Rogues don't wander unescorted in my territory."

I need answers before she leaves.

I roll my shoulders back and relax my clenched fists. She bats her long, dark lashes, and her pleading hazel eyes capture my interest.

"It was a mistake coming here," she whispers and breaks eye contact. "May I pass through your territory?"

My wolf responds to hers, but I'm trying to tame and control the urges. Through the mindlink, I tell my guards to stand down. When they heard a rogue had requested to talk with the Alpha, my men circled the house to watch the perimeter for signs of danger.

"Let's go," I say and reach for her upper arm.

I'm interested in what she has to say, but not until we both calm down.

The mindlink is flooded by comments from pack.

"Just kill her already."

"Kill the rogue and be done with it."

"What are you waiting for?"

And then finally one from Sabrina. "Showing us your soft side, Alpha?"

That one makes my blood boil. This is not about weakness.

Before snapping the mindlink off, I declare for all to hear, "There's been enough bloodshed as it is. I have...*other* plans for this one."

And none of them are as good as she's surely hoping.

CHAPTER 3

LUCINDA

THE ALPHA GRABS my upper arm, but his touch is eerily gentle as he guides me outside and down the porch.

I'm no fool. I know the calm before the storm all too well, and energy buzzes beneath his skin. He's feeling anything but gentle right now.

We walk toward the tree line, and to my surprise, no one follows. I expect wolves to emerge from all directions, ready to attack. It is a standard pack rule—Alphas do not like rogues because we threaten their authority.

But it's just us, which means he ordered them to stand down. Either he doesn't see me as a threat or he's confident enough he can handle me without help.

Judging by the sheer size of him, he's probably not wrong about that, and I find myself wishing the rest of his pack was nearby. At least then there'd be witnesses to whatever he is about to do to me.

"You can run it off," he says as his biceps flex.

Is this when he will kill me? I return an intense stare and lift my chin in defiance. Who does he think I am? A silly little girl foolish enough to ask how high when he says jump?

"With me," he adds. "I'm in need of a good run myself. But since we won't be able to communicate, stay by my side." He gives me a stern glare with his sapphire eyes. "Don't leave my side. Do you understand?"

What other choice do I have? I nod.

"Good, let's go—"

Before he is able to finish his sentence, I begin to shift. My muscles constrict as my fangs tear through my mouth. My arms and legs contort into four muscular legs built for running. My torso and head are last, the vital organs being the most delicate part of the transformation.

Every facet of my body is broken and reconstructed, and my clothes rip from my changing body as I fall onto the forest floor. For the young, old, or weak, it can be a long and painful process. I am none of those things, so my transformation is quick and effortless.

Living alone in the wild for as long as I have, I am constantly looking over my shoulder, worrying if I will live to see the next morning. My rogue lifestyle demands that transforming into my wolf be second nature, so my shift happens within the blink of an eye.

I glance at the Alpha, who has already shimmied out of his jeans. A slight grin forms on his lips before he shifts into a striking white wolf.

Standing in amazement, I admire the creature.

The man is attractive, so I should've known his wolf would be equally breathtaking. And his massive size. I always thought at five feet tall on four legs, I was a decent size, especially for a female. But standing next to him, my solid black wolf is dwarfed in comparison, and I feel like a mere pup.

He motions for me to follow, and the fur on the back of my neck stands erect. My wolf takes control, heightening my senses, searching for signs something is amiss. But as we hike deeper into the forest, all appears quiet, and she eventually relaxes.

It is a peaceful wood, full of oak trees and evergreens. Our pace quickens until we are running at full speed. I stay next to him, careful to follow his lead.

As we run, the sounds of the forest echo behind me, and I take comfort among the chirping birds and scurrying squirrels. And then black wings weave in and out of the canopy overhead, staying parallel with us.

That damn bat! Why won't he leave me alone?

Ignoring the bat, I close my eyes and let the wind ruffle my fur. I revel in the freedom. Running unrestricted through the woods is heaven and was always my favorite pastime as a child.

But as a rogue, I quickly learned an important lesson: running through uncharted territory is dangerous. If you value your life, don't do it. Fortunately, I'm fast and have been able to escape the chance encounters with the lawless wolves who wander unclaimed territories.

At this moment, running with the Alpha through his land, an exhilarating rush of excitement ripples through my body.

After a while, I glance at the Alpha and inwardly snicker. *Let's see just how fast you are, Alpha.*

I surge ahead, succumbing to the need to stretch my muscles, pushing myself to the limit. I've always been fast, so when he strolls up next to me, not even panting, my ears pull back.

Who is this guy?

Looking at him, I expect to see dark and dilated pupils, but instead, his eyes are clear blue. My heart bursts with excitement; he's not mad, he's amused.

We run until the sun is low in the sky. As we enter a clearing, we slow our pace, then stop at a stream. I take a long drink of the cold mountain water, peering up at him.

He's watching me. His eyes narrow, and tiny lines form on his forehead.

Is he still trying to decide if he'll kill me?

There's something familiar about him I can't explain. But I know we've never met. Lowering my head again, I take a slow sip of the refreshing water. *If he wanted to kill me, he would've done it already, right?*

I reach my paws out in front of me and lower my chest, keeping my back still in the air. It feels good to relax and stretch my muscles.

As dusk approaches, he motions with a flick of his head for me to follow. I sit, swatting my tail, and stare off into the distance. I can't go back to the Pack House. Not if Dylan's there.

The Alpha in his wolf form towers over me as he moves to block my path.

I turn and walk in the opposite direction.

This time, he struts up beside me and pounces hard on my back, but it is not playful—he is exercising his Alpha dominance. If I were in his pack, I wouldn't be able to resist. Fortunately for me, I'm not in his pack.

But he's blocking my exit, so I lay on the lush green grass instead, resting my head on my paws. Closing my eyes, I think of my next move.

Do I still want to plead my case, now that I know Dylan is here? No pack is big enough for both Dylan and me. *Sigh. When did life get so complicated?*

A warmth spreads through my body, starting at my back. Stretching around to look, I see the Alpha has laid down, brushing against me. Our eyes meet and he gives a slight nod. I instinctively turn into him and nuzzle under his chin.

What the hell? Why did I do that?

Trying to gain composure and redeem myself, I perform a

few spins before curling up next to him again. I need to keep him close to easily track his movements.

With one last glance in his direction, I stare off into the darkness. He hasn't earned my trust, so it's vital I stay alert all night. But once the bright moon shines overhead, my eyelids get heavy and I struggle to stay awake.

I wake in the morning just before sunrise and cautiously look around. The white wolf that engulfs me, demands my attention. He is beautiful, and I stroke the soft, silky fur that tickles my face.

Hold up. I have hands and a face again. I shifted. And I am naked!

Before I'm able to shift back into my wolf, a pair of sapphire eyes find me.

Normally, nakedness doesn't faze me. My family—the Dark Raven pack—cherished it. But I'm naked with a stranger. A male. An Alpha! My stomach flutters with mixed emotions, and heat rises to my cheeks. I divert my gaze away.

"I'm sorry, this has never happened before," I whisper.

He must sense my embarrassment because he flicks his tail, ensuring I'm covered. I pull it close, wrapping it around me like a blanket.

"Thank you." I flash a weak smile.

He nods and motions with his head to the woods.

"No." My head falls forward in defeat. My long chestnut hair cascades over my shoulders and covers my chest. "I can't go back there."

His muscles tense against my flesh, but his tail doesn't move.

I close my eyes and take a deep, controlled breath to clear my mind. He nuzzles the side of my face, and I look up to meet his deep sapphire eyes, which rest only inches from my face. He nuzzles me again. While I try for a weak smile, I fail miserably.

"Dylan…he's my mate," I whisper.

My body trembles, and I cover my face with my hands as unwanted tears reach the surface. A painful lump in my throat makes it hard to breathe, and I slump over.

The soft fur of the wolf's tail that was covering me disappears, and the Alpha shifts into human form. His strong arms wrap around me, pulling my body into a warm embrace. Placing my head on his chest, he holds me while a waterfall of tears streaks my face.

All too soon, shades of pink and orange paint the sky and morning dew glistens in the sunrise. The Alpha says nothing while I sob into his chest; he just gently strokes my long hair.

Talking about Dylan has never made me react this way, but then again, I have never talked about our shared past. I have never said those words out loud.

Embarrassed by my weakness, I dry my eyes and try to pull myself together. When my shoulders stop trembling and my sobs subside, I look up at him.

My heartbeat quickens and I grab my stomach to stop ease the waves of nausea. His intoxicating scent fills my nose, only this time, it is not a calming effect. A tingling sensation courses through my veins.

"It's okay. I won't hurt you," he says. "You're safe with me."

Yeah right. I nod, though butterflies flutter in my stomach.

"Thank you," I say when I finally find my voice. I sit back on the ground and tuck my legs under me.

"Don't mention it, just part of the job description." He shrugs.

That is the worst pickup line I've ever heard. Raising my eyebrows, I smirk and play with my hair. "What's your name?"

"Caiden. And you are Raven or Lux?" he asks, looking at me with a scrutinizing gaze.

"I go by many names, but Dylan is the only one who's ever called me Lux. You can call me Lucinda if you like."

"Lucinda, when did you two meet?" he asks in a gentle tone, testing my emotional stability, I'm sure. The way my name rolls off his tongue sends shivers rippling up my spine, and I lean into him, resting my head on his shoulder.

"We were in the same pack growing up." I stare at the grass under my legs.

"Really?" he asks with a raised voice. "He doesn't speak much of his life before coming here. What pack was that?"

My muscles tense. "The Dark Ravens."

"And he took you as his mate?"

"No, he's my Fated Mate."

Caiden's eyes soften. "How long have you been on your own?"

"Five years. I went rogue on my eighteenth birthday."

He pulls me closer, and I relish in his scent.

"Why did you come here?" he asks. "It wasn't only to seek permission to pass through my territory, was it?"

A slight breeze blows, and a long piece of grass tickles my knee. I pick it up and start tying it in knots. I welcome the distraction because I'm not ready to tell him about Felix, not after telling him about Dylan.

What will he think of me? I can only imagine how that conversation would go.

It's not unusual for an unmated Alpha to claim another as their own, especially if the wolf's mate has died. That is what Felix wants to do with me; he is not my mate, but he wants to claim me as his own. The bond wouldn't be as strong as it would be if he were my Fated Mate, but I would still be bound to him nonetheless.

"I'll allow you to join the pack if you want to stay," he says.

I gasp and my gaze darts up to his, full of question and curiosity. "Why would you allow that? Most Alphas would kill or enslave me."

"First, I'm not like most Alphas. Second, you're my Beta's Fated Mate," he says.

I close my eyes and mutter under my breath, "Beta?"

"You two should catch up. Five years is a long time."

"He doesn't want me," I whisper.

"You just found him. Give him time," he coos. "Stay a few days. See how you like the pack."

I nod, afraid my voice will expose my true feelings.

"Then it's settled. Let's go." He shifts his weight to stand.

"No." I cross my arms over my chest.

"Lucinda," he says with his dominant Alpha voice.

"I'm not ready to see him yet," I say, matching his tone.

After several moments of silence, he says, "I thought you might say that. I opened the mindlink and asked my sister to leave a car, food, and other essentials at a cabin not too far from here. We can stay there this afternoon and drive back tonight."

My lips curl into a smile. *An Alpha that closes the mindlink? Interesting.*

"Deal." I look up at him through my eyelashes. I'll do anything to delay the confrontation with Dylan.

"Ready to run?"

I nod.

But before he stands, he turns back to me and asks, "What did you mean earlier when you said, *'this has never happened before'*? What's never happened?"

"I've never shifted in my sleep," I say. He cocks an eyebrow, so I elaborate, "Being on my own out in the wilderness, in order to protect myself, it was always easier to sleep as my wolf. I've never involuntarily shifted back to my human form while sleeping."

"When you sleep as your wolf, you don't get quality sleep. They're always on high alert to keep you protected. She must've sensed me and knew you were safe."

"Great. Now she's telling me who I can trust to protect me." I roll my eyes and flash a playful smile. She may trust the wolf, but I still don't trust the man, no matter what he says.

Caiden starts to laugh, and I let out a small giggle. *Are we flirting? Damn it. Get a hold of yourself, Lucinda.* I can't slip back into the trusting little girl I once was.

"Ready?" he asks after regaining his composure.

I nod, then we both shift as we stand, and I follow his lead through the forest.

When the forest comes alive with sounds of scurrying squirrels, chirping birds, an urge to play overcomes me, and I rush forward. But Caiden turns and catches me by surprise. I writhe on the ground enough that he cannot get a good paw on me, then I roll out from under him. Standing to face off, a low rumble resonates through my body, and my eyes widen with excitement. A weak rumble radiates from his chest and vibrates up his throat.

Sweet memories of long-ago flash through my mind—a simpler time when I would play fight with other pups.

Holding my rear high in the air with my chest low to the ground, I wiggle my fluffy black tail.

I quickly scan the area. Thick forest surrounds and shelters the clearing. A stream runs down the mountainside, cutting through the pines. We are safe here, time for fun.

While stalking toward him, I watch his every move. He lowers his head, and I take the opening, pouncing on his exposed back.

He anticipates my move and catches me in midair. Then

we're dancing, predicting each other's moves and matching pounce for a pounce. As if we were pups or long-lost friends, we tumble playfully through the clearing for the rest of the afternoon.

When we get to the cabin, there is a car out front, and I stalk to the door to peek through the window. Saliva pools in my mouth at the freshly baked cookies sitting on the counter.

Caiden doesn't hesitate. He pushes the door open and walks in, motioning with his snout to a door in the rear of the cabin. I brush past him to the bedroom door. Once inside, I find an overnight bag on the bed.

After shifting into human form, I plunder through the bag, finding a pair of black leggings and a gray scoop-neck T-shirt alongside modest black lace undergarments. *Perfect.* I head to the bathroom with the bag of toiletries for a quick shower to freshen up.

Once dressed, I stroll back into the main room, and Caiden turns to me from the small kitchen, holding two plates with sandwiches and cookies.

"Hungry?"

"Yes, please." My eyes widen and I grab my stomach as it grumbles. He chuckles and my heart flutters. I could listen to his laughter all night.

He sets our plates on the coffee table in the middle of the room, and we sit on the floor in comfortable silence to eat.

"This is nice," I say, breaking the zen moment of tranquility. "Does anyone live here?"

"It's my place. I stay here sometimes when I need to get away."

"Get away from your pack?"

He cocks an eyebrow and takes a bite of his sandwich.

"Aren't you the Alpha?"

His lips twitch and the vein at his right temple pops out. Clearly, I hit a nerve.

If I could stay here, alone, far away from Felix's wrath and Dylan's misery...

"Can I stay here?" I ask. "It's quiet and peaceful."

He smiles, but then his cheerful disposition fades and his lips pull into a tight line. "No. This is my place."

He smashes his mouth full with another bite of his sandwich.

I play with the hem of my shirt. "Any other places around like this?"

"You can't run from your fate. The bond between Fated Mates is surreal."

I pick at the sandwich on my plate, studying the perfectly melted cheese dripping down the sides. "How would you know?"

Caiden grunts and shoves a cookie in his mouth.

"And, I'm not running from Dylan." I taste the cookie; it's soft and tender. "I'm not running from my fate. I'm chasing my destiny."

"That's not how it works." He brushes his hands over his plate, and a few crumbs fall. "You need to see and spend time with Dylan again. Let him touch you. He'll feel the pull of the mating. It's not something you can ignore."

"Oh. No, that's where you're mistaken." I take the last bite of my cookie and savor the gooey chocolate while blinking back tears that threaten to escape.

I refuse to shed more tears because of Dylan.

A deep crease in Caiden's forehead forms, and his nose scrunches up in question.

CHAPTER 4

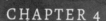

LUCINDA

"Dylan already knows about the bond." My voice trembles and a whimper slips out. "He's known for nine years."

A sharp splintering sound fills the room. Caiden's knuckles turn white as he grips the coffee table, and the wood cracks under his pressure.

"Caiden?"

His pupils dilate and the irises begin to swirl a cloudy black. A low growl escapes from his throat, causing me to flinch.

I place my hands on top of his and rub circular motions on his rough skin with my thumbs. With a rapid pounding pulsing through my veins, I start to hum a steady meditative chant. This is how I would calm my father when his anger would get the better of him.

"Calm down." I pry Caiden's hands off the edge of the table and place them against my cheek. Leaning into his palm, I coo, "It's okay."

He closes his eyes, and when they open again, they are clear and ice blue.

"I want to know everything." He strokes my cheek with his thumb. But even though his eyes meet my stare, his gaze is unfocused. I don't have his attention.

"Fine, but on one condition."

He cocks an eyebrow and my heart flutters.

"I stay here, at least tonight," I say.

He nods, and my lips pucker into a playful smirk.

"But I'm staying too," he says.

Snapping my gaze away from his, my smile deepens, and the butterflies in my stomach return.

"But won't your pack miss their Alpha?" I ask.

"It'll only be two nights since I've been gone. I've been gone longer." His voice trails off into a whisper and he shrugs.

The glassy-eyed look on his face tells me he has spaced out again, somewhere other than here. *What type of Alpha leaves his pack for long periods of time to escape into solitude?*

We finish eating in silence, I clean up the mess from the coffee table incident, then I make hot apple cider while Caiden starts a small fire in the fireplace. It is early spring, but the nights are still cool.

Grabbing a blanket draped over the back of a chair, I curl up on the couch. When he sits next to me, I place my legs across his lap.

"Are you comfortable?" he asks.

I nod, and he watches me, waiting for me to begin my story.

"I'm not sure where to start." I shrug and bite my lower lip. "I've never talked about my life before."

"Start from the beginning. Where are you from, and how do you know Dylan?" he asks in a steady, calming tone.

Licking my lips, I take a deep breath through my nose, and my chest rises until it is full of fresh air. Holding it for a count of three, I release it through my mouth in a controlled fashion.

"Dylan and I are from the Dark Raven Pack. He's three years older, but that never mattered. We were best friends growing up—our parents said we were inseparable." I smile as fond memories flash through my mind…play fighting as pups, skipping school and running through the woods, camping out overnight during full moons, as the memories flood my heart aches.

I've never allowed myself to think of the past—to open Pandora's box. I am not sure why I do now, except Caiden's Alpha is a big security blanket wrapped around me.

Taking a deep breath, I continue, "When Dylan turned seventeen the bond struck us—"

"He's older, but the bond struck you too?" Caiden cocks an eyebrow.

"I was fourteen. The bond struck us at the same time."

His eyebrows rise, creasing his forehead into small rolls. "The bond must be strong. Fourteen is a young age for the bond to spark."

Crossing my arms over my chest, I say, "Yeah, well, you can imagine what it was like to watch him date every female his age."

Caiden shakes his head. "When you find your mate, the urge to consummate the bond is strong and powerful. But you only get satisfaction from your mate. Why did he fight it?"

"He said I was too young, so I agreed to stay away. Two years later, I approached him again, but he said I was still just a kid. I thought he was looking out for my best interest. I was so young and naive."

Caiden brushes a single tear from my cheek.

Laying my head on the soft couch, I stare at nothing in particular. "On my eighteenth birthday I went to him, and he rejected me in front of the Alpha and Beta. The Beta told Dylan that he would accept me or be cast out of the pack. Dylan said he'd leave that night. Then the Alpha told him that he would accept me or I'd be cast out too."

A sharp pain stabs my heart, and a relentless ache spreads through my chest. I remember that day as if it were yesterday.

I twitch my nose, and my shoulders slump. I close my eyes to stop the welling tears that threaten to fall.

Taking a short breath, I continue, "Dylan said, *'not my problem'*."

Against my best efforts, tears stream down my face. I have never said those words out loud. I accepted my fate and moved past it, but nothing could have prepared me for the onslaught of emotions now coursing through my body from voicing those words.

Caiden's strong arms wrap around me. He pulls me into his chest and rubs my back. "Why would the Alpha and Beta do that?"

Between sniffles I lean back and meet his questioning gaze. "We were the future Alpha and Luna of the pack. When Dylan rejected me, he rejected the pack."

Rubbing the nape of his neck with his right hand, he tilts his head to the left and looks at me. "Dylan's never mentioned any of this. Why did you leave your pack?"

Sighing, I say, "The Alpha gave Dylan too much credit. He thought Dylan's affection for me would outweigh his fear of commitment. He hoped that by putting my future—my life—in danger, Dylan's wolf would kick in and take control. He was wrong."

"And the Alpha stood by his word? Even after it backfired?"

I nod and turn into his chest.

"What did your parents do?"

"The Alpha was my dad," I mutter.

"And your mom?"

"She died giving birth to me."

"And Dylan's parents? They stood by and did nothing?"

"Dylan's father was the Beta."

Caiden's arms tighten, and my body melts into his embrace.

"Is that the last time you saw Dylan?" he asks after several minutes of silence.

Biting my lip, I nod.

"What aren't you telling me, Lucinda?"

"We both left that night. I was only eighteen and scared, so I followed him. He didn't want my company, so when we came across a group of rogues, he traded me to them for safe travel through their camp."

Caiden's grip tightens on my forearm.

"Caiden, stop." I twist within his embrace and loosen my arms enough to take his face between my hands, forcing him to look at me. His eyes turn solid black, and his upper fangs protrude over his lower lip. I jerk my body away in an attempt to free myself. "Please calm down. You're hurting me."

Shaking his head, he blinks several times and releases me.

His eyes widen at the red mark left on my forearm, then he looks down at his open palms. After a moment, his gaze drifts to mine. We're only inches apart; his sweet breath warms my face and tingles spread through my body.

"Lucinda, I'm sorry. I'd never hurt you," he whispers in my ear.

Goosebumps ripple up my spine. *I know.*

Caiden leans back, pressing his lips together. "What happened with the group of rogues?"

"I don't want to talk about it," I say.

His arms tense and a vein in his forehead bulges. Turning

my back to him, I curl into a tight ball and watch the flames dance in the fire.

I don't want to think about those dark times. But at least one good thing happened that night: I met Cody.

My throat's dry and my nose twitches while I fight back more tears. *I miss Cody.*

I open my eyes, my heart pounding in my chest, and I scan the darkened room for any sign of danger. Caiden lies in bed next to me. He must have carried me here after I fell asleep on the couch.

Pressing my lips together, I swallow several times and try to calm the churning sensation in my stomach. But *she*, my inner wolf, does not let me panic. *She* continues her steady hum, vibrating deep in my chest. It keeps the dark, narrow tunnel that dances at the edges of my vision at bay.

I close my eyes and take a deep breath, and then another. *Her* constant hum calms my heightened nerves, and my body relaxes. Caiden would never hurt me. He is different from the other Alpha's I have met. *But do I trust him?*

"Are you okay?" Caiden asks, his breath tickling my ear.

"Yes." It is true, at the moment I am okay. I snuggle closer to him, and he tightens his grip around my waist. My eyelids droop and I drift off to sleep again.

A bright light fills the room, and I squint as a ray of sunshine hits my face. I sit up, swing my legs over the edge of the bed, and stretch my arms above my head just as Caiden walks in.

"Good morning," he says with a smile.

"Good morning." I grin, diverting my gaze from his rueful stare. "What time is it?"

"Midmorning. As soon as you're ready, we'll hit the road. I need to get back—they're complaining again."

"Are you sure I can't just stay here?" I fiddle with my fingers.

"It'll be fine. Come on." He closes the distance between us, then he lifts my chin, forcing me to look at him. A small smile crosses his face and my heart warms.

Why does he have this effect on me? I stand to ready myself.

There isn't much to pack, so we clean up from dinner the night before and make sure the coals of the fire are extinguished. And then, hanging my head low, I walk toward the car that will take me back to my nightmare of a Fated Mate.

Standing with one foot inside the car and one out, I study the exterior of the small cabin one last time. It has become my symbol of security and protection. The Alpha in Caiden calms my nerves and keeps the relentless craving for my mate at bay, and for that I am grateful.

Collapsing into the front seat of the car, I close my eyes and bow my head.

The sound of the engine purrs in my ears.

"Let's get this over with," I mutter.

CHAPTER 5

LUCINDA

TAPPING my fingertips on my thighs, I glance out the window and scan the forest. Looking over my shoulder has become second nature.

Caiden cracks his knuckles as he grips the wheel. I study him in silence. I know that look all too well; my father had the same face whenever he received bad news. Caiden must have opened his mindlink to the pack again.

"Is everything okay?" I ask.

"Why did you come here? You told the patrol member it was a matter of life and death." He cocks an eyebrow.

"I'm looking for someone." I fiddle with the hem of my shirt.

"For Dylan?" he asks.

"No."

"Who?"

"A friend." Why is it so difficult for me to talk? It is true that I am looking for my friend. But that is not the life-and-death situation. I release a loud sigh and slouch in my seat.

"And does this friend have a name?"

"It's warm in here." I fan myself, crack my window, then lift my face to catch the cool breeze.

My stomach churns and I wring my hands together in my lap. Caiden's penetrating leer bores into my soul. I force a swallow down my dry throat.

"What's the life-and-death part? If you don't find your friend, you'll die?" Caiden asks after an uncomfortable silence.

"Maybe?" I stutter.

"These types of answers will not win over the pack." Caiden's voice is strained, and his knuckles whiten from his stern grip on the steering wheel.

Taking a deep breath, I close my eyes and place my hands on the dashboard for comfort.

"I'm hoping my friend can help me with something." I look to Caiden under a veil of dark lashes. "I need to hide from someone."

He nods. "It's easy to get lost in the Blood Moone pack. Our territory is one of the largest, and you'll be safe with me until we find your friend."

"So, what's the plan when we get back? Where will I stay? Is there an apartment I can rent or something?"

"No." He glances at me. "You'll stay at the Pack House."

Squirming in my seat, I bite my lower lip and frown.

"You're an unmarked and unclaimed rogue. I can't have you wandering around my territory unescorted."

I bob my head back and forth to let him know I heard him. But I don't agree. I can take care of myself. Most importantly, how am I supposed to find Mia if I need a babysitter?

"Until the pack votes and formally accepts you, you need to stay close," he adds.

"Vote?" I ask.

He nods.

I gaze out the window and watch the tall evergreen trees pass by in a blur as we drive. "How long is the ride?"

"Five hours, give or take."

I squint and my forehead tightens. "That long?"

Caiden laughs. "I don't like the interstate. It takes longer on backroads."

The rest of the trip is peaceful, and I drift in and out of sleep for a few hours. While I am awake, we engage in small talk, and Caiden tells me about the Blood Moone pack and his territory.

We should be around half an hour away when Caiden says, "Our territory includes several small human towns and also many of their major cities. A lot of pack members live among them, hiding their wolf from the humans and mingling as best they can. Others members prefer to live in wolf-only towns, usually in the rural areas."

I have never been one to shy away from humans. Hell, I even found comfort in one for a while. That was after I left Felix, the first time. A shiver runs through my body just thinking about him.

When I first met Felix, my blood boiled with raw passion. He was like a drug, and I needed him in every way. He filled the void that was left when Dylan rejected me as best he could. But then I saw him for who he really was—a psychopath.

I left him and his hodgepodge band of rogue wolves and spent a year among humans in Chicago. And then I met Mia as I was traveling west.

After a few months, she found her Fated Mate, Gavin, and they were headed back to her pack—the Blood Moones. I was to follow after a while, as she thought the Alpha may let me stay.

But Felix found me first.

I shake the eerie feeling that creeps over me just thinking

of Felix, and my heart hangs low with grief. *No. I will not think of those things, not now.*

Closing my eyes, I try to sleep the rest of the ride….and fail. But, the quietness helps to ease my troubled heart. Before long, we drive up a long dirt driveway and I recognize the Pack House from before.

Once we park, I get out of the car and stretch. My muscles are tight from being cramped in one position for so long. It's eerie, but I sense his presence before smelling his signature scent of cumin and freshly cut grass.

The pit of my stomach flutters, telling me my mate is near. Turning around, I stiffen and a little bit of vomit rises in my throat.

"Glad you could catch up to her. She can be quite elusive when she wants to be," Dylan says as he struts down the porch steps.

I cross my arms in front of my chest and glare at him. "I didn't run."

Caiden steps between us. "Any news?"

"Another border attack," Dylan says in a business-like manner.

"Rogues?" Caiden asks.

Dylan nods.

"Injuries?"

"Five, but nothing fatal this time," Dylan says. "They said they were looking for someone."

Caiden nods, shifting his weight and rolling his shoulders, signaling the end of their conversation. When he glances in my direction, our eyes meet. I wipe my clammy palms on my pants as my heart races. *Did Felix find me so soon?*

I follow as Caiden turns and walks toward the Pack House.

Dylan holds out his arm, stopping me with a sly grin, then

calls to Caiden, "I'm glad you returned in one piece. She's known to be difficult. Did she attack you? She doesn't respond well to authority."

"What?" My voice rings in my ears.

"It wouldn't be the first time you attacked an Alpha." Dylan glares at me.

I roll my eyes and try to maneuver around him.

Dylan winks at me, his smirk deepening.

I turn quickly on my heels and shoot him a glare that says more than any words could.

"So feisty." His lips curl into a wicked grin as he touches my cheek. "And yet, you're still just a rogue. Shall I have you whipped for disobedience?"

I slap him hard across the face, leaving a dark red welt on his skin.

He catches my hand and holds it firm. His grin widens, and a tingling sensation spreads through my body from the touch of our bare skin.

"You've always liked it rough, haven't you?" His eyes taunt me and my body warms, remembering the nights we spent together. Leaning closer, he whispers, "Maybe I'll tie you up before the whipping, and then we'll see what else you like."

Heat spreads from my chest up to my neck and to my cheeks. His words excite parts of my body, but I will never let him know that. I concentrate to keep my heart rate in check.

The sly grin suddenly falls from his face as he tilts his head and squints.

Shit. Can he smell my arousal?

Out of the corner of my eye, movement on the porch steps catches my attention. Caiden's body tenses, and the dark-haired girl from before walks past him to head straight for Dylan. She drapes her arms over his shoulders from behind and stares at me with big pale-blue eyes.

"Who's this?" she whines.

"No one of consequence," Dylan says, keeping eye contact with me.

"You're that girl, the rogue, right?" she asks. "I'm Sabrina, Dylan's girlfriend."

Clenching my jaw, I say, "Lucinda."

"And she was just leaving." Dylan turns his back on me and smashes his lips into Sabrina's. He picks her up and feverishly kisses her with no shame.

Heat rises in me and burns my cheeks. I clench and unclench my fists several times before Caiden rests a hand on my arm. His dominant Alpha calms my wolf as he leads me toward the front door of the house.

Walking into the Pack House for the second time sends my emotions into high alert. There's two dozen or more people crammed into the house and I have to force my feet to move as we make our way from the entry foyer into the living room.

Fear of rejection and humiliation causes me to stumble. I need to get a grip on these emotions—wolves smell fear and prey on those weaker. Fear makes us weak.

Wiping my sweaty palms on my pants, I stand taller, roll my shoulders back, and hold my chin high. I am an Alpha's daughter, and I was to be the future Luna of my pack. Time to act dignified.

Caiden squeezes my hand, and I raise my eyes to him under the cover of my lashes and smile.

A sandy-blond-haired guy with bright emerald-green eyes walks toward us with a big grin. *My escort.*

"Here's the little vixen that kept our Alpha away for two days," he says.

"Where is she?" a high-pitched female voice calls out from the back. Making way for the speaker, the crowd in the living room parts.

Who is it, his Luna? I'd be pissed too if my mate took off for two days with another woman. *Oh, wait, my mate does that daily.* My stomach twists in knots.

"Cinda!" the female exclaims as she reaches into my view, a huge smile on her face.

My heart expands and I can't help but rejoice in excitement.

A mischievous grin curls my lips as I inhale her wonderful scent of cinnamon and honey. I've missed her dearly. "Hey, Mia."

"I knew it was you. As soon as—"

"Who knew it?" A male walks up behind her.

"Gavin," I whisper, and my lips pucker before melting into a grin.

"Hey, darlin'." He pulls me into a big hug and snickers. "I knew it was you as soon as we heard our Alpha was chasing a female rogue."

I relax in the familiar scent of leather and tobacco.

"Yeah, whatever," Mia says with a giggle. "I smelled you as soon as we got back to the Pack House—your scent was everywhere."

She pushes Gavin aside and pulls me in for a long embrace.

Glancing over Mia's shoulder, I get a good view of the room. Three couches are positioned in a U-shape and two recliner chairs at each corner. Off to the side, there's a chaise. I've always loved those. That will be my spot. A one-sided smile tugs at the corner of my lip. Maybe this will turn out okay.

"I've missed you," I say, tightening my grip around Mia's shoulders.

"I've missed you too." She pulls away. "I'm so glad you're here. Have you found your mate?"

I glance to Caiden and hope he won't say anything as I shake my head.

Wiggling her eyebrows, she smiles. "No worries. We have many unmated males. Maybe he'll be here. And if he isn't—"

"Yeah, where else could he be?" Dylan walks through the front door with his female leech, Sabrina.

His tone challenges my wolf, and the hair on the back of my neck spikes. I tap my fingers against my thigh and narrow my eyes at him.

"He could be dead," I say under my breath. This earns a playful smile from Dylan and woes from the crowd.

Dylan leans over and whispers into my ear, "Oh, how I've missed your smart-ass mouth."

His lips brush my earlobe, and his warm breath on my neck sends an electric vibration coursing through my soul. I despise the involuntary response my body has toward him.

Sabrina steps closer—too close. I let loose a snarl. Dylan places his arm around Sabrina and kisses her on the head.

I glare at Dylan and hold his stare. If they don't get out of my personal space immediately, I will lose control to my wolf.

CHAPTER 6

CAIDEN

Watching Mia and Lucinda embrace, I rack my brain for a memory of how they know each other. My shoulders tense, and I focus on their interaction. I flash a look to Mia with furrowed brows.

She mindlinks me and says, "This is Cinda, the rogue I told you about when I returned home."

Taking a deep breath, I relax. Lucinda has to stay. Not only is she my Beta's mate, but she saved Mia's life.

I stand only a few feet from Lucinda, and it's hard not to stare at her big smile. Her guard is down; she's the most relaxed I've seen her since we met. Her laughter is contagious.

Sammy asks through the mindlink, "So, find out anything interesting about the vixen?"

"Someone Mia met during her time away," I say.

"Is she going to stay?" he asks.

I glance over my shoulder at Sammy and shake my head, I know what he's thinking. His wide-ass grin causes me to roll my eyes. He hasn't found his mate yet, and maybe if he finds the right person he would be happy—but no, Lucinda is not the right person for him.

I give him my signature Alpha look that says *this conversation is over.*

Sammy and I were best friends growing up. Some would say we were inseparable. Everyone thought I would name him my Beta when the time came. But through the years, we drifted apart, and when the time came, he wasn't there.

I know he has hard feelings over my decision—choosing an outsider over one of our own. And he's not the only one with those thoughts. But I did what I did for the good of the pack. I can't explain it, nor do I need to defend my decision.

Sammy is an honorable man and a good friend. I know he will always stand by my side, no matter what life throws at us.

If only he knew all the horrible things life is capable of.

After a minute of silence, Sammy asks via the mindlink, "Can we trust her? With the number and severity of rogue attacks on the rise—"

"Enough." I glare at him and raise my hand to silence him.

Sammy's eyes darken and a deep crease forms in the center of his forehead. "Whatever you say, you're the Alpha. I'm not second-guessing you, but is that the smartest thing? She's a rogue. And just this morning, a group of rogues that previously trespassed said they were looking for someone."

"How quickly your mind changes. Just a minute ago you were drooling over her."

"Yeah, yeah. But do you honestly think it's a coincidence?"

What do I know about her, other than what she told me? Which could all be a lie. Is Dylan actually her Fated Mate? I've known him for four years, and he has never mentioned it or spoken of his past. Not that I have ever asked about it; sometimes, some things are better left in the past.

Whatever reason he was wandering stray when he found

me makes no difference. What he did for me... No lawless, cruel rogue would've done what he did. But no one else understands because they don't know the whole story, nor will they ever. Nevertheless, he earned his position with the loyalty he showed me that day.

Dylan has been a stand-up Beta, but if everything Lucinda said and the things Dylan has done is true...

Shaking my head, I close my eyes and lick my lips, the taste of bitterness filling my mouth. If what she said is true, actions like that against a Fated Mate are not the traits of a Beta I want in my pack. We don't turn our back on our Fated Mate.

"Look," Sammy says. "I'll stay until we get the rogue attacks under control and our borders protected. Then I'm leaving. I need to at least try and find my mate, or any mate if I'm being honest."

Nodding, I keep my attention fixed on the ground. We've had this conversation several times over the past few years. As much as I don't want him to leave, I won't stop him.

Power flows through the room, overpowering everything else, and I'm pulled from my thoughts. I sense a struggle between Lucinda and Dylan. They're locked in a stare, him with amusement and mischief in his eyes and her with pain and anger.

"He could be dead." I flinch at the harsh words that linger in the air.

I take in the scene unfolding, and narrow my eyes. Dylan and Sabrina are inches from Lucinda.

Stepping closer to her, I place my hand on her lower back. The power is radiating from her. I sniff the air around her, then I stare at Dylan and smirk—she is a strong wolf with Alpha potential. *How did I not notice before?*

Dylan runs his hands through his hair and tugs at the back of his neck.

So, is that it? He can't handle a woman more powerful than him.

I hope that's not the case; it's so childish.

I grab Lucinda's waist, pulling her closer to me, allowing my Alpha to calm her inner wolf.

"You're her, aren't you?" someone asks from the group.

Looking around, Eva steps forward. My eyes involuntarily close, and I take a deep breath. This close to Lucinda, it causes me to inhale her intoxicating scent. She smells of mint and honey. I've come to take comfort in the fresh, sweet smell that radiates off her.

Opening my eyes, I study Lucinda's face.

"Who?" Lucinda asks, stiffening as her smile fades away.

"The girl from Mia's stories. The one who's searching the country in hope of finding her Fated Mate." Eva's eyes sparkle with admiration. She's a romantic, and I fear if she doesn't find her Fated Mate in our Pack within the next few years, she'll leave to search for him. Eva will never survive on her own.

"Not everyone is meant to find their Fated Mate," Lucinda says. "Sometimes you have to go forward and create your own destiny."

"What about fate?" Eva asks, her high cheekbones dropping to a slim, flat surface. "The Elders—"

"I know what the Elders say. That we have a mate who's been marked for us by fate—someone that drives our desires. When the Fated Mates bond, their union will make them stronger and more powerful." Lucinda takes a breath and the entire room is silent, waiting for her to continue. "But why sacrifice your lifetime searching for a fate that you may never find? You should live your life and forge your own destiny."

Eva blinks back tears. Everyone else in the room averts

their gaze to somewhere other than Lucinda, and a low murmur drifts in the air as people contemplate her words.

Tugging at Lucinda's hand before anyone has a chance to debate her, I say, "Come on, I'll show you to your room."

"Room?" Dylan asks, letting go of Sabrina.

"Yes, she'll be staying with us for a while." Rolling my shoulders back, I dare him to challenge me.

He turns and drags Sabrina into the kitchen. Sabrina glances over her shoulder and blows me a kiss as she walks away.

"We'll go shopping tomorrow, okay?" Mia pulls Lucinda into another embrace.

Lucinda nods, but the smile on her face doesn't reach her eyes. *What is she hiding?*

"Come on, it's been a long day." I guide her upstairs and down the hallway, pointing to the doors as we pass. "Mia and Gavin's room is the first door on the right, and Dylan's is next. You'll be staying in the third room on the right. It's the guest room."

I slide the door open and gesture her inside.

As soon as we enter, she turns into my chest and slumps in defeat. I wrap my arms around her, not knowing what else to do.

CHAPTER 7

LUCINDA

Turning into Caiden's chest, I whisper, "Thank you."

If I'm being honest with myself, which these past few years I haven't been, I miss Dylan and seeing him physical with Sabrina shatters my soul.

"Things will get better," he says, squeezing me one last time before holding me at arm's length. "Now, get some rest. If you're going shopping with my sister tomorrow, it will be more exhausting than running in the forest with me."

Tilting my head, I let one side of my mouth rise into a half-smile. "Your sister?"

He nods. His stare plunders through my soul as if he is searching for something. When his focus intensifies, a bead of sweat drips down my spine and I divert my attention to the ground.

My fingers find the hem of my shirt and I begin to fidget. "Mia is the friend I came to find. She told me she had a brother, but didn't mention he was the Alpha."

"I wasn't Alpha when she left," he whispers.

Studying his face, a fine stubble of his five o'clock shadow covers his jaw. *Damn, that is sexy.*

"Who is it that you're running from?" he asks in a steady tone.

"Someone I don't want to see again."

"And does this someone have a name?"

I don't want to talk about Felix, not now, not with Caiden. Now that I've found Mia, I need to talk to her first.

Crossing my arms over my chest, I set my jaw and narrow my stare. "Does it matter?"

The deepening crease in Caiden's forehead and small twitch on the left side of his jaw are the only signs that this was not the response he wanted.

"Unlike a rogue lifestyle, I have an entire pack to look after. I am responsible for their well-being and ensuring their safety," he says, and his eyes soften around the edges.

"You're worried I've put your pack in danger by coming here." My shoulders slump forward, and I stare off into nothingness behind him. If Felix finds me here, God, help this pack.

The light touch of his fingertips on my chin sends small electric shocks speeding through my body. A small twitch in his right eye lets me know he felt it too. He lifts my chin, bringing my face only inches from his. His eyes are wide, and his pupils are fully dilated—the Alpha in him is demanding my attention.

"Yes, you're correct. I am worried about endangering my pack. I like to know who and what is a threat. I don't like being blindsided." He takes a deep breath. "But you saved my sister, the only family I have left. And for that, I promise I will provide protection from whatever or whoever it is you're running from."

He lets go of my chin and takes a step back. A chill runs down my back at the distance he put between us.

"Now get some rest. We'll talk more tomorrow—if Mia

allows it," he says with a smile. "She has an entire day of shopping planned for you two."

The tension between us lingers in the air. His Alpha doesn't like being denied, and he wants to know about Felix. *Sigh.* No, I can't talk about Felix with Caiden, not yet.

Trying to ease the pressure in the room before he leaves, I whisper, "I don't like shopping."

His laugh echoes in my ears. It's a gentle sound, relaxing and peaceful. It's also contagious, and before I realize it, I'm giggling too.

"If you need anything, let me know, I'm just across the hall," he says, giving me one last smile before walking out the door.

Looking around the room, I take in my surroundings.

The bed is huge—the largest I have ever seen. An urge to dive into the pile of pillows and curl up in the fluffy white down comforter overtakes my sanity. But the extra-large window above the bed catches my attention and a warmth radiates throughout my body with a soft drumming in my chest. *I will still be able to sleep under the twinkling lights of the night sky.*

There are two doors to the right—one is a walk-in closet, and the other is my own bathroom. *Heaven.*

I smile at my reflection in the mirror, then splash cool water on my face. *Things could be worse.* I take comfort in the softness of the towel as I pat my face dry. It has been a long time since I've had such luxuries.

But my mood sours as his familiar earthy scent infiltrates in my nostrils. The hair on the back of my neck stands up and my muscles tense. Turning around and peering through the bathroom doorway, I meet his green eyes and lopsided grin as he lounges on my bed with his arms tucked behind his head.

"Lux, what are you doing here?" Dylan asks. His grin fades and his eyes fall into a distant and empty stare.

Exiting the bathroom, I stroll closer to him and he sits up, but his shoulders slump forward.

After everything he's put me through, why do I even bother with him? I curse the sentimental side of my damned heart. *Stay strong.* Even if he is all I have left from home, he's still an ass.

"I didn't follow you, if that's what you're thinking." I cross my arms in front of my chest and stop a few feet from him.

"It did cross my mind." His plucks feathers from the seams of a throw pillow.

"How did you become Beta? You're such an ass."

"Only to you." Lying back down, Dylan puts his hands behind his head and looks to the ceiling.

Glaring at him, I clench my jaw. Over the years, I've learned to control my temper. I had to in order to survive on my own, especially since I crossed paths with Dylan so often.

Each meeting was by chance; nonetheless, it was always the same song and dance. He pushed me away, we were best friends, we were more than friends, and then he turned into an egotistical jackass. *This time will be different. Because this time I don't give a damn.*

"I feel so special," I mock. "And why is that again?"

Dylan growls. "You know why."

"Tell me again, how does it help you feel better?"

He pounds his fist on the bed. "It just does, okay!"

Rolling my eyes, I throw my hands in the air. "You're impossible."

"And irresistible." He smirks.

"Don't push your luck," I say.

His smirk turns into a boyish grin, and he flashes his dimples. This is his signature smile that always sets my heart on fire. *Sigh.* Why does everything have to be so complicated?

"So, why are you here?" he asks.

Studying his posture, the whitening of his knuckles, and clenching jaw—his inner wolf is not happy.

May as well get it over with and deliver the bad news.

Shrugging, I say, "I have nowhere else to go."

Dylan releases a breath. "Why don't you go home? After all this time, I'm sure your dad will let you—"

"He's not Alpha anymore," I whisper.

This is harder than I thought it would be. I stare at the ceiling and blink back the tears, but I'm exhausted from keeping my emotions in check and being strong for so long. My arms hang heavy at my side as the tension in my back eases.

Dylan opens his arms out wide, reaching for me.

Crashing into his chest, I release all the tears that have built up on this subject—remorse and guilt over the incident that led to a massacre.

"What happened?" He rubs my back. All the nonsense about mates is forgotten and we are childhood best friends once again. After all, they were his pack too—his friends and family.

"A few weeks ago, they were attacked by a band of rogues. No one survived."

His body stiffens, and he wraps his arms around me tighter, pulling me closer. I knew one day I would see Dylan again and would have this conversation. But I'm not prepared. I'm not ready to tell him how his father died and that it's all my fault. *I can't tell him the truth, not now.*

Dylan rests his chin on my forehead and rocks us back and forth in slow motion, as if he were rocking a baby to sleep.

My entire body ignites with an internal flame. Sharp tingles roll over my skin, causing goosebumps to run rampant. My wolf begins to take over. My heartbeat quickens, and the surging connection between our wolves draws me closer. I nuzzle into his neck with my nose.

"Lux," he whispers in his smooth, sweet voice. Our faces are only inches apart.

I raise my eyebrows, blinking away any remaining tears, and lean closer to him.

He rests his forehead on mine, our noses brushing each other. He closes his eyes and his chest rises, pressing against mine as he takes a deep breath. Opening his eyes again, he places his hands on my shoulders and gently pushes me away.

"This," he says, motioning between us with his thumb and pinky finger, "isn't going to happen."

My head falls in defeat.

"I know." My pained voice is barely audible, and I fight to hold back my wolf's despair. I'm frustrated that I allowed my wolf to take over and shameful that he knows I still care. I snap myself out of it.

"What happened to us?" I ask. He stares into my eyes, and his deep green orbs probe my soul—searching for something. "We were best friends growing up—inseparable."

"Things change. People change." He reaches for my hand, rubs circles on the back with his thumb, and pulls my hand to his lips. He softly kisses my knuckles before letting go and taking a step away from me.

"How long are you staying here?" he asks. All prior tenderness is gone from his voice.

Dylan the asshole has returned.

"If I stay, are you leaving?"

He nods.

I would love nothing more than to stay. With or without Dylan, in all honesty, his presence is only a minor irritation. But I know I cannot stay more than a few days, a week at most.

And that's stretching it. Who knows where Felix is?

Caiden is right, he has a whole pack to worry about. I can't take the chance of Felix finding me here, or this pack will meet the same fate as my own.

"I'll be leaving soon," I say, "but not just yet."

"Why?" He tilts my chin up with his index finger, making me look at him. Blackness streaks through his green eyes, and I know he is fighting to stay in control.

His wolf wants his mate.

Knowing the pain he must be going through right now, caused by denying his wolf of his mate, makes my heart a little lighter.

I lean against the edge of the bed. "Mia wants to go shopping tomorrow."

What I don't say is that I want the security that Caiden promised me.

"Fine," he says with a strained tone. "Just keep your distance."

His fists clench and his body tenses. On instinct, I reach out to stroke his chest, trying to calm him down. He grabs my wrist and holds it for a minute before pushing me away.

"Don't. Please don't touch me again." Narrowing his eyes, he walks past me and closes the door behind him.

I collapse on the bed. Tears pool up, but I refuse to allow them to streak my face.

CHAPTER 8

CAIDEN

When I walk back downstairs and enter the main room, I'm pleased to find that Mia and Gavin have ushered almost everyone out of the Pack House. Only a few stragglers remain, and Mia is talking with them.

Through the mindlink I say to Mia, "Thank you."

"You owe me," she says back. "Kitchen. Now."

When Mia takes that tone with me, I know something is up.

Upon entering the kitchen, I grab a stool that's tucked up under the counter to sit on and wait for my little sister. The brief silence is calming.

Mia walks through the doorway. Running to me, she lunges for my midsection and wraps both her arms around me in a tight hug. "Caiden!"

"Is everything okay?" I ask.

"Everything is better than okay." Mia tightens her embrace.

Wrapping my arms around her, I give her a squeeze just as Gavin walks through the doorway.

"Am I interrupting something?" Gavin asks, and I begin to laugh.

Mia lets go and slips into the seat next to me. "Caiden, I'm just so happy that you finally met Cinda."

Gavin chimes in, "Yeah, she's pretty cool. She'll be a great asset to the pack."

"You'll let her stay, won't you?" Mia asks.

I shrug. "It's not up to me, remember? The Pack Elders will want to interview her, then she'll need to meet each member, and in time she'll be brought to a vote."

Gavin grumbles under his breath, "That whole thing is so stupid."

"Yeah, why did you even agree to all that?" Mia asks. "Oh wait, I remember. You weren't around so they kinda did it without your permission in the first place, right?"

Crossing her arms in front of her chest, Mia wrinkles her nose and sticks out her tongue.

Even when you are the Alpha, little sisters will always be little sisters. I shake my head.

"What's done is done. But we can help her through the process by preparing her as best we can," I say.

"And how do you propose we do that?" Mia asks.

I lay my hands on the counter and spread my fingers flat against the hard top. "Tomorrow when you're shopping, you have to talk to her and find out what type of trouble she's in."

"Why do you think Cinda's in trouble?" Gavin asks.

"She said she was running from someone."

"Really? Who?" Mia asks.

"If I knew that, then I wouldn't need— Oh, never mind!" Sometimes my patience doesn't extend very far with my sister.

"Lighten up, Caiden." Mia reaches across the counter to rub my arm. "Just because she's running from someone, doesn't necessarily mean she's in trouble."

"Mia's right," Gavin says. "She could be running from an ex-boyfriend or something."

My pulse increases thinking of Lucinda with someone else.

Mia shrugs and puckers her lips into a sassy pout.

If she wasn't my little sister I'd reprimand her.

I stand with more force than intended and dart for the door. As I pass behind Mia, I say, "Just find out what you can."

Leaving the kitchen, I turn to head upstairs.

Long black hair whips around and smacks me in the face.

"Oh hi, Caiden," Sabrina says. "I'm sorry, I didn't see you there."

Sure.

"Sabrina." I nod and continue past her to the stairs.

Reaching out and grabbing my hand, Sabrina says, "Caiden, I've been meaning to talk to you. Do you have a few minutes?"

"Can it wait until office hours in the morning?"

"Are you actually going to have them tomorrow?" Sabrina asks. "It's been about a month since you've held office hours. It's been two months since you attended a weekly council meeting. And I can't remember the last time I saw you at a monthly pack meet—"

"Is this what you want? To review my attendance record?"

"No—"

A low growl escapes and I narrow my eyes. "Then hurry up and get to your point."

"We need to talk about a plan to deal with the border attacks—"

"There is no *we*," I say. "Dylan, Sammy, and I have a plan."

"Then what is it?"

"It doesn't concern you."

"But—"

Stepping closer to Sabrina, my nose brushes hers. "Let's get an understanding. I tolerate you because you are Patrick's niece. He was an honorable Beta to my father, may he rest in peace. But that is as far as it goes."

I clench my fists at her wide-eyed stare.

She begins to open her mouth, but I've had enough of this conversation. Rolling back my shoulders, my wolf shows his dominance. Sabrina is powerless and has no choice but to submit.

Letting out a deep breath, I storm away from her and continue up the stairs. Brushing past Dylan in the hall, I shoot him a glare and say through the mindlink, "We need to talk later."

I head straight for my room.

Lying down on my bed, I watch the small golden flame of my oil lamp dance in the air. It calms my nerves and eases my tension.

My father gave me the lamp, saying it was an old family heirloom and he hoped one day I would pass it to my son. He told me, *your eye is the lamp of the body.* I've never understood what he meant.

But as long as the flame of my lamp still flickers, then I will keep pushing forward through this meaningless existence. No matter how hard it is to wake up every day and look at the shell of a man in the mirror staring back at me, life goes on.

Closing my eyes, I slow my breathing and try to relax.

My eyes flash open as I'm startled awake by a loud banging noise. My scalp tingles, but the alarmed Alpha within me soon calms once I realize it's only Dylan and Sabrina.

They must be having one of their kinky sex nights.

Gritting my teeth, I roll over and pull a pillow over my

head, but it doesn't drown out the constant moaning of Sabrina's annoying voice.

I hear a light tapping on my door and sense someone in the hall. If someone needs me, why wouldn't they use the mindlink?

Getting out of bed, I quickly throw on a pair of flannel pants and open the door in time to see Lucinda slipping into her room.

I run my hand through my hair. "Lucinda, is everything okay?"

"Oh, hi. I'm sorry to wake you," she says, shying away from my gaze. Her chest rises as she closes her eyes and takes a deep breath. "It's nothing. I'm fine."

When she opens her eyes, she blushes as she notices my clothes, or lack thereof.

"Ahh! Ooo! Dylan!"

Lucinda flinches at the moans and growls that break through the silence of the night. She flashes me a weak smile and starts to close the door.

I get it.

Crossing the hall, I shut her door, take her arm and say, "Come on."

As she follows me into my room, she warily looks around. *What was she expecting?*

She raises her eyebrows at the soft light of the oil lamp that still glows on the nightstand. I shrug. And then she traces the top of the glass with her fingertips.

"Get some sleep," I say.

She crawls into bed and lies down on her left side. I crawl into bed behind her and drape my arm over her body, allowing the Alpha within me—my wolf—to calm her and put her wolf at ease.

She soon falls asleep, and I'm not far behind her.

I wake up inhaling an intoxicating and sweet scent. Notes

of nectar and peppermint drift through my nostrils, causing my lips to turn up at the corners. Opening my eyes, I gaze at this heavenly creature resting peacefully in my arms. *How can Dylan reject her?*

When her eyes flutter open, I say, "Good morning."

She rolls over to face me, and a light shade of pink rushes to her cheeks.

"Good morning," she whispers and diverts her eyes away from mine. An uneasiness rumbles in the pit of my stomach, and I push it aside.

"First off, let's get something straight. I'll always protect you when you need it, but let's not make this—" I gesture at our current situation. "—a habit. I don't want anyone to get the wrong impression."

Her eyebrows raise and her eyes widen. "OH! Right, of course."

Sitting up, she starts to scoot off the foot of the bed. A blush rises to her cheeks as she plays with the hem of her shirt. Damn it, I've embarrassed her.

"Did I see Dylan coming out of your room last night?" I ask.

She freezes and turns to look at me. With a cautious tone, she says, "Yes."

"What did he want?" My stare penetrates her hazel eyes.

"To talk." She shrugs and turns her back to me. Her long chestnut hair whips over her shoulder, causing her delightful scent to flood my senses.

"You two can be civil with each other?" My breath catches in my throat.

"When we're alone, he's different. He's tender and caring, almost like we're friends again. It's only when we're in a crowd, especially around other guys, that he's an asshole." She glances over her shoulder. A faint smile plays at the edges of her ruby lips, then her face hardens and the tender smile falls from her face. "I guess we have a love-hate relationship. Well, mostly hate. We're rarely alone."

Staring at the ground, the realization hits me as the meaning behind her words sink in. A low rumble of laughter erupts from my throat. Her surprised look tells me she hasn't figured it out. I quiet my laughter.

"Lucinda, the connection to our Fated Mate is like a double-edged sword. Just as we're hardwired to love our Fated Mate, we're also very possessive of them." I choose my words carefully.

"For some unknown reason, Dylan is trying hard to reject your love. But in doing so, he hasn't the strength to control the possessive nature of his wolf. His hostile behavior is the backlash. His wolf wants his mate, but Dylan won't allow it. Therefore, he is doing everything he can to push you away, so, unfortunately, you suffer the consequences."

My own heart yearns as I speak about mates.

Lucinda nibbles on her lower lip and fidgets with the hem of her shirt. "How do you know so much about Fated Mates?"

"I found mine," I whisper, looking away.

I can't talk about my mate. Not now. Not with her.

CHAPTER 9

LUCINDA

CAIDEN TENSES at the mention of his mate. Staring into his deep blue eyes, I search for answers to my unasked questions. But all I see is remorse and wistful longing before he diverts his gaze away from mine.

"I should go before everyone wakes up," I say.

He nods and his eyes remain fixed on the ground, so I stand to leave.

In the doorway, I stop and give one last glance to Caiden. The morning light shines through the window behind him to outline his body. His silhouette is heavenly. Paired with the backdrop of the English ivy climbing the tree outside, it is a truly surreal moment.

A sorrowful pain surges through me as I close the door. I just witnessed the Alpha at his lowest. A broken man sitting on the edge of his bed, head resting in his hands. My chest tightens with grief for an unknown reason.

A low growl draws me from my thoughts I was lost in. I quickly turn to find Dylan standing in front of his door and he glares at me. I scoot across the hall and slip into my room. *It's too early to deal with his mood swings right now.*

After freshening up, I head downstairs and seek out the loud voices I heard from the stairs. Entering the kitchen, I find Mia and Gavin laughing while Dylan sits brooding at the table.

"Cinda!" Mia says. "Perfect timing—"

"Are your ears burnin'? Because we were just talking 'bout you." Gavin flashes me a mischievous grin.

"Oh yeah?" I glide my fingertips across the top of a chair as I cross the room.

"Pull up a chair. Gavin was just about to tell the story of the first time you all met," a male voice says.

I turn to see the man with sandy-blond hair and emerald-green eyes. *My escort.*

"Hi. I'm Sammy." He extends his hand.

"Cinda." I firmly shake his hand.

"So, as I was saying," Gavin continues, "the first time I met Cinda, she saved my life. Dylan and I were out hunting when a band of rogues sprang on us. They were out for blood and went straight for the kill.

"Dylan went down, and a huge beast was headed straight for me. I took a second to ask Dylan if he was okay, and that was my mistake. The beast was faster than I thought, and he caught me by surprise." Gavin's hands and arms strike in the air as he talks.

"During his attack, I lost my footing, and we both fell to the hard ground. I was on my back with him on top of me. He was huge and I couldn't shake him, then next thing I know, he sunk his teeth into my shoulder. I started to fade out."

Gavin kneels on the ground and begins to act out his story.

"But Dylan pounced on the guy, knocking him off me, and they rolled a couple of times, landing a few feet away. Dylan stood, placing himself between me and the other wolves—he was protecting me."

I glance to Dylan, but he's staring at the floor.

"There were seven of them, and they had us pinned against a tree with no escape route. I was useless, lying on the forest floor, blood gushing. Then, out of nowhere, a black wolf leaps through the air and stands next to Dylan. A menacing growl escaped the black wolf, and was baring lethal fangs. I could feel the power radiate off of this newcomer, and I knew this wolf was a strong Alpha."

Sammy taps his foot against the ground and scoots to the edge of his seat. "Go on."

"But I felt something else too. I looked at the tree line to see the most beautiful silhouette of a female wolf." Gavin stands back up and pulls Mia close to him to place a kiss on her forehead before continuing. "As you can guess, it was Mia."

Sammy jumps from his seat and waves his hands around in the air. "And? What happened with the black wolf and the rogues?"

The door opens and my new favorite scent swirls in the air as Caiden strolls into the kitchen.

My eyes flit away as he turns toward me. A low growl rumbles through the room, and I know it's from Dylan sitting in the corner.

Sammy says to Caiden, "Gavin's telling the story of how he met Mia and Cinda."

Caiden smiles and nods.

Gavin clears his throat and continues his story. "Well, let's just say I was terrified by the mysterious black wolf as I watched it shred the band of rogues to pieces. Dylan held his own against a couple of the rogues, but I was in awe of this newcomer. But this new wolf had not only skill, strength, and speed, but also grace. It was the most amazing and utterly terrifying fight I've ever witnessed."

Gavin is the most dramatic storyteller. Sammy's leg bounces as he sits on the edge of his seat. Caiden, leaning against the counter stares transfixed on Gavin, raising his eyebrows waiting for the story to continue. Mia crosses over to me and squeezes my hand.

Everyone is transfixed, lingering on Gavin's every word. Well, everyone except Dylan. He's still pouting in the corner.

"In one swift motion, the black wolf lunged in and ripped out the throat of the rogue leader. After his lifeless body fell to the ground, the other rogues scattered into the trees."

"And then what?" Sammy asks.

Gavin shrugs. "And then I passed out."

"Seriously? What type of story ends like that?"

Gavin laughs. "Who said that was the end?"

"Then hurry up and continue, you damn fool!" Sammy jokes, and we all laugh.

Gavin's lips turn up into a wide grin. "When I woke up the next morning, I was in a cabin with Mia by my side. I was in too much pain the day before to think much about the black wolf, so you can imagine my surprise when I found out the black wolf was Cinda."

Sammy gasps and I chuckle. Gavin's face that morning had been priceless—a golden moment worthy of framing.

My gaze wanders to Dylan. He stares at me, intently watching my every movement. But then his eyes soften around the edges as they meet mine, and I'm pulled into the bittersweet memory of that night. The night my wolf finally got what she always wanted, and then lost it, again.

I had fought before, but that was my first kill. So, I was shaken up after killing those wolves, especially in such a brutal manner. Since then, I've discovered that my razor-sharp canines are my best defense and my weapon of choice. But that night, I was a mess. Dylan's strong arms had wrapped around me to calm my frenzied nerves.

Heat rises along the back of my neck as I remember other events of that night—his warm breath flowing over my chilled skin as he nuzzled the sweet spot behind my ear. I remember the pleasure of his soft lips on mine and the gentleness of his touch against my bare skin.

Since Mia took care of Gavin, Dylan and I were left to our own devices. There was not much talking. Except right before I fell asleep in the security of his embrace when he whispered, *I love you, Lux. I always have and always will.*

My heart swelled with joy that night, only to be crushed the next morning when I woke to a cold bed and found him gone. No note, nothing—just gone.

Pulling myself back to reality, I lock my gaze with Dylan's, a fire burning in his eyes. I know he was remembering that night too. And then Caiden's fingertips brush against my lower back ever so gently as he passes behind me. I turn toward him, and a shy smile tugs at my lips.

Dylan abruptly stands, causing his chair to fall over, and he storms outside. Mia raises her eyebrows at his outburst.

Shrugging, Gavin says, "You know he's moody."

"Hey, Cinda," Sammy's voice cracks and a light blush rises to his cheeks. "If you're not doing anything today, I'd love to show you around."

"Sorry, Sammy, but she's booked the entire day," Mia says. She stands and reaches out to me.

I flash a small smile to Sammy. He seems like a nice guy.

"But, she's free tomorrow." Mia winks and the grin falls from my face.

"Great." Sammy presses his hand upon his chest and bows his head. "Then I'll see you tomorrow."

My eyes widen, and I turn to Caiden only to find his brow line pulled taut.

"Mia, if you're going shopping, you should head out soon," Caiden says. "And be back before dark."

"Yes, Alpha Sir," Mia says with a salute.

Caiden shakes his head. "Mia, I'm serious."

"I know, and it reminds me why I find you so cute," Mia says.

I doubt an Alpha wants to be called cute, even if it is by his sister.

Mia gazes at me. "Cinda, are you ready?"

I nod and try to hide my grimace at the thought of an entire day of shopping. Caiden chuckles, and a smile that melts my heart lights up his face.

"Hey, girls." Gavin's eyebrows draw close together, and he clears his throat. "Be careful, okay? There's been more attacks. Please be on guard and be back before dark."

We nod, and to his delight, we each take a cheek and give him a big kiss.

"Yes, Daddy," Mia and I say in unison as we turn to leave.

Stepping outside, Dylan stands on the porch. He turns to face me as I approach.

"Can we talk a minute?" he asks.

I nod and walk down the porch steps away from the others.

Scratching the back of his neck, he asks, "What are you doing?"

Rolling my eyes, I cross my arms. "What do you mean? I'm going shopping with Mia, remember?"

Was that a little harsh? Nah, after the bittersweet memory I just relived, I currently despise the man in front of me. The feeling will pass, it always does. *Stay strong, Lucinda.*

"No. What are you doing with Caiden?" He pinches his lips together after returning the stern tone.

"That is none of your business," I say under my breath, earning me a low growl. *What am I doing with Caiden?*

"Actually, it is," he spits through tight lips.

"How do you figure that?"

"You're my mate. You're MINE!" Dylan growls, his hands shaking with rage.

"Oh yeah? Since when?" I turn on my heels and head toward Mia's nightfire-red metallic Mini Cooper.

After I slide into the passenger seat, Mia speeds away. Through the cloud of dust left in our wake, Caiden appears on the porch. I'm sure he observed my little argument with Dylan.

Oh well, damage control will have to wait.

Out of the corner of my eye, a flash of golden-brown streaks the green grass as it heads toward the woods.

Dylan's wolf.

CHAPTER 10

LUCINDA

"Finally!" Mia squeals as we drive down the road. "I can't believe you're here."

I flash her a wicked grin. "I know, me neither."

What am I doing? I need her help, but I've also endangered her life if Felix finds me here. I shouldn't have come.

Taking her hands off the steering wheel, she waves them around, doing a little party dance.

I roll my eyes and shake my head. "Please keep your eyes on the road and hands on the steering wheel."

Just then, a bat comes out of nowhere, heading for our windshield. Mia grabs the steering wheel, swerves the car, and the creature flies away unscathed. But my stomach and nerves are rattled.

Mia slows the car to the speed limit. "That was crazy."

"Yeah." Is all I can muster. That damn bat creeps me out. *Is it a warning sign?*

"Well, it's about damn time you got here." She adjusts her weight in the seat. "Where have you been? What took you so long? Why didn't you—"

"Whoa! Slow down, one question at a time."

"Fine. What took you so long?" Mia eyes me carefully, the smile dropping from her face. "When Gavin and I left you, we made a deal. Remember? You were going to come join us within a month."

Slouching in my seat, I shift my weight. I don't have the heart to tell her I won't be staying long.

"That was three years ago."

Covering my face with my hands, I groan. "I know. I uh, I, well you see…" The words twist in my dry mouth. *What can I tell her? I can't tell her the truth.*

"I was worried sick. I thought… Do you know what it was like when I returned? What had happened to my pack? My brother—" She slammed her palm on the steering wheel. "Damn it, Cinda! I thought they killed you too!"

Tears begin to stream down her face.

"Hey, I'm okay. I'm a hard nut to crack, remember?" I flash a weak smile as if that will cure everything. "I'm fine, really. I'm sorry it took longer than I said it would. I ran into an old acquaintance."

I change the subject before she asks for more details.

"But what happened to your pack?" I ask. "And what happened with your brother?"

"It was a slaughter," she says in a low, monotone voice. The tears leave wet streaks marking her pale face, and she enters a trance-like state. "Gavin and I arrived home just after it, so we only heard stories. But there was an unprovoked rogue attack. We weren't prepared and suffered many losses, my parents among them."

My stomach churns as I think of my own pack. "I'm so sorry. Do you know why they attacked, or who it was?"

It reminds me of Felix.

"The Elders think they just wanted to kill, and they succeeded. It was a massacre."

"That's not unheard of, but it still sounds so strange, don't you think?"

"I don't know what to think. Caiden thinks there must be more to it, but he hasn't been able to find anything."

"So that's when Caiden became Alpha?" I ask.

She nods and then her eyes light up. The playfulness in her voice returns. "Speaking of Caiden, what's up with you two?"

I've missed her mood swings.

Shaking my head, a few pieces of my hair fall loose and cover the blush that is rising to my cheeks based on the heat in them. "Nothing's up, we just met. He's a good Alpha. Different than most. He's nonjudgmental, caring, and understanding. This pack is very lucky to have him."

"Yeah." Mia's fingers fidget with the leather steering wheel.

"Spill it."

"He, I don't know. He isn't the same. I can't blame him after everything that's happened, but he's put distance between him and the pack," Mia says. "He goes off for days, sometimes even weeks, and turns off the mindlink so we can't reach him."

"Do you know where he goes or what he does?"

"No, but you two seem to be friendly," she says, and I nod, hiding a grin. "That's good. He needs more friends."

I would like to have friends too. Unfortunately, my friends usually die.

"Well, I wouldn't be a good friend."

"And why not? Aren't we friends?" Mia asks, raising one eyebrow at me.

"Yes. You're my best friend," I say. "But he's an Alpha, and I come with a lot of baggage that he shouldn't have to deal with as an Alpha."

"Well, he has a lot of baggage too. Maybe you two can

ship your luggage down the river or something?" She snorts, and I let out a full-on belly laugh. It feels good to relax and be happy.

When I first met Mia, she was traveling alone, looking for her Fated Mate. She had no business being out in the wild by herself. And since I was wandering aimlessly through the country and lonely, I took her under my wing and we soon became best friends.

But when she asked me what I was doing out in the wild alone, I couldn't bring myself to tell her the truth—that I was rejected by my Fated Mate and kicked out of my pack. So I let her believe I was doing the same thing she was. And she never questioned how far I had traveled, nor how long I'd been out on my own.

Thank goodness she's more of a talker.

When I think about how I ended up in this part of the county, all the way to the mountains in the east, it's a mystery. I wasn't trying to follow Dylan, not after that first night we left home. Those rogues he traded me to were rough and vulgar, but after a few days they warmed up to me. I stayed with them for a while and learned as much as I could about taking care of myself as a rogue. That was the first time I met Felix. But eventually, I had to go.

I hadn't a clue where Dylan was, and frankly, I didn't care.

That's why it always amazed me when I would run into him. As often as I stumbled upon him, I started to look at it as a sign that we were meant to be together. I started to think that the feeling I had was a string tied from my soul to his, pulling me along as he ran. Pittsburg, Indianapolis, Kansas City, Denver—and that's the last time I saw him.

Each time I showed up, he would be surprised but then relieved that I was still alive and doing well. Then we'd get into an argument or a physical fight and I'd leave. After a few weeks, that deep pull inside me would return.

It was my compass through the wilderness, which guided me to Mia. I can't be more grateful for having her as my best friend.

The car ride is short, and we arrive in the parking lot of a crowded mall. Mia drives around for ten minutes—the entire time she dodges humans casually strolling by the parked cars —and then she finally finds a place to park.

We head to the main entrance, and Mia asks, "I noticed you didn't have a bag—"

"Right. I left in a hurry."

Mia gives me a suspicious look. "Are you in some kind of trouble?"

I smile. "You can say that."

"Does it involve a male—that acquaintance you ran into? Did you think I missed that tidbit?" She smirks.

I shake my head, and a few loose pieces of hair fall into my face again.

"Is he human?" she asks.

Rolling my eyes, I say, "Oh no. I wouldn't be running from a human."

"Good. Don't worry yourself, I know how to deal with the non-humans." She giggles, but quivers race up my spine. I pray she never meets Felix.

Mia stops and turns to face me. "Okay, we need a plan of attack if we are going to buy you a complete wardrobe and still be home before Gavin and Caiden totally freak out."

"No, I just need a few different pieces," I say, biting my lip. *How do I tell her I won't be staying long?*

She glares at me. "Fine. A few pieces of classic clothing that can be mixed and matched to give the illusion of a full wardrobe. But—"

"One small problem," I say.

Mia raises her eyebrows and puckers her lips, waiting for me to finish.

"I have no money." A small smile tug at my lips and I shrug, hoping that will be the end of it.

"Oh please," she says. "No problem at all. I've got plenty."

Mia spends the next few hours dragging me in and out of every store. While I despise shopping, I haven't done it in so long that I'm honestly enjoying myself. Except Mia insists I try on everything.

I blow the hair that's fallen loose from all the changing out of my face, then I study myself in the mirror. And then I step out from behind the curtain to show Mia.

"That one is perfect!" Mia squeals and claps her hands together in front of her face.

Changing back into my jeans and T-shirt, I grab the clothes and head to the checkout. Mia collects all the bags of previously purchased items and follows.

"All this isn't necessary," I say as we wait in line.

"What do you mean? Of course, it is."

"Do I really need a weekender bag?"

"Yes." Mia hands her credit card to the cashier.

We take a break from shopping and buy lunch in the food court. I'm relaxed among the crowds of humans milling about, ignorant to the fact otherworldly creatures surround them.

It's these creatures, the other wolves, that cause my wolf to perk up and stay alert. All the other wolf shifters stop to speak with Mia, and in turn, she introduces them to me.

And then I smell it. The familiar scent of vanilla and pine. My heart skips a beat and I scan the crowd. My gaze falls upon a brown-haired man, and his hazel eyes stab me with daggers when they meet mine.

Cody.

"Cinda? What are you doing here?" I hear Cody's voice in my head.

Damn. I guess Felix hasn't released me from the mindlink with his band of rogues yet.

The other packs will never view him as a serious Alpha with an established pack, not after what happened to his prior one. It's a good thing I've learned how to be selective with the mindlink and block everyone except Cody.

My heart drops, and waves of nausea ooze through me.

"You shouldn't be here!" Cody screams through the mindlink. "Leave. Now!"

But it's too late. An iron grip tightens on my shoulder.

CHAPTER 11

CAIDEN

WELL, that was entertaining. A grin creeps across my face as I watch Dylan run into the woods. So, he does care. Getting them to accept each other should be easier than I previously anticipated.

Assuming that's what I want.

My stomach tightens.

What am I doing? He doesn't deserve her. But he is her Fated Mate. Everyone deserves a second chance. I should go after him; maybe a good fight is what he needs to kick some sense into him.

As I take a few steps toward the tree line, I reach out to Dylan in the mindlink. He shuts me down.

Ouch! What the hell? A blast of coldness runs through my body, sending chills down to the bone.

"Don't." Dylan's voice echo's in my head. "Let me be. We'll talk when I return."

He is a lot more powerful than he lets on. I grind my teeth against each other as my muscles shake with rage. I've trusted him with my life—with the lives of my pack—and he doesn't have the courtesy to tell me the truth about him and his past.

Granted, I never asked, but he should've mentioned something like this. Is he trying to keep secrets from me and suppress his strength to hide his true power? I thought I knew him, but maybe I don't.

Standing on the porch seething, I say through the mindlink, "Yes, we will talk when you return."

I open the door with such force, the hinges rattle, then I storm into the Pack House and head straight to my office. As I rife through the cabinets, someone coughs behind me.

"What's up, Caiden?" Sammy asks.

"Just looking for the old pack records," I say.

"For something specific? I thought you already knew everything there was to know about our history?" Sammy stuffs his hands into the front pockets of his stonewashed denim pants.

"Not our pack." Taking a deep breath to calm myself, I turn toward a new cabinet and pull the drawer open. "I'm looking for the history of another pack. All of the Alphas before me kept in touch with the other packs, and my father and grandfather kept an extensive collection of detailed notes, journals, and correspondences."

After the death of my father in the massacre, I should have continued communications, but I wasn't in the right state of mind. And the annual Alpha Retreat and Elders Convention has been canceled. The attacks on our pack and several others has spooked everyone.

Sammy steps up beside me. "Okay. What are we looking for?"

"I'm not exactly sure. Anything to do with the Dark Raven pack." I have a feeling something happened in their old pack that forever changed the lives of Dylan and Lucinda.

Maybe Dylan doesn't know about it. Or maybe it is another secret kept and a lie told.

"Is this it?" Sammy asks as he holds up a spiral notebook with *Dark Raven* written across the front in ornate gold calligraphy.

Snatching the notebook from Sammy, I hurry to sit at my desk and stare at the writing on the cover. It is my father's cursive handwriting, and the memory of his death flashes behind my eyelids: him kneeling over my mother's bloody body, crumpled on the dead grass stained red with her blood, his palms covering his face as he wept.

Watching from across the field, I yelled to him. I saw the rogue behind him preparing a fatal blow. *How could he not know he was there, and why was he blocking the mindlink?*

Father looked at me as the claws of the attacker wrapped around his neck. With one swift motion, the attacker severed my father's head from his body. That one look told me everything I needed to know, and it haunts me every day.

This is why I haven't touched these books since becoming Alpha.

Shaking my head to erase the painful memory, I brush my fingers over the word, *Raven*, etched into the center of the leather-bound notebook.

Raven, an omen of death and destruction.

The memory of my parents' final moment flashes again, only this time, I focus on the shiny black raven perched on a nearby tree, watching their demise with an uncanny interest.

My fingers begin to curl, but I relax and start flipping through the notebook. Each page is recorded as a journal entry with a date.

I figure starting at the end will be more beneficial, so I skip ahead to where the writing stops. Interestingly enough, the last entry has no date, but it is titled.

Dylan named next Alpha.

A grunt escapes my lips, and I look to Sammy. "The last entry is about Dylan."

I pull up a chair and motion for Sammy to sit next to me as I begin to read the entry aloud.

"A wandering caravan of gypsies traveled through the territory after the announcement of the Alpha selection. The young pups loved them reading tarot cards, offering palm readings, and all the other fortune telling games. One woman offered something she called 'special gifts.' Fortunately, few people took her up on this offer because the one person that was known to have accepted her gift died instantly. Be wary of the traveling gypsies."

I look to Sammy as I furrow my eyebrows.

"What does a caravan of gypsies have to do with Dylan?" Sammy asks.

"I don't think anything, why?"

Shrugging, he looks down to his feet and a warm glow rises to his cheeks. "I don't know. I guess since the title was about him being named Alpha, I thought maybe there was a connection. Did he ever tell you he was named Alpha?"

"No, he didn't."

"Do you think there could be a connection? Maybe he had his palm read and didn't like what it said," Sammy says.

"Maybe." *Doubt it.*

"The question is, why is he here and not still with the Dark Ravens?" Sammy asks. "He's supposed to be their Alpha, right? So why is he here, as our Beta?"

Because he rejected Lucinda, his Fated Mate, and the Alpha kicked Dylan and Lucinda out. But I can't tell Sammy that. It's not my secret to tell.

Instead, I focus on the journal and flip through a few more pages. Looking for Lucinda's name, I find an older entry. Though, it doesn't give much information, only that her mother died during childbirth when Lucinda was born. The pages before and after this entry have been torn out.

"Hey, do you remember that soothsayer that showed up on your birthday one year?" Sammy asks, interrupting my thoughts.

Turning to glare out the window, I nod. I don't want to think about that night. Soothsayer my ass; she was a fucking witch. A low growl vibrates my throat.

Sammy ignores my mood and continues to talk. "She read my palm but wouldn't tell me what it said. She spat on the floor and threw my hand back at me. What a quack!"

Before I can say anything, Dylan saunters into the room.

"Dylan." I nod with a grunt.

"Caiden. Sammy," Dylan says. He looks refreshed. The run did him good. Unfortunately, I didn't run.

Anger boiling inside me, I ask, "What happened the summer you were named Alpha?"

"What do you mean?" His eyes narrow and his lips curl into a snarl.

"Specifically, with the gypsy," I say.

At the sound of the word gypsy, all expression falls from Dylan's face and his complexion grows pale. For a second, I worry he might faint, but fueled by anger, my sympathy stays hidden.

"Who died?" I ask.

Dylan's eyes swirl black and power radiates off him to ripple through the room.

"Answer!" I pound on the desk and let loose a deep growl. He is strong, but I am stronger. I exercise my alpha dominance over his willpower, and he finally closes his eyes with a sigh.

I study his posture for any indication of subordination, but when he opens his eyes, they are once again pure green.

"My mom," he whispers in a strained tone and hangs his head low.

The corner of my right eye twitches as fear floods my

body. Closing my eyes, I ball my fists so tight that my finger-nails dig into my skin.

"Caiden? Are you okay?" Sammy asks, placing a hand on my shoulder.

Shaking my head, I begin to filter through all the mindlinks in the pack, looking for the person projecting this predominant feeling of fear.

My heartbeat quickens and my stomach twists in knots as I find her.

"MIA!"

Gavin rushes into the room and screams, "Mia!"

My eyes open wide, and I look to Gavin for answers. His breathing is heavy and beads of sweat roll down his temples. He's wide-eyed with a crazed look on his face.

"Let's go," I command, rushing past him and out the door to my black Hellcat. I reach out to Mia in the mindlink, but she doesn't respond.

Gavin, Dylan, and Sammy climb into the car, and they barely have their doors closed when I step on the gas and peel out of the driveway, leaving a cloud of dust behind us.

"Gavin, can you reach her?" I ask.

Glancing in the rearview mirror, Gavin's eyes widen in alarm.

"We need to hurry!" he shouts.

"What's going on?" Dylan asks.

"I'm not sure. She's so frantic her thoughts are all jumbled." Gavin clenches and relaxes his fists.

I taught him that. It is an old trick my dad taught me to help control my wolf in times of stress and anger.

"Is she still with Lucinda?" I ask.

Gavin's eyes are closed and he bites his lip, but he nods.

"Don't worry, man. Lux won't let anything happen to her." Dylan's chin rises in praise as he says her name, a smile slowly spreading across his face.

"It's not Mia I'm worried about," Gavin whispers. His voice is barely audible and full of despair.

My chest tightens and my pulse races. If it's not Mia then it's Lucinda.

I glance at Dylan, who is sitting next to me in the passenger seat. His face is like stone—emotionless—but his fists are clenched tight, and his knuckles are white as hell.

CHAPTER 12

LUCINDA

WHEN I TILT my head toward the hand on my shoulder, the familiar stench of cloves and bayberry permeates the air. At one point in time, I yearned for his scent, but now I dread it with my life.

I take a deep breath, extinguishing the butterflies and settling the queasiness in my stomach. As I exhale, I wink at Mia to calm her nerves. Her eyes are wide, and the distinct scent of fear rolls off her body.

Turning to face the man standing behind me, I let his name roll off my tongue. "Hello, Felix. To what do I owe this honor?"

His deep brown eyes stare into mine. Feeding off power and dominance, he holds my gaze and waits for me to falter.

I will never give in to him.

"Lucinda, what a wonderful surprise," he says in his haughty Queen's English accent. His lips curve up to the right, forming his classic smirk.

Both of us are unwilling to back down.

He begins a deep, rich laugh. "Glad to see you haven't changed. Still so stubborn."

I let lose a deep, gratifying sigh. *I won that round.* Yet, the lightness in my chest doesn't last long. *I wonder what it will cost me in the future.*

"You do realize you're trespassing on pack territory, right?" Mia interjects, her last word catching in her throat as Felix takes notice of her for the first time.

"Am I? Oh, what a shame," he says in a controlled tone. "I don't pay much attention to pack business or territories."

"The Alpha is on his way." Mia's cheeks are bright red, but she does not sway under his harsh glare.

My gaze darts around, looking for Cody. He's standing near the bottom of the escalators a few yards from my location, the same place he was when I first spotted him. But now he starts walking toward us.

"Cody, why are you here?" I ask through the mindlink, careful to block Felix and any of his other misfit wolves that may be lurking nearby.

"We got a tip that someone we're looking for is here," Cody says. "What are you doing here?"

"Running away from Felix, just like we planned." As soon as the words leave my mind, a small grin appears on Cody's face, brightening his creamy hazel eyes.

"To me, it looks like you're shopping," he says with a wink as he passes me to stand next to Felix.

"Felix, you should leave," I say. They need to leave before Caiden arrives—that will only cause trouble for everyone.

"Not yet."

Knowing the drive is only a short distance—and that's driving at the speed limit—I send Cody a message through the mindlink. "Cody, please persuade him to leave."

"Sorry, he's determined. No changing his mind." Cody frowns. "And too late."

"They're here," Cody says out loud.

My heart skips a beat as ripples of power surge through

the air, declaring the presence of the Alpha. From the corner of my eye, I glimpse Caiden and Dylan walking side by side. Their lips are drawn in hard, straight lines, and their eyes are solid blocks of black. They're fighting for control against their wolves.

This is not good.

I've always known Dylan was powerful, but seeing him now, next to Caiden—his tense jaw and broad shoulders—the two could be related. And I sense the power that emits from him. This is really not good.

Being the daughter of an Alpha, I am dominant myself, as is Felix. I can't tell if he is more domineering than Caiden, but he has no control over his power-hungry nature. He once confided in me about a witch that cursed him. I didn't believe it until I witnessed his wrath firsthand.

Having so many formidable wolves in such close proximity will not end well.

"Lucinda," Felix says, bringing me out of my inner thoughts. "Come with me willingly and there will be no trouble."

I search his eyes for anything to tell me that he is sincere, but I find nothing. My time with Felix taught me two things. Felix is not a man to cross, and you shouldn't enter a fight with him if you value your life because you will die.

"No. She's not going with you," Mia says, pointing her finger at him.

"Kitten, we've been through this before. You're a mighty Alpha and you deserve a mate as strong as you—someone like me. Come back with me," Felix coos in a calm voice.

I bite the inside of my bottom lip to soothe my rampant nerves. Glancing to Caiden and Dylan, I notice Sammy and Gavin have joined their flank.

"She's not going anywhere with you," Mia seethes.

There's a flash in Felix's eye a split second before his hand crosses his chest. I step in front of Mia and grab his forearm, successfully blocking his backhand slap.

I have been the unfortunate recipient of those too many times.

As our skin touches, a tingling sensation surges through our bodies, uniting our power as one. I quickly release his arm and stumble backward a step, my eyes wide as I watch Felix.

That's new.

Strong arms catch me from behind before I fall flat on my ass. A warmth spreads across my limbs and settles in my chest at the scent of cumin and fresh-cut grass.

Looking up from under my eyelashes, Dylan smiles down at me. His eyes soften for a moment and then turn cold as he lifts me to a standing position.

"You're trespassing. Leave. Now." Caiden's voice snaps my head to him. He stands a foot in front of us, face-to-face with Felix.

Caiden, I hope you know what you're doing. Be careful, I plead to myself.

"Gladly. I'll just take what's mine and we'll be on our way," Felix says, his eyes glued on me.

Caiden and Dylan both turn and give me a once-over.

While Caiden tilts his head at an awkward angle, watching me, Dylan raises one of his eyebrows and a small smirk forms.

Rolling my eyes, I cross my arms and flash Felix the best evil eye I can conjure. Through the mindlink, I ask Cody, "How many times do I need to say no until he understands— I am not his."

Cody looks to the ground, then flashes a playful grin before saying, "Yeah, I don't think he got that memo."

Well, this will play out one of two ways—neither of which is good for me or the Blood Moone pack. *Sigh.* Why did we have to go shopping?

Chills race through my body, causing goosebumps on my arm.

He doesn't know I found my Fated Mate—not that he would care. And although it's shameful to turn your back on and reject your Fated Mate, I have accepted Dylan's decision and hope one day I will understand his motives.

However, it doesn't mean I want Felix as my mate. No. With the wicked things I've seen him do, I would rather be dead than be bound for life to that controlling and psychotic monster.

CHAPTER 13

LUCINDA

DYLAN SMIRKS, and his eyes gleam with mischief. That look means trouble—I know it all too well.

When we were younger, before he pulled away from me, we would get into all sorts of trouble together in school. Then after school, we would run to our secret hideout in the woods before our fathers could punish us.

The last time we were in our special place wasn't because we were hiding. Well, we were hiding, but not because of trouble. Dylan was nervous; it was right before the announcement of him as the new Alpha—the successor to my dad. We went and stayed there for three days.

Everyone looked for us, and we could hear them calling our names, but no one found us.

Our hideout went against a wolf's natural instinct—only cats climb trees—and we vowed never to tell anyone about our little secret. *Why? Who knows.* The vow was Dylan's idea.

At the time, I thought it was because he was ashamed of hiding and being nervous. But now I wonder if he knew how handy it may become in the future.

Reaching forward, I grab his arm. I need to defuse this

situation before it erupts into something deadly. And by the look on Dylan's face, he's on the verge of losing control.

Think fast and calm his wolf. There are too many innocent bystanders.

"Hey, I'm not his," I say in a soothing voice, studying Dylan's eyes—the pupils restrict and dilate, completely overtaking his beautiful green irises.

He leans forward and whispers in my ear, "I know."

The warmth of his breath on my neck sends chills down my spine. I turn to look at him and my nose brushes against his jawbone.

Sweeping my hair off my shoulder, Dylan examines my neck. With his calloused thumb, he traces the sweet spot where my collarbone meets my shoulder. This is the location where wolves mark their mate to claim them as their own and bond their wolves together forever.

My palms begin to sweat, and my mouth goes dry. My heart quickens as his fingertips brush against my bare skin.

"Calm down, Cinda," Cody says through the mindlink. "And slow your heartbeat. All the wolves within a mile can hear that thumping."

I swallow hard, ball my hands into fists, and focus on slowing my pulse. Dylan gives me a slight nod. *Was it a nod of approval?*

"It would appear she doesn't belong to anyone," he says and turns to show Felix my unmarked neck.

That's right, still unmarked and unwanted. Let's broadcast it to the world. Sigh.

Felix's smile fades to a grimace. "No. Not yet. I have special plans for her tonight."

Dylan clenches his free hand into a tight fist and a low growl penetrates my ears; my shoulders quiver.

Only my wolf can prevent him from the path he's heading down.

I step closer to him, taking his hand in mine and holding it against my chest. Looking up at him, I smile and bring his fist up to my lips, kissing his knuckles. I need his wolf to calm down so Dylan can regain control before he does something stupid and gets us all killed.

"Remember our secret hiding place when we were younger?" I whisper.

Staring at me with the dark, onyx eyes of his wolf, he nods.

"I'll be fine. He won't touch me," I say.

He squeezes my hands one last time before walking away. A low growl rumbles behind me, and I turn to find Caiden watching Dylan walk through the crowd and down the long corridor, heading toward the mall exit.

"She's not going anywhere." Caiden's voice cuts through the silence, projecting his dominance and authority.

I startle at the sound and sway on my feet from the power he's emitting.

"Why do you protect a mere rogue?" Felix taunts.

"Is she what you came for?" Caiden asks.

"You didn't answer my question," Felix says.

"You're trespassing on my land. I'll be the one asking the questions." Caiden's voice is deep and rough.

My breath hitches as Caiden and Felix continues their unrelenting stare. Mia said Caiden has been mentally unstable since the attack a few years ago.

Oh, Caiden, hold it together. Don't let Felix see your weakness.

Caiden clenches and unclenches his hands while the vein running across his temples throb. Felix, on the other hand, with his witty remarks and bemused smile is enjoying himself. He lives for these moments.

Reaching out to Cody in the mindlink, I say, "Cody, please stop this."

Cody steps forward to answer Caiden's questions. "No. She's not what we came for."

"Of course, she isn't the reason we're here. But finding her is a nice surprise. She's a bonus to our successful mission." Felix flashes a wicked smile and winks at me.

"Mission? What is your mission here?" Caiden puffs out his chest.

"We've been hunting a witch." Felix flicks his wrist in the air.

My gaze darts to Felix. "The witch that cur—"

"Yes!" Felix snaps. His eyes narrow into tight slits. "And I'll kill her this time."

"You're hunting a witch?" Caiden asks.

"We picked up her trail a few weeks ago and followed her here."

"I haven't heard any reports of a witch in my territory."

"Witches excel at disguising themselves. Unless you're intimately familiar with their putrid stench, you wouldn't know a witch from a human."

"You've captured this witch?" Caiden asks.

"Yes. And it was on our way out that I picked up the mouthwatering aroma of mint and honey." Felix's gaze roams over my body, and he licks his lips.

"Cinda, he's putting everyone on alert," Cody says through the mindlink.

Damn! Felix is ruthless—he doesn't care who lives or who dies, or about innocent human bystanders. I can't let a fight break out. I take a deep breath and know what I must do.

With a roll of my eyes, I step between the two Alphas who continue their struggle for control of the situation. I place a hand on each of their chests, but curl my fingers in repulsion as they touch Felix's body. "Fine, I'll go with you as long as you leave this Pack alone. Deal?"

A smile spreads over Felix's face, and Mia's whimpers flood my eardrums.

"Wise decision, kitten. Let's go." Felix extends his hand to me.

His long and twisted fingers disgust me, so I turn my back to him and instead search Mia's eyes that are filled with tears.

"Hey, I'll be fine. Don't worry about me, okay?" I flash a grin.

She nods once before burying her face in Gavin's chest.

"Cinda, what are you doing?" Cody says through the mindlink. "You escaped once. He won't let you escape again."

I send back, "I know what I'm doing."

I hope.

CHAPTER 14

CAIDEN

"Lucinda." I grab her wrist to stop her. "You don't have to go with him."

"It's okay. I wasn't going to stay here much longer anyway," she says with a slight shrug.

"I told you I'd protect you." I step forward and close the distance between us.

"I know," she whispers, dropping her gaze to the floor.

Hooking her chin, I tilt her face up to look at me, and her eyes penetrate deep into my soul. I look for something—anything—to tell me what she's thinking.

She rises on her tiptoes and kisses me on the cheek. The touch of her moist lips against my skin sends a frenzy of emotion into my heart.

"Thank you for everything," she whispers.

She turns and walks away with Felix. His arm drapes over her shoulders and stabbing pains shoot through my chest.

Lucinda slaps Felix's arm off her and shoves him away.

"Touch me again and you won't live to see the sunset." I faintly hear her say, and the pain in my heart alleviates ever so slightly.

"Caiden, do something!" Mia sobs behind me.

I stand, frozen in shock. My mind races with emotions, and I can't breathe. The last time I felt this dreadful pain, I lost my mate, Elizabeth. The memories of those dark times rush forward.

During the rogue attack several years ago, after my father was killed, the rogues stopped fighting and retreated. They took a few captives back to their camp for entertainment.

Elizabeth and I were among those captured.

Chained in silver, my wolf was repressed, my strength drained, and the mindlink with my pack was cut off. We were isolated and on our own.

They tortured Elizabeth for several days before she was brutally slaughtered.

They forced me to watch.

Powerless to help her, each whelp, cry, howl, and whimper rang in my ears. The image of her swollen eyes is forever etched into my memory—tiny pieces of my soul shattered with each tear she shed.

The agony that overcame me when she took her last breath sent me into a wild and crazed rage. I'll never know who they were or what they wanted from me because they're all dead.

For days, all I saw was red.

That's when I met Dylan. He found me in the wild, stumbling around aimlessly. We were close to my pack territory, so he guessed I was from there. He took me to the outskirts and awaited one of the guards, who instantly recognized me.

I had not shifted out of my wolf form for days. Dylan said I was a feral creature and had regressed to my wolf's primitive statehood, more or less—a crazed beast.

He doesn't know how right he was.

In the following days, Dylan stayed close, keeping watch over me to ensure I would not snap and attack my own pack members. He didn't trust my members to be able to kill me if needed since I was their Alpha. They would have hesitated, whereas Dylan had no connection and would not blink an eye if it came to that.

During this timeframe, Dylan became an invaluable part of my pack. He showed the courage and leadership I needed in a Beta. Our friendship quickly grew, and I named him as my Beta just as Mia and Gavin returned.

I don't remember the details of the incident that took place before Dylan found me in the wild, but each time Elizabeth's name was mentioned, I froze and zoned out, blocking the mindlink with my pack and sometimes going off for days with no pack interaction.

Sometimes I just need to be alone.

Mia still worries about me—she has ever since we were younger. She worries I suffer from PTSD, post-traumatic stress disorder, and she suggests I see a doctor. But I know it's not PTSD. My mind is shattering from the bond breaking with my mate.

Not everyone can survive the break and keep their mental state in check.

I went to see a doctor, though, to keep Mia happy. He said my subconscious blocked the details from my memory. Probably for the better. I don't want to remember the raging beast I transformed into.

The same heart-wrenching pain I felt after losing Elizabeth washes over me now. I don't know what connection Lucinda and I have, but I am drawn to her, and not just because she is my Beta's mate.

"Caiden?"

I shake my head to erase the dark memories that invaded my mind. My vision clears, and Mia's standing in front of me with tears streaming down her face.

"Oh, Caiden!" She wraps her arms around my midsection,

burying her face in my chest. "You had that look in your eyes again. I thought I lost you for good this time."

"No, I'm still here," I whisper in her ear as I hug her back.

Turning to Gavin and Sammy, I ask, "Where's Dylan?"

"The Pack House." Sammy's voice quivers when our eyes meet.

I untangle myself from Mia's embrace and storm toward the exit, blazing a trail through the crowd and leaving everyone to follow behind me. I climb in the car and Sammy jumps in the passenger seat. Gavin and Mia climb into her car.

"Hey, Caiden?" Sammy asks.

I grunt.

My vision's going bleary, and I begin to see black.

How could Dylan just leave like that? Disgraceful. Even if she wasn't his mate, a Beta never turns their back on someone in need.

"What's going on?" Sammy continues.

"I'm not sure." I let out a breath I didn't realize I was holding.

"Who was that guy?"

"I don't know."

"How did a nice girl like Lucinda get mixed up with the likes of him?" Sammy asks under his breath.

I grip the steering wheel tighter. *Yes, I do wonder.*

CHAPTER 15

LUCINDA

IT PAINED my soul to watch Dylan walk away, but turning my back on Caiden was the hardest thing I've ever done. My heart, which I thought hardened years ago, is ripping through my chest, yearning for the calming bergamot scent I have come to love.

Why does he affect me this much?

My pulse races, and my hands grow clammy. Straightening my shoulders, I hold my head high.

I can do this.

Felix drapes his arm over my shoulders, and a rush of anger pours over me.

"Touch me again and you won't live to see the sunset," I say through gritted teeth.

A low rumble erupts from his chest.

I curl my fists tightly, causing my nails to cut into the delicate skin on my palms.

"Still so feisty," he whispers into my ear. "This will be more fun than I thought."

"Well, one good thing will come out of this," Cody says through the mindlink.

"And what's that?" I ask.

"I can finally get rid of your stuff," Cody says with a wink.

My personal belongings. I thought I'd lost them forever. I could kiss Cody for keeping them for me.

Turning the corner, I steal one last look over my shoulder. Caiden is standing in the same spot where I left him, pale as a ghost. His eyes are glazed over, dazed, and unfocused. Now I understand what Mia means when she said he checks out of reality sometimes and it's eerie.

"Is something going on between you and the Alpha?" Felix asks, nudging my shoulder.

"No," I snap.

"Oh, you two seem rather cozy." Felix raises an eyebrow. "Of course, then there's the Beta too. You appear almost intimate with him."

"We're friends. Period." I pick up my pace and shuffle ahead of him and out of the mall exit.

"What a pity. Both of them appear worthy—"

I snap around to face him. "Leave them alone." My growl fills the silence.

Felix dismisses me with the wave of a hand.

"I mean it, Felix!" I stomp my foot firmly.

Felix tenses and steps into me. The look in his eyes causes the hair on the back of my neck to stand up.

"You will submit to me," he says and grits his teeth.

"Maybe in the next life, but I don't plan on visiting Hell—"

"Let's hope it doesn't go that far."

Felix's eyes turn a darker shade of black than I've ever seen. Our eyes meet, locked in an unwavering stare, neither one willing to submit to the other.

Cody clears his throat. "It looks like the Alpha's got his act back together."

Cody has always been good for breaking the tension between Felix and me. Bless him.

"Yes, it does," Felix says under his breath.

"Interesting company he's keeping, too," Cody says.

"We'll have to pay closer attention to him."

"What do you mean?" I ask.

"Oh, you don't know?" Felix drums his fingers across his bottom lip. A smirk creeps across his face.

I know it's a bait trap, and I'm like a mouse attracted to the sweetness of peanut butter. But I can't help it—I want to know more about Caiden, so I walk right into the trap.

Lowering my gaze to the ground, I show submission. In a soft tone, I say, "No."

"That's a good girl," he chides.

I hold back a growl as Cody holds open the car door for me, and I climb into the back seat.

Felix sits next to me. "Let's just say he's been a little unstable since the loss of his mate. Rumor has it they were Fated Mates."

"What happened?" My shoulders drop and my stomach ties in knots.

"It was rather beautiful—a clever plan I must say. I'm a little jealous I didn't think of it." He stares out the window, and his lips curl into a wicked grin. "If you can't physically dominate your opponent, break them mentally."

"What does that mean?" I ask.

"The things they did to that poor girl are unthinkable... repulsive even for me. The kicker is they made him watch, chained to a tree, bound by silver and powerless to help."

Heat radiates through my body, and a strange sensation spills over my soul. I feel weightless, as if I'm floating in midair.

My heart yearns to soothe Caiden's pain.

I know how ruthless Felix can be, and for him to say

repulsive, then I can only imagine the horrors she endured. I shudder as images of my pack flash through my mind. The most revolting things Felix did to my father—

Power surges through me, rippling over my burning skin.

"You assisted in torturing Caiden and his mate?" Venom drips off my words, sticking to my lips like sap on a tree.

"Oh no, no. Nothing like that." Felix carefully studies my eyes. "I watched from afar, curious to see how the Alpha would react."

"How he would react?" I ask.

After a moment of silence, Felix dismisses my questioning gaze with the flit of his fingers. "Yes. The attackers planned a well-thought-out strike. They were looking for someone or something."

"How do you know that?"

Felix brushes my cheek with his thumb. "Oh, my dear kitten, you are so naive in the ways of our world."

"Naive?" I slap his hand away. *Right.* I roll my eyes and glance at Cody who sits next to Felix. "No, I think I grew up pretty quick on my own."

"That may be so, but you are still ignorant of everything going on in the world around you."

"What is that supposed to mean?"

"You know nothing of the company in which you keep," Felix says.

"What are you talking about?"

Cody slices his hand through the air, cutting an invincible barrier between Felix and I, "The Alpha, his Beta, and the other one—"

Felix raises his hand. "Kitten, you are oblivious to the true nature of the men you surround yourself with. You are also ignorant of the impending war between the Nation and the Coven."

Crossing my hands over my chest, I turn to look out the

window. He is right; I have no idea what he's talking about. The Wolf Council stays out of the Vampire Nation and the Witch's Coven business. What is Felix involved in?

I turn back to Felix. "So, how did he react?"

"What?" Felix asks.

"You said you wanted to see how Caiden would react. So, how did he react?"

"He became crazed with power," Felix says. "And I'll admit, it frightened me. It took all my strength to turn my back on that display of power, but—"

I throw myself at Felix. Craving vengeance and an outlet for my pent-up rage, I raise my fists in balls of burning desire. My fury sees no justice as I strike him over and over again.

The car jerks to a stop, and I fly off the seat and onto the floor.

Why am I so angry at him? Because he watched them torture Caiden's mate and drive Caiden insane.

Felix glowers upon me with solid black pupils; the strength of his power stifles the air around me. Wiping his lip, he peers at the back of his hand and licks the blood.

"You will do good to learn your place," Felix says.

A solid object smashes across my face, followed by intense throbbing pain. There's a sharp stab to my stomach, accompanied by a snapping in my chest.

I hunch over in my seat and grab my stomach as waves of nausea roll through me.

I'm vaguely aware of Felix exiting before two strong arms grab my shoulders, yank me from the car, and drag me across the loose gravel.

Finding my footing, I stagger and try to run, but another blow meets my jaw, causing my head to spin.

Felix strikes my head hard, and I collapse to the ground. He kicks my stomach and face before stomping on my chest.

I gasp and struggle for breath around a loud crack and crunch.

My ribs.

I look up to Felix, and his smile makes the hair on my arms stand tall. Pushing myself to my knees, I grit my teeth against the pain and find my footing. I draw upon the strength of my inner wolf and after a few stumbles, I stand tall, face-to-face with Felix. His mouth is moving, which makes me think he's talking, but I'm not listening. I'm too focused on keeping my pain hidden.

I will never show weakness to him.

Felix steps closer to me, and I spit a pool of blood at his feet. His long fingers wrap around my neck. As he growls in my ear, he lifts me a foot off the ground until my feet dangle below me.

Grabbing at his hand, I gasp for air.

"You're pathetic. Why would anyone fear you?" Felix laughs. "They want you dead. But not yet, I have a better idea."

A stabbing pain shoots through my chest, rendering me unable to move. However, my inner wolf will never allow me to give up, no matter how much pain there is. I claw at Felix's forearm and kick my legs, unsuccessfully trying to wiggle loose.

My senses become hazy. My ears itch, my hearing is fuzzy, and my vision begins to dim. Grayness encloses my line of sight.

I reach out to Cody in the mindlink. He's the only one that is ever able to calm Felix. "Please."

Cody steps forward, whispers something into Felix's ear, and Felix lets go of my neck. My body crashes into the cold earth, and Cody rushes to my side.

"Cinda, you'll be okay." Cody puts his arm around me for support while lifting me to my feet.

A deep pain spreads through every part of my body. Wincing, I raise my head to the sky, and a lone bat drifts overhead.

Damn bat.

Felix walks away, leaving Cody to help me up the porch, down the hall, and into my holding room. Luckily, the dimly lit room isn't too far away. I know the room well; I have spent much time here.

Cody steps away from me. "This will only be temporary. We plan to travel soon."

Perfect. Traveling is the perfect time for an escape.

Cody must see my small smile forming and know what I'm thinking. "Cinda, if you trust me, then please don't do anything stupid."

My smile opens the wounds on my lips, causing fresh blood to pool. I lick the blood away. "Yeah, okay."

If I get the chance, I'm gone.

Cody heads toward the door. Through the mindlink, he says, "Oh, your stuff is in the box under the bed."

The big wooden door closes behind him with a loud clank, signaling he locked the deadbolt.

Guess you're not helping me escape this time.

I take a step toward the small bed that lies in the corner of the room. Purple eyes stare at me from the darkness.

I'm not alone.

CHAPTER 16

CAIDEN

When I pull up to the Pack House, I sense a mass frenzy of fear and confusion. I open the car door to step out and pause to take a deep inhale. As I breathe out through my nose, I release a howl and exit the car.

"Hey, man." Sammy presses a hand against my chest to stop my forward motion. "Stay calm, okay?"

With my fists clenched, I brush past him and stride toward the house.

I make a brief hesitation when I reach the front door, unsuccessfully trying to clear my head and shake the image of Lucinda walking away.

A piercing pain stabs my heart each time she turns her back—a sign she declined the pack.

As I open the front door, my senses kick into high gear, and I swivel my head, searching for any sign of danger. An uneasiness washes over me, and my hands begin to shake. A handful of pack members sit idly in the living room, and their eyes widen.

"Caiden," a young voice says, cutting through the awkward tension hanging in the air.

My fangs flash under my lips as loud noises erupt from upstairs. A familiar scent lingers in the air, and my heart plummets into my stomach. The faint sweetness of mint and honey tease my senses.

I cast a glance down at my hands; they are shaking uncontrollably.

Sammy places a reassuring hand on my shoulder from behind as I close my eyes and clench my fists, wrestling with control of my inner wolf.

"Dylan's gone mad," the young voice whispers to Sammy. "He stormed into the Pack House with a crazed look in his eyes. He's been smashing things in his room ever since."

In a heartbeat, I bound up the stairs and find myself in front of Dylan's room. Pounding once with my fist projects enough power to send the door flying off the hinges. A low growl escapes me as the scene unfolds.

Sabrina is lying on Dylan's bed, half-naked, with a smirk plastered on her face. Dylan jumps to the middle of the room as I snarl.

"Sabrina. Leave," I command.

I do not take my eyes off Dylan, though in the corner of my eye, she raises her eyebrows to Dylan without moving.

"Now!" My voice vibrates across the room, laced with my Alpha dominance.

She flinches, instantly grabs her clothes, and exits the room.

Dylan and I stand a few feet apart. His body is as rigid as a washboard, and his fists are clenched into tight balls, mimicking my own. The scowl on his face only fuels my anger.

"You're pathetic," I spit through clenched teeth.

Narrowing his eyes, he asks, "How so?"

"You walk out on Lucinda"—he flinches at the sound of

her name—"and you run to Sabrina! She won't fulfill the needs your wolf wants—"

"You don't know what you're talking about." Dylan rolls his shoulders back to puff out his chest.

"Oh, I know exactly what's going on between you and Lucinda." As her name rolls off my tongue, an ache pounds in my chest.

Warm liquid runs down my palms. *Damn.* I frantically try to retract my claws before they pierce all the way through my palms.

"It's an old childhood crush, nothing more," Dylan mutters.

"I've seen the way you look at her—the way you watch her as she crosses the room."

Dylan's fist makes contact with my jaw. A throbbing pain erupts, and I stumble to the floor.

He has a nasty right hook.

I slowly stand and square my shoulders, turning to face him.

"She's your mate." I spit a mouthful of blood on the floor.

This time, I'm ready when his fist comes swinging. I meet his arm in the air with my own, successfully blocking the punch. I raise my fist and land a solid hit to his gut with a snarl. He stumbles backward before finding his footing.

Charging me again, his strong legs propel him through the air. My muscles ripple under my skin, and I jump, catching him midair. I wrap my arms around him in an iron grip. I squeeze.

"You think you know—" He chokes and struggles against me as I hold him firm against my chest. He coughs. "She's wrong—"

His eyes start to roll back into his head, and my vision blurs and fades to black...

"CAIDEN!" A voice pulls me out of my trance.

I release Dylan, and he slumps to the floor. He lands on all fours and looks up to me in defeat.

"Stop! Whatever's going on, just stop." Mia storms across the room and buries her face in my chest.

I stand tall and tense, not moving to comfort her.

"What are we going to do?" She cries. "What are we going to do?"

Grabbing her arms to steady her, I say, "Mia, there isn't anything I can do. She wouldn't accept the pack."

Saying these words sends a chill through my body and freezes my heart.

"So that's it? You're just going to leave her with him?" Mia asks.

The thought of leaving Lucinda with Felix pains my soul. My frozen heart shatters into several little pieces.

Rubbing the bridge of my nose with my thumb and index finger, I steady the black void that is threatening to overtake me.

"I can't endanger the pack," I mumble as my shoulders slump and my head falls forward, resting my chin on my chest.

"There isn't anything else we can do?" Mia asks.

"Mia, there isn't anything in the world I want more than to go after them. But I am the Alpha, and my duty is to protect the pack. Lucinda is not part of the pack."

Why is that so strange to say? The words stick in my mouth as if they were peanut butter.

"That's right, she's just a rogue." Sabrina's voice echoes in the silent room from her position eaves dropping at the door. "And if you were to endanger your pack by running off after her, then—"

"Who the hell do you think you are?" Mia rushes toward her in a fit of rage. "Cinda isn't just a rogue, you b—"

Gavin grabs Mia's hand before it makes contact with Sabrina's face.

"Mia, stop. Cinda wouldn't want you fighting like this," Gavin says.

"Sabrina, I thought I already told you to leave," I say. "If I have to tell you again, you'll regret it." She has some damn nerve and I'm at my wits end. She is becoming bolder every day. Does she think I don't notice? I need to watch her more closely.

Sabrina's smirk fades into a pout, and her eyes open wide as she attempts to mimic sad puppy-dog eyes and fails miserably.

"Out," I say through the mindlink and flare my nostrils, holding in a snarl.

"Fine, I'm leaving. But mark my words, if this pack becomes the target of a psycho rogue wolf, then—"

"Then what, Sabrina?" Dylan thrusts his fists down by his side and jerks his attention to her.

"Are you threatening the Alpha?" Sammy's voice overlaps Dylan's.

With one last look to me, Sabrina leaves the room, but I'm not satisfied she's left until the front door slams and her car peels out of the driveway.

Mia's gaze wanders the room until it lands on Dylan.

"You!" Mia storms over to him. "What do you know of Felix?"

"Nothing." Dylan shrugs.

Mia's hand is quick, and she hits Dylan with a thundering smack.

"What's that for?" Dylan rubs his reddened cheek.

"For Cinda," Mia huffs. "I don't know what happened between you two that night, but I've never seen her look so vulnerable. In the morning when you were gone, she was—"

"What does that have to do with anything?" Dylan snaps.

"When I met her, she was running from something or someone. I don't know who, or what, but I have a feeling it was Felix." Mia's face turns a slight shade of red.

"You don't know that. It could have been anyone," Dylan says.

"You left her back then, just like you're leaving her now!" My little sister begins to tremble with rage.

"Mia, why do you think it's Felix she's running from?" I ask. Placing my hand on her shoulder, I apply pressure, allowing my Alpha to calm her wolf. "He's an arrogant SOB, and I don't like him, but I don't think Lucinda would've gone with him if—"

Mia turns to face me; her eyes are glazed over. She's looking at me, but not truly seeing me. I brush away a tear that rolls down her cheek.

"Mia?" I ask in a soothing tone.

"You...you..." She sniffles several times. "You didn't see her face when he first approached us in the mall."

She falls into my chest. This time, I wrap my arms around her, holding tight, providing the comfort she needs and taking comfort for myself as well.

"What do you mean?" Dylan asks.

"She paled—white as a ghost," Mia whispers. "It wasn't long before she hid it. But I saw the fear in her eyes. I've never seen her look so vulnerable."

The thought of Lucinda stepping forward to leave with Felix when she's terrified of him sets my skin on fire. Why would she risk her life like that? I grunt at the mere idea of him touching her.

"There is one way." I turn my attention to Dylan.

"No," he says with a clenched jaw.

"No?" I boom. "You're willing to leave her with the likes of Felix?"

"She's strong and clever. She'll be fine." Dylan rubs the back of his neck.

My grip tightens around Mia's waist, and a slight yelp escapes her lips.

"I'll go." Gavin's voice enters the room, catching us all by surprise.

Mia runs to him, flinging herself into his arms. A strong yearning for mint and honey washes over my body.

I give Dylan my Alpha stare. "He can't go alone."

CHAPTER 17

LUCINDA

"Hello, my child," a gravelly voice says. The older woman with tan leathery skin sits on the floor a few feet from me. Her hair and clothing remind me of a nomad, but her purple eyes tell me she is anything but human.

She looks vaguely familiar. Though, with my blurred vision and diminished visibility, almost anyone would look familiar.

"Who are you?" I ask, my voice rough and scratchy.

"Have we met before, my dear?" she continues as if I did not speak.

"No, I don't think so." I rub my throat, and it burns as I swallow.

Her deep piercing gaze makes my palms sweat, and I shuffle my feet to calm the eerie sensation coursing through my body from her scrutiny.

"I remember all my visitors. But you, I do not remember," the woman says.

"Right," I mutter and head over to the bed. She doesn't seem like a threat.

Kneeling next to the bed, I look under it and pull out an

old canvas-covered stateroom trunk. I unlatch the lid, then open it slowly and peer inside.

My heart warms when I find my hobo sling bag. I have always been fond of this bag. It was the only birthday present I received when I turned nine years old. However, I couldn't be certain about why it carries so much importance—whether it's because this is the last gift I ever received or because Dylan gave me the present.

That is something to ponder another time.

Either way, I've come to find this bag the perfect companion for my lifestyle. Its versatility lends it to limitless options. And since it is soft, flexible, and washable, it's easy to use as a human but also to tote around in wolf form. I can carry it in my mouth, or even with a little struggle, I can sling it over my neck.

Emptying the contents of my bag, I find my wallet, smartphone, and favorite lip gloss, in addition to a few other pieces of clothing. I grab the phone and press the on button, but nothing happens. *Of course.*

While I haven't missed my phone in the past few weeks, in a time like this, it would be helpful since I have no mindlink with Dylan, Mia, or Caiden. Not that the mindlink would help even if I did; the distance is far too great.

My shoulders sag as I let out a deep sigh.

"This is peculiar because you have the aura of my touch upon you. And yet we've never met," the woman muses and begins to giggle.

I turn my head to look at her, and my eyes narrow. The way she is crouched in the corner and strumming her fingertips together gives the appearance of someone that recently escaped from a mental institute.

A creepy sensation I can't explain rushes through the air, and goosebumps ripple on my forearms.

My eyes dart around the room. I need to get out of here. *I can only imagine what Felix will do to me, and this woman gives me the creeps.*

Shivers prick my skin like shards of ice stabbing me.

I pull myself to my feet and stumble around the room, looking for a way to escape. Standing up too long takes its toll and causes my head to throb with a dull pain. I lick the dried blood off my lips, close my eyes, and hope the room will stop spinning soon.

The old woman mutters, "You have an uncanny resemblance to—"

"To whom?" I ask, keeping my eyes closed and resting my head against the cold wall.

"Raven."

Upon hearing my family name, my eyes shoot open. But my vision is blurred and it takes a moment to focus.

The woman stands across the room from me with perfect posture and her head held high.

"What did you say?" I ask.

"You are the daughter of Raven, are you not?" She speaks with more strength behind each word and takes a step toward me. "No need to answer, I understand now."

She sits back down.

"Understand what?" I ask.

"Everything." The woman closes her eyes as if she were sleeping.

Whatever. This woman is a lunatic.

"You're not planning to leave us so soon, are you dear?"

I glare at her.

"Felix won't let you escape so easily."

That's what you think.

"And I'm sure your brother is excited to know that you're still alive—"

"My brother? I think you have the wrong person."

"I know exactly who I'm speaking to, Daughter of Cornelia."

"Well then, I am sorry to share the bad news, but my brother died at birth." I once asked my father why pages were missing in the Pack Journal, and after a long pause, he simply said, *'You had a twin brother who was stillborn, and he killed your mother.'* He never mentioned it again, so I never asked more questions.

"Yes, I heard that as well," she says. "But it's—"

"Hold your tongue, witch!" Felix's tone demands my attention as he stands in the open doorway, his Alpha declaring his presence in the room.

"Son of Tiergan, so nice of you to join us. I was just catching up with this dear child. I must say, I'm a little surprised to see her still alive." The woman's words linger in the air.

"Enough. Out." Felix demands, and the witch hobbles across the room. Felix follows, slamming the door behind him.

The flame of the single candle in the room flickers from their movement and I watch the shadows dance on the floor. The woman's words echo in my mind. *Still alive.* I gulp and wince at the raw, dry pain throbbing in my throat.

If Felix wanted me dead, he would've killed me many times over. Although, he did say someone wanted me dead, right? Cringing as I swallow again, I try to remember what he said during his attack.

He has a better idea.

I'm not going to sit around and wait to find out what that idea is.

My gaze searches the empty room. I've been here before in this exact situation. The last time I escaped, I went home to my father for protection.

I will not make the same mistake again. As much as my

wolf yearns for the safety in the spicy scent of bergamot, I will not put Caiden and his pack in danger.

Tracing the stone wall with frantic fingers, I search for the hidden passage. The last time I was held here, it took weeks to search for a way out, but I finally found the key. I shake my head and give one last push against the marked stone in the wall so that a small passageway reveals itself. This historic house was used in the Underground Railroad.

Thank you, history channel.

I reach up to climb into the little space. Pain washes through my chest, and I wince, grab my ribs, and fall to the floor. I should remain still so my bones heal properly, but time is not a luxury I have at the moment.

Shifting during the healing process can really mess up your bone structure too, so as a common rule, we stay human while we heal. Unless we were injured as a wolf, then depending on the extent of the injury, it may be best to remain a wolf to heal.

Dim light peeks from the tiny opening above me, and I pull myself up the wall, groaning as I climb into the compact location. I know I'll have to re-break my ribs to set them properly, but that can wait. Sometimes the rapid healing ability is a blessing, but right now it's not.

I shimmy on my belly through the dark tunnel. The thick air sits heavy in my chest and I choke back a cough. Beads of sweat drip down my temples, and the ground is damp against my fingers. My shoulders brush against the wall and stir up layers of dust and I sneeze.

As I crawl farther, the narrow space widens, opening into a larger tunnel. Finally, I am able to stand and drag my body along the wall of the corridor, heading to freedom.

And the woman said it wouldn't be easy.

My lips turn into a smile, but the joy doesn't last long. I muffle a cough as the foul, stale air fills my lungs.

I reach the last obstacle that keeps me from escaping Felix's captivity. The iron door.

From past experience, when opened, this door creaks loud enough to alert an army. My fingers quiver as I touch the rusty door. The coolness is moist against my hands. I take a deep breath and slowly press upon the door, careful to only open it a few inches before the squeaking begins.

As I squeeze through the narrow opening, the door slips an inch further open and creaks. Voices drift in the air. *Are they looking for me already?*

My heart pounds and I quickly slip through the remaining doorway. Taking a quick glance around, shadows of men appear just around the corner. I bit my lip and dart across the open field to the nearby treeline.

Once in the protection of the forest, I look around and wait for my eyes to adjust. I came from pure darkness into a dark forest; however, the full moon provides some light here. Raising my face to the sky, I bask in the glowing radiance and power.

The urge to howl simmers deep within me, but I hesitate, not wanting to give away my location. I am exhausted from the climb out, and my body is worn from the beating I took earlier. I need to rest.

My wolf blood provides the ability to heal quickly, but the damage that's been done by Felix—a very powerful Alpha —will take a few days to completely heal.

I hobble to the nearest tall tree and climb. Each movement I make takes all my strength in order to move from tree to tree, concealing myself in the thick branches.

Eventually once it's safe enough, I relax my tense muscles and allow myself to acknowledge the searing pain rolling through my body. I've used the strength of my inner wolf to compartmentalize the pain up until this point. But now the adrenaline is wearing off.

I settle down on a sturdy branch high above the ground, am drift off to sleep—or rather, I pass out from exhaustion and excruciating pain.

My wolf stirs inside me, begging me to wake. A hushed voice calls my name, and my heart flutters as I inhale the familiar scent—cumin wraps around me, enveloping me in his embrace.

"Lux, please wake up." Dylan's voice cracks, and a tear drips onto my cheek.

CHAPTER 18

CAIDEN

"CAIDEN," Mia warns in the mindlink, "Sabrina is here."

I pound my fist on the office desk, and my papers ruffle from the force. This morning I received a request from Sabrina to meet with the Alpha on official pack business. At a time like this, she wants a meeting.

Swiping at the table with my forearm, I send all my paper and books crashing to the floor.

There's a knock on the office door.

"Caiden," Mia says.

"Don't bother him. I'll let myself in." Sabrina pushes the door open and charges past Mia.

I nod to Mia, and she closes the door behind Sabrina.

"What do you want, Sabrina?"

Her lips curl into a brilliant smile. "As the pack liaison—"

"The what?"

"The pack liaison." Sabrina slinks across the room and drops a stack of papers on my desk. And then she slides into the leather chair in front of me.

Under the desk, I clench my fists. "We don't have a pack liaison."

She raises her hand to cover her mouth, and her eyes widen. "Oh, haven't you heard?"

Miss Drama Queen at her best. My gaze bores a hole into her dark pupils.

"I'll take that as a no," she says. "If you would've attended some of the monthly pack meetings, or the weekly council meetings—"

I stand and lean over the desk toward her. "I have my reasons."

"Yes, yes. Dylan always gives your excuse of the day. And since the Alpha isn't available during these said meetings, they elected a pack liaison. They thought it would be easier for me to meet with you than for everyone to try to get an audience."

My nostrils flare and a growl escapes. Why is this the first I'm hearing of it?

"It's your fault." Sabrina stands and lounges on the edge of the desk, causing me to take a step back. She will think I stood down from a power struggle, but she couldn't be further from the truth. I will never give in to the likes of her.

Crossing my arms over my chest, I ask, "What is?"

"The position you're in."

"And what position is that?" My inner wolf is not happy. It's taking all my concentration to resist the surging power he's emitting.

"Caiden," she says, and her eyes soften. She walks around the desk, closing the distance between us, and she places her hand on my forearm. "You're losing your pack. Ever since Eliza—"

"Don't ever say her name." I jerk my arm from her touch.

"You haven't exactly lived up to the Alpha we thought you would be," she says.

"I protect the pack, strengthen our borders, train

warriors, and patrol the borders." I clench my teeth. "What more would you have me do?"

"You don't socialize or communicate—"

"I didn't realize that was a requirement."

"It is." Her smile is haunting, and her tone is low yet stern. "Never underestimate what socializing and communicating with the pack members can achieve."

Did she just give me a warning?

Folding my arms over my chest, I ask, "Is this the pack business you came to discuss?"

"No. That was just food for thought." She slides the stack of papers toward me. "Here are the grievances from the pack members."

I take the papers from her and flip through the several dozen pages.

"And a suggestion, if I may?" she asks. "Each member that took the time to write a grievance will expect a timely written response from the Alpha himself."

I hold back a growl that threatens to surface. As much as I don't like Sabrina and dislike her new pack position, she's right. I should make this my number one priority.

"Thank you, Sabrina. I will begin reviewing them immediately. Is there anything else?"

"One last thing," she says.

Lifting my eyes from the stack of grievances, I give her my full attention.

"I can't find Dylan. Do you know where he is?" she asks.

"He's running an errand. He'll be back soon."

Her eyes harden and her pupils dilate. "I noticed that rogue is gone too."

"And?" I drop the grievances on my desk and roll my shoulders. *She will not portray dominance in my presence.*

A snarl slips from between her glossy ruby-red lips.

"Sabrina, leave." A rumble billows in my chest.

She casts her eyes down and turns to leave.

Once the door closes behind her, I take a deep breath, walk across the room to the window, and gaze out into the forest. After several seconds, or maybe it's minutes—every day it seems I lose track of more and more time—I return to my desk, ready to review the stack of grievances.

The door creaks open, and I glare at the intruder. I drop the letter I was reading, but nod for Elder Charles to enter.

I'll never get these damn things done.

With a deep breath, I clench my fists several times. "Elder Charles, to what do I owe the pleasure of this visit?"

The old man slips into the room and stands across the desk from where I sit. He extends a courteous bow. "Alpha."

"Please sit."

"No. This will be short."

Elder Charles is one of the oldest members of the pack, and he knows our history better than anyone. He was good friends with my grandfather, though that relationship didn't travel down to my father. He and my father never agreed on anything. This is the first audience I've had alone with him since becoming Alpha, and I'm already annoyed.

I offer a curt nod for him to proceed.

"You're playing a dangerous game."

"I'm not playing any game."

"The rogue—"

"What about her? Have you learned something of interest?"

"We've been through all our records, both pack and personal, as well as memories, notes—"

"Get on with it."

"We shouldn't get involved."

"Involved in what exactly?"

"The rogue's life."

"Why not?"

"The Blood Moone pack has never been an ally with the Dark Ravens. We have no allegiance. We owe her nothing."

"I appreciate your council, and I am fully aware of the situation."

"Don't let your personal feelings interfere with your duties as the Alpha of this pack, or you may find yourself…"

"Are you threatening me?" My biceps flex as I clench my fists.

"You're introducing the potential for a power struggle. Do you realize that? Either between her and your Beta or even with you." He huffs out a large breath.

"Yes, she is powerful with Alpha potential. But—"

"But what? But nothing! Do you trust her?"

"Yes."

Elder Charles throws his hands in the air and tilts his head to the ceiling. "You're a damn fool. I pray to the Moon Goddess to save us all."

My chest tightens and I roll my shoulders forward. "I think we're done here."

Elder Charles turns and steps out of the room.

I take large strides to the speed bag in the corner and give it hell. After successfully letting out my frustration at the day, I return to my station at the desk and pick up a pen and another grievance letter about how bad of an Alpha I've been.

"Hey, Caiden, do you have a minute?" Sammy's voice echoes through the empty room.

I drop the pen onto the hard wooden desk, and I glance up to find Sammy standing in the doorway of my office.

"Hey Sammy, come on in and take a seat." I rub my left temple with my fingertips.

Sammy sits on the edge of his seat and keeps his eyes cast down. "Caiden, I feel a pull. I think my mate is close."

I lean back in my chair and cross my arms behind my head. *I know where this is going, and I don't like it.*

"Caiden, I want to follow the pull. I want to go find my mate," Sammy says with wide eyes.

I run my hands through my hair and massage the nape of my neck. "Sammy, you are one of my closest and most trusted friends. I want nothing more than your happiness. But right now, I need you here to help protect this pack. When—"

"When what, Caiden? When Dylan returns, then what?"

"Then maybe—"

Sammy throws his hands in the air. "Maybe? Then maybe I can go? You'll just have another reason—another excuse—for why it isn't the right time."

"It's not like that and you know it," I say through my teeth. But it is. Sammy could have left years ago, but I always thought of a reason for him to stay.

"Whatever. I get it." Sammy stands with such force that his chair tips over. "Thank you for your time, Alpha."

The way he says *Alpha* stabs a dagger deep into my soul. However, Sammy will get over it, eventually. His wolf is hurting and angry, but Sammy will survive.

After he leaves, I stare out into the forest once more.

"Caiden," I hear the soft voice of Mia calling me from the other side of the door. I knew it would only be a matter of time before she wanted to speak to me too.

"Caiden," she says again, opening the door this time. "They found her…but Gavin said it's best they camp tonight and journey home tomorrow."

My nose twitches. "Why are they camping? They should get as far away from Felix as possible. I don't trust him."

"Well, if you would open your mindlink, you would know why." She crosses her arms, giving me the look only a sister would give an Alpha.

I growl. "I'm not questioning the judgment of your mate, I just think they'd be safer back on pack territory and under our protection."

"Well, she, um…" Mia licks her lips and blinks back tears. "She's not walking so well. She needs to rest and heal a bit before traveling."

Why does hearing that pain me so much? Remorse that I allowed her to go with Felix, and guilt that I'm not the one to save her fill me. I regret I was not able to protect her from this. It is like—

No, I cannot go there.

But the images of Elizabeth are dredged up.

My shoulders roll back, and my chest rises with the intake of a deep breath. I begin to shift.

Brushing past Mia, I head for the back door in a hurry. I need the solace of the woods tonight; it will be a long night of hunting to satisfy my cravings, which will never be appeased.

CHAPTER 19

LUCINDA

"Hey," I croak as I open my eyes. "You…you came for me?"

At this moment, looking at Dylan, I see my best friend from childhood sitting next to me in the tree.

Lurking in the treetops, high above everything else below, I feel like we are in our secret hiding place again, spending endless nights hiding, gazing at the stars, and talking about anything and everything until we fall asleep. I miss my best friend and the old days of carefree nonsense.

But I can't stop a nagging feeling. I should be happy that Dylan, my mate, came for me, but my heart skips a beat at the thought of the tantalizing scent of Caiden. Even though I didn't want either of them to come, part of me wishes it were the Alpha here with me now.

What is wrong with me?

"Don't think too much of it." Dylan turns away from me and wipes his eyes. "I didn't volunteer. Caiden ordered me."

The sound of his name brings a warmth rushing to my cheeks, and I divert my gaze before Dylan notices.

After a moment of silence, I turn back to him and whisper, "What happened to us?"

Staring straight into his eyes, he shrugs and looks away.

"We were so close, until your mother—"

"Stop!" he snaps, "I told you, things change."

"They didn't have to. I would've been there for you, whatever it was you were going through. You didn't have to go through it alone."

"Yes, I did," he whispers.

"Dylan." I reach up and gently brush the backs of my fingers down the side of his cheek. A slight tingle rush through them.

"Don't." He removes my hand and places it back down at my side. "Can you walk?"

I nod but wince as I try to move.

"How did you find me?" I ask, as Dylan wraps his arm around me and helps me slide down the tree.

"Gavin's an excellent tracker," he says with a sly grin. "But like most wolves, he doesn't like heights."

There's a faint snicker as our feet land firmly on the solid ground.

"What?" Gavin says with a shrug and a crooked smile. "There was a distinct burnt tire aroma that lingered in the air from Felix's car. It was intoxicating."

His sense of smell and tracking ability never ceases to amaze me. But I guess when you are raised in the wild, your senses aren't dulled by humans. At least, that's what Gavin told me once.

"Cinda, get over here!" A huge grin crosses Gavin's face.

He extends his arms out to me but before he engulfs me in his trademark bear hug, I throw up my arms to stop him.

"Go easy on me," I whisper as I rub my ribs.

Gavin's eyes soften and the smile falls from his face. He gently drapes his arms around me.

I let his comforting smell of leather and tobacco wash

over me. *Sigh.* I relax and take small comfort in the strong arms of a dear friend, my body sagging in Gavin's embrace.

I am safe with these two here, though I know it won't be long before Felix discovers I'm gone.

"Thanks for coming for me," I mumble into his chest.

Stepping back, he holds me at arm's length by my shoulders, and his scrutinizing gaze examines my body.

"I'm fine, I'll heal." I attempt a weak smile.

"Oh, Cinda—"

"Stop!" I hold up my hand. "I said I'm fine, so leave it alone."

"We need a place to camp tonight," Dylan says, clearing his throat. "You'll walk better in the morning after some sleep."

Hopefully, tonight I'll heal enough to walk comfortably since I don't want to shift yet.

"I'll go see if I can find a safe place to camp for the night," Gavin says.

Dylan and I squat down near a bush and wait. After a few minutes, Gavin returns.

"I found the perfect place," he says. "It's not too far from here."

Gavin and Dylan help me hobble over to this little gem of a place. It's beautiful—a little opening tucked away in the earth on the underside of a hill. The side of the hill has eroded over time, but the roots of the large tree on top remain intact and create a secret dwelling underneath.

"Go on you two, I'll take the first watch." Gavin motions to Dylan and me. He walks a few feet away and disappears behind a tree.

I groan, realizing he'll be talking with Mia tonight. I will have to do serious damage control with her tomorrow.

Shaking my head, I sit down on the cold, damp earth and watch Dylan sit across from me. He half reclines against the wall, and I try to lie down. This is a small shelter, so when I lie down, I end up near his feet. When I begin to toss and turn on the hard ground, and groan at the sharp pains of discomfort, Dylan lets out a deep sigh.

"Come here." He holds his arm open for me to snuggle next to him.

Just the reaction I was hoping for.

When we were younger, our families went camping together, and I could never sleep on the hard ground—ironic for a wolf, I know. So, I always snuggled into Dylan's chest and slept as sound as a baby.

Sitting next to him, I concentrate on slowing my pulse. It's been a long time since we've been so intimate and civil with each other—and alone. My head finds the soft spot on his chest, and his arm wraps around me, creating a warmth on my arm where his hand rests.

"Thank you," I whisper.

His body tenses underneath me. "I'm only doing what is expected of my position as a Beta."

"So that's it. We aren't even friends?" I ask. After a few moments of silence, I sit up and look him straight in the eyes. "Surely we can still be friends, after all that we've been through."

"No, we shouldn't be. It wouldn't be good for either of our wolves. They'd be frustrated all the time."

"I can handle it, can you?" I challenge.

"It's not just about handling it," he starts.

"Then what exactly is it? We were best friends one day, then the next you threw it all away. You turned your back on me as if you were rejecting me right then, almost as if you knew—" A burning question pops into my head.

"Don't be silly. That's too young to find your mate," he scoffs.

"And yet you pushed me away, just like you did when you found out."

"Coincidence. If I knew before it struck, that would be like cheating fate, right?" He cocks an eyebrow at me.

"How would that be cheating fate? Unless you found out early and did something to alter it." I say through a yawn. "But we all know you can't alter who your mate is, right?"

"Go to sleep, Lux." He guides my head back to his chest.

"Good night, my friend." I snuggle into his arms.

"We are not friends," he says, which brings a smirk to my lips.

"Then we agree to disagree on the matter of friendship." I yawn again.

"Sleep," he says again, and a faint chuckle rumbles in his chest.

Waking in the morning, a smile creeps across my face before I open my eyes. I linger in Dylan's warm embrace, trying to remember the dream that left me feeling lighter than air.

I open my eyes and look up at Dylan. His eyes are fully dilated—jet black. I draw a sharp breath. *This is not good.*

"Whoa! Dylan, calm down." Slowly sitting up, I move out of his embrace.

"What's going on with you and Caiden?" He growls.

"What?" My cheeks burn as my dream pours back into my memory—flashes of Caiden.

"You were whispering his name in your sleep." He snarls and leans toward me.

"Umm, I was? I don't know." I stand up and take a step away. How embarrassing. I hope he doesn't tell Caiden.

Dylan curls his lips and let's loose a low growl. "How close are you two?"

"Not that close," I say, taking steps backward as far as I can go.

"Then why are you dreaming about him?"

"I don't know! Something about him makes me feel…safe."

"SAFE?" He roars. "And I don't?"

"Well, you haven't really given me any reason to—"

"I'm your mate!" Standing up, he rushes toward me, pinning me to the back of our little hideaway.

"Since when?" I growl.

He lifts my chin, and I look up into his eyes. I clench my jaw, bracing for a fight.

Dylan leans in close, nuzzles my neck, and sniffs my hair. Pausing over my shoulder, he kisses the sweet spot. My heart starts pounding in my chest, and little tingles shiver up and down my body.

Is this it? Is he going to claim me?

"Mine," he growls.

There's a slight quiver in my legs as his lips graze the sweet spot again.

"Oh yeah? Prove it." I let out a breath I didn't realize I was holding. *Do I want this? Do I honestly want Dylan?*

He starts to shake, and his fists ball up. He's fighting for control; I shouldn't provoke him, but he agitates me, which makes me push him harder.

"Never." He steps back and walks away from me.

CHAPTER 20

CAIDEN

SITTING ON THE BACK PORCH, I stare down at my hands. *Blood.*

I close my eyes, resting my elbows on my knees, and my head hangs low. I try to remember the events of last night. My muscles ache from the rage that coursed through my body. It's been a while since I lost total control like that.

What have I done?

I slam my hands down on my knees and curse the soothsayer, or whoever she was, all those years ago. She waltzed into our camp on the eve of my twelfth birthday—the year I was to be officially named the next Alpha. She begged my father to allow her to present me with a gift. He hesitated at first, but eventually gave in.

The gift she wanted to give me was a gift of my choosing. She tried to entice me with thoughts of power, strength, and love. I refused. I didn't want anything given to me, I wanted to make my own future.

She became frustrated, but she continued relentless offerings. After speaking with me for a while, she was able to lure out my deepest and darkest secret: my ultimate fear—failure.

My father and grandfather were strong leaders, and I

didn't want to fail them, nor our pack. I feared that I wouldn't fill the shoes of the great Alphas before me. That I would fail my family's legacy.

Using this knowledge, she inflicted her gift—as she called it—though it is more like a sickness.

She instilled within me a strength equal to no other—greatness I couldn't have fathomed in my wildest dreams. But with most things, it came with a price. The price for this gift is that I can't control the inner beast that rages inside me.

When anger builds up, it needs an outlet. My mind loses consciousness and 'it' takes over my feral side. *The beast.*

The first time it happened I was fourteen, and to this day, the memories still haunt me. I killed a human hiking in the woods.

Grief overtook my emotions when I realized what I'd done. I couldn't remember the events, but my body was caked with blood, much like it is now. A few days later, one of our patrol scouts found the maimed body in the woods. He was a young man not much older than me.

My parents were grateful one of our own discovered the body and not a human. That would've only complicated the situation.

The body was disposed of with no trace, but in the human world, he is still an open missing person case.

My dad blamed it on the Alpha growing within me, though I knew better. I locked myself up for months after that, working on self-control. Since then, the only time I've lost total control was when the bond broke with Elizabeth.

Until last night.

Opening my eyes, I scratch at the caked blood that covers my hands, willing myself to calm down.

Images of Elizabeth flash into view. Her limbs hanging limp, dripping with blood. The deep gashes across her flesh and the parts of her insides that should never be seen oozing from her body like poison. Her swollen face, and her hollow eyes pleading to me for help.

I felt every pain they instilled upon her and the lacerations that penetrated her delicate skin. Every cut, gash, and mark they left on her perfect body. I was helpless to do anything but watch as they slaughtered her piece by piece with excitement in their eyes, getting a thrill with each of her cries.

My muscles quiver, and the darkness nears. Curling my fists into tight balls, I fight against the pull. *The beast wants out.*

"Hey," says a soft voice say.

The door behind me opens, and I get a rush of mint and honey. I freeze in place, unsure of what to do.

I can't let her see me like this.

In the corner of my eye, Lucinda tosses something on the ground inside the mudroom before the door closes behind her.

"Umm…thank you," she whispers, placing her hand on my shoulder from behind.

I flinch at the touch, but it provides a calmness that is much needed. Still, the beast within me is vying for control.

Her hand grazes down my arm as she sits next to me on the porch.

I steal a glance in her direction. Welts remain on her body. *Shit.* I should never have let her leave with Felix. Elizabeth, Lucinda, the lines are blurring, and my strength is diminishing. I'm losing the fight for control.

I stand, careful to keep my back to her, ready to bolt at a moment's notice. "You have nothing to thank me for."

She steps in front of me, but I can't bear to look at her. I can't handle seeing the marks left on her body. Her hands reach for mine. My pulse begins to race, but at the same time, tranquility wraps around me as our skin touches. It is a sensation I've never known.

Strange.

I embrace her hands with my own and gently lift them to my lips to place a kiss on her knuckles.

"Lucinda, please forgive me. I told you I'd protect you, and I failed," I whisper, keeping my head hung low.

The dried blood still clings to my hands, and I cringe. My mind races with all the possibilities for what happened last night.

"Hey." Her soft voice carries through my dark thoughts. "It's been a few days since I've shifted and run, are you up for it?"

"A few days?" My heart pounds at this new information.

"Yes, four and a half days to be exact—since Dylan and Gavin found me," she says.

Shit. The beast has been loose for four days, running wild doing who knows what hellish activities.

"Yes," I manage to say through my clenched jaw. The realization that it's been more than just one night since I lost control hits me like a brick. I'm on the verge of losing it again.

I shift and dart into the woods without waiting for Lucinda.

I need to be alone.

CAIDEN'S SHIFT catches me off guard. And the look in his eyes is daunting; it's screaming for help. Good thing my reaction time is quicker than most. I shift and chase after him. He shouldn't be alone.

Once I catch up to him, I run alongside his wolf, keeping pace with his long strides. He doesn't acknowledge me, other than a low growl that permeates up his throat and out through his clenched teeth.

I don't care what he thinks he wants, I'm not leaving him alone.

Running through the woods is elating. The breeze ruffling my fur, sticks and leaves crunching under my heavy paws, and the sweetness of bergamot filling my nose blinding me from other scents. A soft purr tickles my throat.

The thick forest opens up to a beautiful meadow covered in a blanket of wildflowers. I stop at the edge, staring in awe at the wondrous sight in front of us.

Caiden stops a few feet in front of me and looks back in my direction. He stands next to me for a moment, then darts out into the open. He's calmer, I think. The massive white wolf is rolling on his back in the middle of the field. He stands up and stretches, before giving me a sideways glance.

A butterfly lands on his nose and he jerks away. His quick movement stirs a frenzy of butterflies into the air. Now, he's chasing butterflies, or maybe trying to kill them.

I shrug, snickering to myself, and trot after him.

Caiden turns to me as I approach, but he has a distant look in his eyes. It's almost as if he is watching a memory unfold. He shakes his head and stalks toward me with his tail twitching high in the air.

He reminds me of a young pup wanting to play. My heart soars with excitement. I take off toward him and pounce on his back. He tumbles forward, and we both roll. He recovers quicker than I, but we face off again.

I bow forward, sticking my rear in the air and wag my tail. He lifts his head and bellows out the most beautiful howl that lingers in the air.

We rumble playfully the rest of the afternoon. As dusk approaches, he catches me off guard, and I smash into the hard ground. Having the wind knocked out of me, I shift upon impact. Caiden shifts immediately after and runs to my side.

"Are you okay?" He brushes my head with his fingertips. His blue eyes are full of concern. "I'm so sorry."

"I'm okay," I whisper.

My eyes meet his, and we hold our gaze. My heart thumps, and I nibble on my lower lip. His sapphire eyes turn black with a tinge of red as they hungrily roam over my body, and my breath catches as he traces my neckline with his fingertip.

What was it that Mia said? Elizabeth was the only one that was able to calm him. My heart pounds harder, and my cheeks burn as he lowers his head. My lips throb in anticipation as he descends upon me.

Our lips touch in the softest kiss. His tongue gently traces my lower lip, and his cool breath caresses my burning lips. He skims the sides of my body with his hands, and his thumbs graze my breasts, which sends a frenzy of heat coursing through me from head to toe.

I dig my fingernails into the soft flesh of his back, and our kiss deepens. Caiden's hands move down to my hips, causing an involuntary shudder and a low moan escapes my lips.

Caiden growls in response and grabs my hips, pulling me closer. When his bare skin touches mine, small pockets of heat explode and send an unquenchable fire burning through my limbs. I wrap my arms around his neck and run my hands through his hair.

My throbbing lips leave the warmth of his as I lift my chin to the night sky. He leaves a trail of kisses on my jawline and gently nips on my earlobe before leaving love bites on my exposed neck. I pull his head closer, burying it into my neckline. Every part of my body rings with a passion I've never felt before.

Continuing his trail of kisses down my collarbone, he traces the curves of my breasts with his fingertips, and I arch my back in anticipation. His tongue flicks my nipple to a hardened peak. He looks up to me with a sultry gaze and teases me again. A yearning from deep within overpowers my senses.

I need him.

Sitting up, I roll him over so he's lying on his back. As I straddle him, I gaze into his eyes and stumble backward, falling off his lap. He rises and crouches over me, examining my naked body lying frozen in front of him. His eyes are a deep crimson, and I fear it isn't Caiden in control anymore.

"Caiden?" My voice is barely a whisper traveling on the cool breeze in the night air.

He stares into my eyes and pushes himself off me, falling

onto his back. He lies still and silent. After several minutes, I curl up next to him for warmth and rest my head on his chest.

The spicy scent of bergamot washes over me, though there is no calming sense of protection. His arm doesn't wrap around me as it has before. Instead, it hangs limp on the ground at his side.

Caiden, where have you gone?

I wish I could relax and fall asleep under the moonlit sky, but my senses are on overload, listening to every small noise carried on the breeze. I watch over the Alpha as he lies motionless under my touch.

Sometime during the night, I must have given in to sleep because I wake with my stomach twisting in knots from nervousness mixed with happiness as I peer at Caiden sitting a few feet from me. His elbows rest on his knees, and his head hangs low in his lap.

"Is everything okay?" I ask, touching his shoulder.

He flinches. Crawling around to look at him, I sit back when I notice a glaze in his eyes. My breath catches in my throat as I remember his state last night. But then I take a closer look.

Tears.

"Caiden, what's wrong?" I ask, my heart freezing with worry.

"I'm sorry, Lucinda."

"Sorry for what?" I grab his face, making him look at me. I already know the answer. *Last night was a mistake.*

"Last night—"

"I know. Don't worry about it. It's no big deal."

He looks at me with wide, questioning eyes.

"I know you miss Elizabeth. I'm glad—" I bite my lip. "You've already given me so much comfort, so I'm glad I was finally able to reciprocate."

He closes his eyes and takes a deep breath.

"I'm an Alpha. I shouldn't have done that. I took advantage of you in the most feral way possible. If things would have escalated—" He runs his hands through his hair. "I don't know if I could live with myself."

"Well, you didn't get far," I say with a small shrug.

"How far is far?"

Does he not remember?

"Second base. Like I said, not far."

He nods, but I still can't tell what he remembers.

"I'm sorry. It'll never happen again. You have a Fated Mate. That is a rare gift that shouldn't be thrown away or ignored."

Crossing my arms over my chest, I smirk. "True. I have a mate who denies me every damn day."

"We should head back," he says.

I nod, unable to form words because of the lump in my throat. I knew there was something different about him last night—the look in his eyes. Hell, even his eye color changed. But I still hoped a little part of him was there.

Sigh.

I waste no time shifting into my wolf and Caiden follows.

The run home is different. No playfulness, no racing, just running. Caiden does not spare me a single look the entire run. I thought Dylan broke my heart years ago. Now, the few parts that are still alive just shattered.

Arriving back at the Pack House, Caiden heads in through the front door and straight to his room, I assume.

I decide to enter through the back door since this will give Caiden enough space away from me to sort things out. In the doorway of the mudroom, I look around for something to wear. I reach for the robes the pack keeps hanging by the back door just for this purpose, but no, that will not do. I'm not ready to go upstairs yet.

Instead, I find my tote bag, which I brought back from Felix's, right where I left it. Rummaging through it, I find a pair of black lace undies, a scoop-neck gray tunic that hits me mid-thigh, and a pair of black over-the-knee leg warmers.

Interesting outfit, but it'll work in a pinch.

I throw on the ensemble and head for the kitchen. I laugh to myself as Mia's words echo in my mind. The vulgar things she's sure to say when she sees me.

I stop mid-stride as I enter the room. *Dylan, shit.* His jaw is set tight, and his eyes are jet black.

"Where have you been?" he asks.

"Out running," I say.

"You didn't come home last night." His gaze travels down my body.

I begin to fidget under his scrutinizing stare, but then my inner wolf stops me. Things escalated fast last night and then stopped cold turkey. My wolf yearns with a burning desire I can't quench.

"Yeah, what's your point?" Flipping my hair over my shoulder, I turn toward the fridge. In the corner of my eye, he sniffs the air.

"Who were you with?" His eyes are as solid black as onyx.

"It's of no concern to you."

"I know you were with someone. I can smell your arousal!"

"Well, you see…the beauty of being rogue is that I've learned to take care of myself." I smirk as I stalk toward him, licking my index and middle fingers for added effect. When I'm close enough to him, I run my two wet fingers against his lips. I know what this will do to him. He is a kinky bastard in the bedroom, and I like to push all his buttons. It's wrong to toy with his wolf like this, but I need a release, and Dylan is the best target.

He grabs my hips, pulling me forward and nuzzling his head in the crook of my neck, grazing his fangs over the sweet spot. My heart pounds, my stomach rolls, and my hands tremble under his touch.

"Mine," he whispers against my skin.

I moan with anticipation, and my wolf yearns for his touch.

But he pulls back at the last moment, and I startle at his eyes. Just a few moments ago they were solid black, and now they are his luscious green.

"No. I'm sorry, Lux. No." He pushes me away.

I raise my eyebrows and creases form on my forehead. He sniffs the air again, and the muscles in his face tense.

"Caiden?" he asks.

I freeze and a rush of heat travels up my neck. My lady parts begin to throb, remembering the things Caiden did to me last night.

"What about me?" Caiden asks as he strolls into the kitchen.

The heated look in his eyes as he takes in my appearance makes my insides quiver. My blush deepens as our eyes meet and lock into a stare. He appears refreshed and calm, but there is something different about him I can't pinpoint.

His lips turn up in the corners, giving me a shy grin.

Caiden walks behind me, brushing his fingertips ever so lightly against my lower back. My breath catches as little shocks of electricity spread through my body at his touch.

I turn to look at him, and his eyes are wide with surprise.

He felt it too.

Dylan looks between me and Caiden. His canines extend past his upper lip, and he releases a low growl.

A threatening rumble of dominance and a warning.

CHAPTER 22

LUCINDA

I squint and then glare at Dylan. *What does he have to be upset about?*

My nostrils flare and I roll my eyes.

Dylan's grimaces softens to a boyish grin, and I think of Sabrina and smirk. He only looks at me that way.

I don't think he has given her much time since I arrived. Although, I know he's made up his mind about us, for whatever reason. I just wish he'd tell me why. Then maybe my wolf would settle down and accept his decision as I have.

When Dylan's eyes meet mine, a warmth rushes to my cheeks. He caught me gazing upon him while lost in thought.

Dylan's demeanor has changed and I follow his intense glare. Caiden stands behind the counter making breakfast. Caiden's been busy, while I've been daydreaming. He's already pulled out milk, eggs, spices, bread, and a few things in jars I don't recognize. My tummy growls and Caiden's attention snaps to me.

"Sorry, I guess I'm a little hungry," I say.

A smirk rises to his face, and a low growl escapes Dylan as Caiden whisks together the ingredients.

"Cinda! There you are. I've been looking for you." Mia rounds the corner into the kitchen. "Mmm, that smells delicious. What is it?"

"French toast," Caiden says, shrugging.

"It's your specialty," she whispers. "You haven't made it since Eliza…"

"Yeah, well I felt like French toast this morning."

"How are you?" she asks, crossing the room to him. "Where have you been? I've been so worried. The whole pack's been worried."

"I'm fine. Better now." He glances my way before turning back to work on the stove.

My heart flutters. His face was emotionless, giving nothing away, but I felt his wolf surge through the room to me. Dylan must've felt it too because a low growl erupts from his direction…again.

I refuse to acknowledge him. He's been too much to deal with since the night of my rescue and our little heart-to-heart.

"Hey, Mia, what are you doing today?" I ask. A day hanging out with my best friend is exactly what I need right now.

"Funny that you ask," she says a little too high-pitched. "That's something I wanted to talk to Caiden and Dylan about."

I stand up and get out plates, forks, and knives while she gets the syrup, butter, and powdered sugar. Caiden carries a platter of French toast to the table, and we all sit down.

"We haven't had that cookout I wanted to have," she says, shoveling in a forkful of dripping French toast into her mouth.

I furrow my brows at her.

"You know, so you can meet everyone and see if your mate's here," she says between bites.

I almost drop my fork as my fingers falter. *I wish I never told her that stupid story.*

"Don't worry, Cinda. I know you won't find him there." She glares at Dylan. "But I still think it would be good for everyone to meet you and to see that their Alpha is alive and well."

Great, so she knows. My chest rises, and I let out an audible sigh. "Yes." Caiden's voice breaks the awkward silence that's crept into the room. "It would be good."

He looks at me and worry lines show at the corners of his eyes. What does he have to worry about?

"Hey, sugar." Sabrina enters the room.

I lift my gaze to Dylan, and his shoulders straighten as he sits up taller.

"Hey, babe." He curves his arm around her waist, pulling her onto his lap.

"Sorry I'm late. Did I miss breakfast?" Sabrina licks maple syrup from Dylan's lips.

"Mia, do you mind cleaning up?" Caiden abruptly stands from the table and looks at me. "Dylan and I have some business to discuss."

Caiden leaves the room.

Dylan gives Sabrina a juicy wet kiss, surely for my benefit, before standing and leaving.

Sabrina sits in his seat and grabs a piece of French toast from the platter. Picking it up with her hand, she eats it plain.

"So, what are you girls doing today?" she asks, waving the toast around.

"Not much. Just grocery shopping for the cookout tonight," Mia says as she clears the table.

"Oh, right. I got the message about the cookout," Sabrina says rolling her eyes. "It came through the mindlink loud and clear."

I stand and begin putting away the sugar, syrup, and butter. A burning prickles along my back, and I glance over my shoulder to find Sabrina shooting dagger eyes at me.

"You should shower. You reek," Sabrina says, almost in a snarl.

My heart starts to pound. Is Caiden's scent on me that obvious?

"Sabrina, stop it." Mia walks toward the table with her hands on her hips. "You're jealous so just leave it alone."

"Me? Jealous?" Sabrina snarks through fits of fake laughter.

"Yes, you." Mia lounges on the table with one hip. I remain where I am behind the counter on the opposite side of the room.

"No, little girl. I have no reason to be jealous," Sabrina quips, standing and leaning across the table—only inches from Mia's face.

"It's no secret you've always wanted my brother." Mia holds her stare.

"But now I've got Dylan, and he's more of an Alpha than Caiden's turned out to be," Sabrina says in a hushed tone. "Everyone knows Dylan's the only reason our Pack is still alive. On occasion, Caiden loses touch with reality and then disappears with no warning—"

"Wait, what?" I flick my hands into the air.

Sabrina glares at me.

I saunter across the room. "Do you think Dylan will actually challenge Caiden for the Alpha title?"

Mia's head snaps to me, her eyes wide with surprise.

"He'd be stupid not to." Sabrina shrugs.

I sit down and rest my forehead against the oak table. Forcing my wolf to remain calm, and combat the dizzy spell that threatens to overtake me. My vision narrows, the edges blurry and gray.

"Cinda, are you okay?" Mia asks while rubbing my back. Her voice is a little higher than usual.

"I'm fine." I take deep breaths in through my nose and out through my mouth. After a moment, I sit up and stare at Sabrina. "You're putting him up to this, aren't you? He'd never think of this on his own."

"Oh, he doesn't need too much encouragement. He's just more dedicated to this pack than Caiden is." Sabrina waves her hand in the air. As she says Caiden's name, her mouth twists into a pucker, looking as if she ate something sour.

"How can you say that?" Mia jumps to attention, shaking with rage.

"Calm down, Mia." I place a hand on her shoulder. "She obviously doesn't know Dylan that well if she calls him dedicated."

"Face it. Ever since Caiden lost his mate, he hasn't exactly been the same." Sabrina shrugs and flips her hair over her shoulder.

"You don't know the intense bond mates have, nor what it's like to lose one." Mia growls.

"All the better for Dylan to be Alpha. He found his mate, she rejected him, and he's overcome it."

"Is that what he told you?" I ask with a furrowed brow.

She nods, her lips pursed.

Heavy silence lingers in the air. I turn and stride toward the hallway. "Whatever, I'm going to shower."

Mia turns to follow me out.

Sabrina smirks. "Nice chat girls. We should do it again sometime."

Dylan wouldn't actually challenge Caiden to be the Alpha, would he?

DYLAN and I have been locked in my office, discussing plans on what to do about Felix. The first hour the only idea Dylan offered was to make peace with Felix. But how?

"No." I shake my head. "He'll come for her, and we must be ready when he does."

"She isn't staying much longer, right?" Dylan asks, though it's more of a statement than a question. "Her presence here puts the entire pack at risk against Felix, a powerful Alpha that we know nothing about, is a foolish act."

Rolling my eyes, I turn and gaze out of the only window in this room at the forest—my sanctuary.

The soft leather wingback chair crunches behind me as Dylan sits down. I glare at him, and he leans his head back against the headrest.

"What's going on with you and Lux?" he asks.

I think of her—the first time I saw her standing in the doorway of my house. A moment of silence passes, then Dylan clears his throat.

He raises his eyebrows. "Well?"

I look back to the forest.

"Do you think I don't notice you scenting her every chance you get?" He puckers his lips. "You probably don't even notice how often you do it. But how can I miss your fingers brushing across her back, her arm, her shoulder—anywhere you can touch her—to leave your scent?"

It's true. When I'm near her, I can't help myself. My wolf has an unyielding need to scent her. I can't explain it; my wolf has never had this driving force to scent before. The thought of her sweet scent—mint and honey—floods my memory, and heat rises to my face thinking of last night.

What I did was wrong. I took advantage of her, but in that moment, I only wanted one thing, and that was Lucinda.

Blinking several times, I turn my back to the forest and return to reality. Dylan watches me with a scrutinizing gaze, and my words catch in my throat.

How do I have a conversation about my feelings for Lucinda? I'm not even sure what those feelings are. And to talk about it with her mate of all people. *No.*

We stare at each other for another awkward moment before he speaks again. "I can't explain it, but there's something special between you two. My wolf can sense it. When you two are near each other, the energy that ripples through the room is like no other I've felt."

I have noticed my wolf acts differently around her too; I'm stable and more in control.

"Her strength reminds me of Elizabeth," I say, forcing the whisper from my lips.

"Who?" Dylan asks, and I realize he never knew her.

"Elizabeth was my mate." The look we share says it all—no other words are needed on this topic.

"Caiden, I say this as your Beta and as your friend. Lux is special. The dynamic your two wolves have—"

The door flies open.

I spin toward the intrusion, and a warmth rushes over my

body as her scent swirls in the room to declare her presence. My nostrils fill with her heavenly scent, and I wipe my palms on my jeans as my pulse quickens.

"Lucinda, is everything okay?" I ask, stepping closer to her.

Lucinda and Mia stand in the doorway. Lucinda's lips are drawn into a tight line and her brows are furrowed. Mia tugs at her arm, trying to pull her back into the hall.

What happened to set her off?

"How could you?" Lucinda glares at Dylan, and her eyes begin to swirl black.

Whoa, she needs to calm the fuck down.

"What are you talking about?" I place my hand on her shoulder, extending my dominance to calm her. I have craved those little sparks of energy ever since the first touch. Dylan's right, I can't help but touch her when she's so near.

"We just had a little chat with Sabrina," Lucinda says, clipping her words.

"Come on, Cinda, this can wait until you've calmed down," Mia says, still tugging on Lucinda's arm.

"No, it can't wait. You don't understand! Felix will come looking for me. This pack will be destroyed." Lucinda keeps her eyes glued on Dylan.

"Lucinda," I say firmly, positioning myself in front of her, blocking her line of vision to Dylan, and forcing her to look at me. "I know Felix will come. That's what we've been working on—creating a defensive strategy against him. We're a strong pack with many experienced warriors that will be ready and willing to fight."

Her eyes slowly focus on mine, and the beautiful golden hazel begins to return.

"No, Caiden, your pack is weak thanks to him and Sabrina." She looks back at Dylan, and her intensity begins to rise again. "Do you honestly think you can win against Caiden?"

I tilt my head, unsure I heard correctly. "Against me, what?"

I look between Dylan and Lucinda, and finally to Mia, who leans against the doorframe.

"Sabrina told us all about their little plan for Dylan to challenge the Alpha," Lucinda sasses as she strolls over to Dylan. "You make me sick."

She lunges for Dylan, but she's still within my reach and I grab her waist, pulling her back before her fist makes contact with him. Surprised by her outburst, it takes me a moment to process what she said.

Narrowing my eyes at Dylan, I ask, "Is this true?"

"No." Dylan stands tall, rolling his shoulders back. His pupils restrict and his nostrils flare. "That is not *my* plan."

"See, Cinda, I told you it's all Sabrina. She's been after Caiden since we were kids," Mia says, stepping into the room toward us.

Mia's right. Ever since the first dance in sixth grade, Sabrina has been making my life miserable. I'm not even sure what I did, other than not asking her to dance.

"It doesn't matter if he was or wasn't going to act on it," Lucinda says. "If Sabrina's thought of it, who has she talked to, and how many other people have thought of it?" Lucinda closes her eyes and rubs her temples.

Should I be surprised my pack is on the verge of revolt? With my behavior since becoming Alpha, and also since Lucinda waltzed into my life, no, I am not surprised the pack is unhappy. I've been wearing blinders assuming the pack would respect me because of my family name.

I pound my fist against my desk and clench my jaw.

"I'm sorry, Caiden," she says, her voice cracking. As she opens her eyes, a tear threatens to run down her cheek. "Your pack is broken. There's doubt and a loss of confidence in you, their Alpha. Your pack is weak and vulnerable. I've seen it before. Felix will destroy you."

I want nothing more than to engulf her in my arms, but I have to remember my place. I am the Alpha and her mate is here, so he can comfort her. She has a mate, she has a mate...

"Is that how the massacre happened?" Dylan steps forward and reaches for her hands.

She nods, and another stray tear runs down her cheek.

"You said it was a pack of rogues." Dylan curses under his breath and twitches his nose.

"How else would you describe Felix and his lawless followers? They're just a well-organized band of stray rogues."

"So, you were there?" Dylan rubs his thumb against the back of her hands.

A sharp pain shoots through my arm, and my hands begin to shake. I take a deep breath and smell her lingering scent still mixed with mine from last night. My lips tug up in a one-sided smirk, and my hands steady.

"Yes. I should never have asked for their help and protection, but I had nowhere else to go, so I went home."

"Hold on," I say. "What happened?"

Lucinda takes a deep breath. "I got mixed up with Felix about three years ago, soon after Mia and Gavin left. I needed a little space and time to figure things out. When I first met Felix, he interested me. He was an Alpha, but his band of followers was made up of wanderers. They didn't have a place to call home. They lived a rogue lifestyle, which worked for me."

She shrugs and turns to me.

I nod, motioning for her to continue.

"But then I witnessed his madness," she says, cringing. "He kills innocent people for fun and slaughters humans for sport. He even keeps captives to pit against each other—or worse, against other things for entertainment."

"What type of things?" Mia asks.

"Dark, sinister things. Things I didn't know existed and never would've believed if I didn't see them with my own eyes."

"That doesn't help."

"Bloodsucking vampires—"

"They're real?" Mia eyes grow wide and her complexion pales.

"I wish they weren't." Lucinda's gaze is unfocused as she stares into nothingness.

My father told us stories of vampires when we were young. But we always thought they were just that, stories. I have never seen a vampire, but if the stories are true, then I hope to never meet one.

Dylan squeezes Lucinda's hands to bring her back from wherever her mind wandered. "So what did you do?"

"I left. But I was careless, and I should've known better. He caught up to me as soon as Mia and Gavin left, only this time he was determined to keep me."

I close the distance between Lucinda and I and wipe a lone tear off her cheek.

"He threw me in an old dry well. You should've seen the look on his face when I climbed out the next day." She allows a weak smile to cross her face, then a small shiver runs through her body. "He immediately charged me and we fought. That was when he decided he was going to claim me as his, so Cody helped me escape that night."

"And that's when you went home?" I ask.

She blinks and tears pour from her glassy eyes down onto her cheek. "It didn't take him long to follow me. I should've known better—Felix is one of the best trackers I've ever seen. His pack attacked at night while we were sleeping. They killed everyone they came across. My dad was still the Alpha, and your dad was still the Beta," she says, turning to Dylan. "They ordered me to stay hidden, refusing to turn me over to Felix. He said he would let everyone live if I went willingly, and if not, he'd kill everyone and take me by force."

Mia fans herself with her hands, her cheeks flushed. I walk over to the small fridge next to my desk and grab a bottle of water for everyone. Lucinda takes a quick sip before continuing her story.

"They fought through the night. At sunrise, I peeked out of my hiding place in the treetops, and Felix and his men surrounded a small circle of what was left of our pack. Only a couple dozen was still alive, and so many had died all because of me."

Dylan leans up against the arm of a chair and I toss him another bottle of water. Hearing about his father's death isn't easy.

Lucinda looks down at her hands. And, I catch the water bottle before it crashes to the floor.

"I thought I could save them by giving myself to Felix. But after he bound my arms and legs, he turned and beheaded both the Alpha and Beta with one quick movement. Then his men did the same to everyone else. They slaughtered an entire pack. And the worst part is they drank the blood and feasted on the flesh of my dad, then they burned the rest. Felix gave me some of the ashes in a glass vile and told me I should be happy and grateful for what he did."

As she finishes telling her story, Lucinda's tears dry up and her lips pull tight.

Turning to me, she says, "I'm leaving."

"No, you're not," I counter. "Not with Felix tracking you."

"It's the only way you'll survive." Lucinda's voice begins to rise. "He's not coming to kill the Alpha and lead the pack. He's coming to destroy you and your pack."

"My pack will fight." I clench my jaw. My heartbeat quickens and beads of sweat trickle down the small of my back.

"It'll be a slaughter." Her eyes soften. "Those who haven't lost faith in you will lose confidence when you ask them to fight Felix for a mere rogue."

"But you're not a mere rogue." I rest my hand on her shoulder and smile. "You're my Beta's mate."

Our eyes lock. The energy coursing through my soul sparks, causing little bursts of fire to break out all over my body. Her eyes open wide, and I know she feels it too.

"No," Dylan says. I open my mouth to protest, but he cuts me off. "Lux, you aren't a rogue, and you aren't my mate. You are the daughter of an Alpha—an Alpha that was slain—and a member of an entire pack that was ruthlessly slaughtered by Felix."

Lucinda bites her lower lip as I digest what Dylan said.

Mia breaks the silence. "Yes, that is perfect! It's the truth, and inspiring."

Turning to Mia, I scowl.

"What?" she asks, looking at me and wiggles her shoulders. "Okay seriously, this—" Mia waves her hands toward Lucinda and me. "—is way more confidence-building than that." She motions between Lucinda and Dylan.

"Even if I am an Alpha's daughter, they don't know me," Lucinda protests. "Why—"

"That is exactly why we need to have the cookout tonight," Mia says with a wide grin. She has always loved parties.

"And Mia's right." Dylan clears his throat and motions between Lucinda and me. "This is inspiring. The energy you two give off is enough to rebuild confidence in the Alpha."

"I still think I should leave." Lucinda plays with her long hair, twirling it between her fingers.

I reach for Lucinda's delicate fingers and squeeze her hand. "No. You're staying."

"Something tells me that Felix will attack us even if you aren't here, so you may as well stay," Dylan says.

Now he's thinking and acting like the Beta I know him to be.

"Fine." Lucinda sighs and looks at me. "I'll stay, for now. But only to help you. You need your pack's confidence restored, and I'll do whatever I can to help fix the damage Dylan and Sabrina may have caused with their stupid plan."

I hope I can trust her to stay.

CHAPTER 24

LUCINDA

As I step out of the shower, the latch on my door clicks. I grab a robe and peer into my bedroom.

"Mia? What are you doing?" I ask.

"Caiden asked me to keep an eye on you." She lounges on my bed. "He's worried you'll leave."

"I'm not going anywhere. Not yet, anyway," I mumble.

"Cinda! Don't talk like that." Mia jumps off the bed and staggers toward me. She holds both my shoulders, her face only inches from mine. "Don't run. Stay, please stay. Even if you won't stay for yourself, stay for Caiden."

I tighten and tie the robe's belt around my waist.

"There is something there. You and Caiden..." She releases her grip on my shoulders. While tapping her lips with her right fingers, she places her left hand on her hip. "I don't know. You two just click."

I shift my weight. "I said I'll stay to help him, so I'm staying. I don't need a babysitter."

"I think someone has a little crush," Mia says in a singsong voice.

The sweetness of last night flashes in my memory. And then I remember the poison of his words this morning.

"No, I don't think so," I say matter-of-factly.

"Oh please." Mia waves her hand.

I shrug.

"So, what's going on with you two? And don't say nothing." She looks at me with a stern face.

"Nothing?" I can't help but smile.

"Nothing my ass. Something happened last night—his scent was all over you. I want details."

"Details? Ew! He's your brother." I wrinkle my nose.

"I knew it. I knew something happened." Mia squeals in delight, then turns serious. "I've been so worried about him. The past few years have been hard. I've watched him spiral out of control, and the pack's noticed too. I'm not surprised they've lost faith. It has been Dylan that's kept the pack together—kept a revolt at bay." She blinks back her tears. "But now that you're here, Caiden's different. He's been more stable since you arrived."

"Mia," I say in a soft tone. "We both know I'm not his mate. So I don't know why I'd have any effect on him."

"Maybe it's your wolf?" Mia snickers. "She does declare your presence very loudly when you enter a room."

She's always teased me because my scent is strong; she says it spreads into a room well before me, as if my wolf is announcing I have arrived.

Rolling my eyes, I look away in an attempt to hide a smirk. "Maybe, and that is exactly why it would never work between us."

Mia grabs a pillow off the bed and tosses it at me.

"What? Caiden is a strong Alpha, and I'm sure you've realized by now, that I am too. Two Alphas together would be a disaster. A relationship needs two parts to work in perfect harmony—a dominant and a submissive. The pair are meant to complement each other, not work against each other." I slide down the edge of the bed and sit on the floor. "Caiden and I, we're both dominant."

Mia snorts and squats next to me.

"Can you imagine the chaotic mess two dominant Alphas would cause when they disagree? And I'm sure we would disagree, so we'd would never work. Can I get dressed now?"

Mia's small, sad smile transforms into a wicked grin. "Why do you think I'm here? I've come with gifts."

She turns and waves her hands toward the bags of clothes sitting on the floor next to the door.

Damn. There goes my plan to wear jeans and a thermal to the cookout.

Mia grabs my arm and pulls me toward the bags of clothes. She points to the heap of dirty clothes on the floor. "Do you think I'd let you go wearing those?"

"What devilish plan do you have in store for me tonight?" I ask.

"Me?" Mia giggles.

I sigh. "Let's get this over with."

Mia grabs the bags and begins to unpack, placing several outfits on the bed. When I inspect them, they're actually not that bad. I like the first one: a pair of distressed jeans with a mint-green baby doll top. But I remember how chilly it is at night and move on to the next.

The second outfit is another pair of jeans. I smile because Mia knows what I like. It's a pair of black skinny jeans and a red halter top with a deep plunge neckline. This looks like something Sabrina would wear, so I give it no more time and move on.

Running my hands over the soft gray sweater on the bed, I know this is it. Vintage wash skinny jeans, a black tank top, and the softest gray cropped sweater.

"This one is perfect!" I pick up the sweater and rub it against my cheek; it's so soft.

"Are you sure?" Mia asks. "Red is a more powerful color."

"I don't think I need to give my wolf an extra power boost tonight."

"Gray and black are so drab, though."

"Then why is it here?" I ask.

"Fine. If that's what you want to wear." Mia sighs and turns her back to me. "The boys win."

"What?" My heart pounds against my ribs.

"Caiden and Dylan picked that out. They said it looked the most like you. So while you get dressed, I'll go find accessories." Mia grabs the other clothes on the bed, tosses them into the bag, and heads out the door. Before she shuts it, she turns back to me. "Oh, and dry your hair the best you can. I have an idea."

She closes the door, and I flop onto my bed. All I want to do is crawl under the covers.

But I need to be a social butterfly tonight and win everyone over. I'm doing this for Caiden. Closing my eyes, I see Caiden, his deep blue eyes and perfect smile.

Heat rises to my cheeks as I remember his soft kisses and gentle touch, then I smell that sweet scent of Bergamot. Picking up the sweater, I take a big sniff. He scented the sweater. I hug it and smile.

A creak of a floorboard comes from the other side of my door. I snap my head in the direction of the sound and stand to dress quickly.

"She's fine," Mia says as she opens the door.

Caiden stands in the hall behind her, and I flash him a small smile before he turns into his room.

"How long until we leave?" I ask Mia as she walks across the room.

"A couple of hours, why?"

"So soon? What happened to the whole day?" I whisper to myself.

"You slept and showered?" Mia says.

"Thanks, Captain Obvious." I glare at her, but I can't keep up pretenses for long. I burst out laughing and she follows. Soon, tears run down my face and I can't stop laughing.

I gave her this nickname when we were out in the wild. She was so naive; she had no business being out there. I collapse on the floor giggling as I remember the time she said '*someone camped here*' when we came across an old campfire.

"It's a good thing we haven't done your makeup yet, or else it would be ruined," Mia says, finally regaining her composure.

"Makeup?" I frown. "You didn't say anything about that."

"Just a little. You won't even know it's there."

"Fine. I'm at your mercy." I give her my best devil eyes as I walk across the room to sit in a chair.

After what feels like hours of Mia playing with my hair, she's finally satisfied with a French braid. But not just any French braid. First, she teased my hair to give it volume, then she sprayed it with a sea salt spray to give it texture, and finally, she pulled it into a braid, ensuring it had that messy, unkempt look.

"Perfect!" Mia squeals. "Go look in the mirror. You'll love it."

Walking to the bathroom, my feet move like lead. I like big events almost as much as I like shopping. Mia brings me a hand mirror, and I admire the back of my head. A grin tugs at the corners of my lips; it looks amazing.

"I knew you'd love it. Now, shoes." She walks to a box sitting on the bed, opens it, and holds up a pair of black flat booties. "What do you think about these?"

"Let's see." I take the boots and put them on. "Fashionable, and surprisingly comfortable."

Mia holds up a pair of rose-gold dangle earrings. "And the final touch."

Taking them from her, I study the interlocking loops, which create an infinity symbol. "They're beautiful."

"Come on, hurry up and put them on."

I slide them in place, step back a few feet from Mia, and she looks at me with a scrutinizing gaze. Finally, she smiles.

"You look smashing!" Mia says. "He's going to drool all over himself."

"What? Who?" I ask in a deep voice.

Looking in the mirror, I get lost in thought. I know I'm not all dolled up for a wedding or prom, but for me, this is the fanciest I've been in a long time.

I hear Mia talking, but I'm not listening; my eyes are glued to the young lady in the mirror. *Who are you?*

"Hello? Earth to Cinda." Mia snaps her fingers in my face.

"What?" I ask, turning away from the mirror.

"I was saying, the boys are meeting us there. Since it took so long to get you ready, they went to the store to buy everything for tonight," Mia says. "Just one last thing."

"What's that?" I ask.

Picking up her cell phone, she smirks. "A selfie!"

The cookout is at a pavilion deep in the forest. As we walk along the woodland path, Mia tells me the story of how Caiden and their father built the pavilion.

I try to listen, but the beauty and serenity of the woods is distracting. My pulse quickens—being back in the woods, my wolf is on high alert. She's full of mixed emotions, just as I am, only for different reasons. Well, maybe a few of the same reasons. Letting out a sigh, I relax my shoulders.

"What's up?" Mia asks.

"It's so beautiful out here." I peer around at the last of the sun rays shining through the trees, dancing on the forest floor. I give a small smile. "I think I miss it."

"Caiden likes it out here too," she says, giving me one of those knowing looks.

"Mia." I come to a halt. "I told you earlier, he's not interested, and it won't work. Just leave it alone."

"He's interested." Mia steps closer to me—we're eye to eye. "He just has to get over a few things first."

"A few things? Like what?" I fold my arms across my chest.

"Well…" Mia says in a long-winded breath. "For starters, he holds the bond between mates in the highest regard—it's a little old-fashioned if you ask me. He has feelings for you, but he's fighting it because you found your Fated Mate. To claim you as his own mate in front of your Fated Mate goes against everything he is."

Mia squeezes my hands, giving me a small smile.

"Oh, is that all." I roll my eyes and step past her to continue our walk.

My Fated Mate rejects me, I have a psychotic Alpha that wants to claim me against my will, and the most decent man I've ever met can't get over the fact that my Fated Mate rejected me. If I can accept it, he should be able to too. But why should he? Do I want him to?

While I'm lost in thought, we arrive at the cookout.

The pavilion demands my attention first. Stopping on the outskirts, I admire the massive structure. It's an Adirondack-style pavilion, complete with rugged woodland accents. But next, I admire the backdrop. The view is stunning. As the sun sets, purple, pink, and orange color the sky, and fireflies add a magical element as they twinkle in the air.

"Come on." Mia tugs at my arm to get my attention.

My eyes leave the beauty of the pavilion, and I survey the

pack members who are standing around. I know Caiden has a large territory, though I've never asked how many members are in their pack. By the looks of it, I'd estimate a few hundred—double the size of my father's pack. My heart pounds hard in my chest.

As we draw near, the pack members chatting amongst themselves turn to Mia and me, and it gets so quiet you can hear the hum of the tree frogs.

Scanning the crowd, I find Caiden at the grill with Dylan and Sammy. A few other men are chatting with them too. I smile, and a rush of adrenaline flows through my body, leaving me breathless.

I know as soon as he senses my presence because he stands taller and his head twitches, but he doesn't turn around.

Dylan is the first to turn in our direction, and smirking, he walks toward me.

"Nice outfit." He hugs me and whispers in my ear, "Tonight will be hard, but I'm going to try. Don't think anything of it, okay?"

"Yup," I say as cheerfully as possible, a fake smile on my face.

"Hey, Mia," Dylan says, backing away from me.

Sammy jogs over. "Hey, Lucinda, glad you could make it."

"Thanks, I'm excited to be here," I say, this time with a genuine smile.

"You're wearing makeup." Sammy grins.

Tugging at the hem of my shirt and rubbing my palms on my pants, I sigh. "Is it that obvious?"

"No, you look pretty."

My cheeks flush.

He tugs on my arm. "Well, come on, let's go meet the pack."

I glance to Mia for help, but she shrugs and turns in the

opposite direction, heading toward Gavin in the distance. *Figures.*

Dylan only laughs before walking away.

How could they leave me? I'll be eaten alive in a crowd this size.

CHAPTER 25

LUCINDA

S<small>AMMY FIRST GUIDES</small> me over to a group of women that appear to be in their early twenties. Their fake smiles and high-pitched voices prove to match their attitudes. After giving me a once-over, they turn their attention back on themselves.

It took all my control to be polite to them. *Sigh.* This will be a long night at this rate.

Next, Sammy takes my arm in his and navigates me through a massive crowd congregating in the center. He introduces me to people as we pass, and luckily, he doesn't stop for small talk.

I catch a glimpse of the young girl, Eva, who asked me about the journey in finding my Fated Mat. I wave in her direction. A man standing beside her takes notice and pushes his way through the crowd to reach us.

"Who do you think you are?" he says in a deep voice.

"Excuse me?" I ask.

"Filling a young and naive girl's head with silly nonsense about giving up on Fated Mates and pursuing your own destiny," he says.

"Hi, Mr. Willow." Sammy extends a hand. "Have you met Lucinda? She is our guest—"

"I don't need to meet her. I've heard enough about her already. You should be ashamed of yourself." He turns back into the crowd.

Ouch.

After that, it becomes harder and harder to put on a happy face and mingle with the pack members. The warm welcomes include hugs and kisses, while the cold shoulders include insults. Some people are even blunt enough to ask about my relationship with the Alpha.

The nerve of them.

Dylan finds us and motions to Sammy.

Thank you.

Sammy turns to me and says, "It's time."

I take a deep breath, and for the first time since I arrived, I look to find Caiden. His eyes are already on me as we approach.

"Welcome, Lucinda." Caiden smiles. "Are you ready?"

"Yup, let's do this," I wipe my sweaty palms on my legs and straighten my hem line.

"Hello everyone," Caiden says over the crowd. "Thank you for coming out tonight on such short notice."

"Where've you been, Alpha?" a man shouts from the crowd.

"Yeah, where've you been the past few days? We needed you," another voice calls out.

"You left with no word and no trace."

One voice turns into many.

"You left your pack again, unguarded."

This pack is more broken than I thought.

"And you!" Someone in the crowd turn to point at Dylan, "You were nowhere to be found either!"

"Usually we can depend on you when we can't depend on our own Alpha! But not this time!" an elderly man yells.

"Yeah, when Caiden pulls his disappearing act, you're the one we turn to. But you weren't here," another man says, and the crowd roars.

I bite my lip and scan the crowd. I find Sabrina leaning against a tall white pine tree on the outskirts of the crowd. She's smirking at a group of young men wearing brightly colored polo shirts in the center of the crowd, not too far from Caiden. Every single one of them has their hair spiked up with gel, and they have their backs turned to Caiden to shout into the crowd.

Heat flushes the back of my neck. How can they be so disrespectful? I clench and unclench my fists to calm myself down.

Caiden's voice brings my attention back to him. "Everyone, calm down."

A wave of power rolls through the air.

He points to me. "I'd like to introduce you to our guest, Lucinda. She needed Dylan's help earlier this week—"

"You chose a rogue over your own pack?" the crowd yells.

"No," Caiden booms over them. His jaw muscles tighten. Running his hands through his hair he says, "She isn't a rogue—at least not by choice."

Dylan surprises me by stepping forward. "Lux, or Lucinda, is a childhood friend of mine. We grew up together in the same pack."

"But this is your pack now! Where does your allegiance lie?" the crowd demands.

The corners of Dylan's lips cast down in disgust. This is not the response he was expecting. He steps back, and Caiden turns his back to the crowd, speaking with Dylan and Mia.

Out of the corner of my eye, a quick movement and flash

of color catches my attention. I leap and shift in midair, pouncing on one of the young men from the group I spotted earlier as he charges toward Caiden.

A sharp serrated knife drops from his hand as my big paw places pressure on his wrist. A low growl vibrates from my throat, and I bare my teeth.

I extend one of my claws so the tip is close to puncturing his skin, but a warm hand rubs my head and leaves behind the most wonderful scent of bergamot. My growl becomes a low rumble, and I sit up, freeing the young man. He scoots to a standing position with a pale face and wide eyes, then runs back to his buddies.

Caiden growls into the crowd. "Is there anyone else that would like to challenge me? If so, please be honorable and challenge me to my face."

I nuzzle against his leg, and he flashes me a smile.

"Now, as we were saying before," Caiden speaks again, "Lucinda is no mere rogue. She's the daughter of an Alpha— an Alpha that was slain—and a member of an entire pack that was slaughtered."

The pack members shrug and shake their heads. Although, some members look horrified.

"We know the pain of losing pack members. We've been through it and survived," Caiden continues. "But we didn't survive all on our own. If our neighboring packs hadn't provided us with assistance, what would've happened to us? Now we're in the reverse situation and another pack is in need of our assistance—even if it's only one member because that's all that is left. Are we to turn our backs and not provide help when needed?"

Caiden's speech is inspiring. His emotions roll through the air and crowd, wave after wave. Pack members wipe their eyes, dab their noses, and shuffle their feet.

"No decisions need to be made tonight. Tonight, is a night

of celebration—a celebration of life," Caiden says, flashing a smile to the pack while Mia cues the music.

The chemistry of this pack interests me.

There is a clear division and two types of members. Those that lived through and had their lives permanently changed during their rogue attack; these members are standing as stone statues. And the others—the young or those not affected at all—they're laughing and joking with each other, eager to eat, dance, and party.

I rub against Caiden. This is a hard pack to lead—having to please two types of people. I flip my tail to get his attention and nod toward the woods, trying to tell him I'm going back to the Pack House. I think he understands because he doesn't try to stop me when I turn to leave.

Life would be easier at times if I could communicate with him while in wolf form, but that would require being accepted into his pack, and I'm not ready for that yet.

Back at the Pack House, I look through the clothes Mia bought me during our shopping trip, trying to decide if I want to get dressed and join the pack again or lounge here and relax. The flannel pants win. I'm better off here anyway. Caiden needs to restore not just confidence in his pack but loyalty too. He needs to do that without me by his side.

I head downstairs and crawl onto the soft and comfortable chaise I've had my eye on since I first arrived. Grabbing a blanket and the TV remote, I get lost channel surfing.

A small creek and I throw the remote across the room. Whipping around, the front door swings open. A smile creeps over my face when Caiden enters and closes the door behind him. I was so caught up in the movie on TV, I didn't even notice how late it had gotten.

"I brought you some food," he says, holding up a bag.

"Thanks. I'm starving." My stomach growls as I smelled the food.

He walks toward me and takes out all the food to place it on the coffee table. I kneel on the floor and begin eating.

"Lucinda," Caiden says, "I want to thank you for what you did earlier. Pouncing on that punk—"

"Don't mention it." I shrug.

"Your sleek transformation caught everyone's attention. That's all anyone was talking about after you left."

"Awesome," I say in a dry tone, and Caiden begins to laugh.

"I'm sorry you weren't able to enjoy yourself," he says. "There was music and dancing after you left."

I lift my head from eating and raise my eyebrows. "Oh yeah?"

"Would you like to dance?" he asks.

"Here? Now?" I wipe my mouth with a napkin.

He nods and stands, extending a hand out to me.

I place my hand in his, and those little sparks of electricity run through my arm as he helps me stand. He changes the TV channel to a music station, and we begin to dance.

His right hand curls around my waist, and his left holds my right hand at a ninety-degree angle in the air. I place my left hand around his waist.

With each step, our bodies move closer until my chest is flush against his. His warm breath blows on the back of my neck, sending electric sparks rolling down my body. And I try to steady my shaky hands as I lay my head on his chest.

"Lucinda," Caiden whispers in my ear.

"Yeah."

"Most people have agreed to fight," he says.

Pulling away from his chest, I look into his eyes. "Most people?"

"There was more talk about me being a fit Alpha." His fingers fiddle with my hair. "Maybe I'm not. I haven't been a very good Alpha."

"What? Don't talk like that."

"It's true. I've done nothing but cause trouble. Dylan's always been there for everything—to clean up my messes." He sighs. "Maybe I should just give the Alpha seat to Dylan."

I shake my head and squeeze his hand, pulling him closer to me. I lean my head against his chest once more. "That won't be good for anyone."

"Do you think Felix will leave this pack alone if you and I both leave?" He rests his chin on my head.

"I doubt it. He's power-hungry. He'd hunt us down and then attack this pack. You have plenty of strong members that he'd want to devour."

"What do you mean *'power-hungry'* and *'devour'*?" Caiden asks, pushing me away from him so we're face-to-face. My wolf is giddy with excitement at the proximity of our lips.

"Remember the witch he's tracking?" I ask. "He told me a story about the night Felix was named the next Alpha. He said a soothsayer came bearing gifts for the new Alpha-to-be, and her gift was one wish of his choice. Felix, in his youthful pride, wished to be a mighty and powerful Alpha."

I adjust my weight to get more comfortable before continuing.

"Cody said the soothsayer turned out to be a witch that cursed Felix. She gave him his wish but turned him into a power-hungry Alpha with no control. Anyone more powerful—or as powerful as he is—must die. Felix killed his father, the Alpha, that night. He was his first kill."

Shivers run through my body.

Caiden pulls me so close our noses almost touch, and I can't stop myself from glancing at his lips. My pulse quickens, and my palms start to itch. I lean up and softly brush my lips against his. Gaining no response, I pull my lips away and warmth rushes to my cheeks.

I try to turn away, but Caiden holds me steady, not letting me escape his strong arms. His blue eyes bore deep into my soul, and my wolf howls at the intensity of his stare. As his eyes swirl black, he smashes his lips into mine.

He feverishly kisses me in an animalistic rage. I melt into his touch, and his hands grab my hips, pulling me closer so our bodies intertwine as one. He growls as my hands roam his head, and I run my fingers through his blond hair.

When his lips leave mine, my wolf whines. But she is cut short when warmth radiates over my skin as he trails kisses along my jawline and down my neck. Digging my nails into his back, I lean into his kisses and moan in delight.

The front door opens, and we jump apart. I smile at Caiden and bite my lip. He looks at me, running his right hand through his hair, then struts past me toward the back of the house and disappears down the hall.

Mia calls through the silence, "Hey, Cinda!"

I turn to face her, Gavin, and Dylan in the doorway.

"Was that Caiden?" she asks.

"Oh hey. How was the cookout?" I ask.

CHAPTER 26

CAIDEN

I SPLASH cold water on my face and stare into the mirror to gain control of myself.

"What are you doing?" I ask myself. "She has a mate, damn it! Stop making it harder for the both of us."

I grip the sides of the sink top and growl into the mirror. I don't recognize the man reflecting back.

Turning around, I lean against the sink and try to steady my shaking hands.

"No, not now. Calm down," I whisper. "Calm down."

I refuse to lose control tonight. With every deep breath, my pulse slows, and I think about my curse.

And then a delightful laughter drifts from the living room and distracts me. I walk out of the bathroom and down the hall. Before I round the corner, she laughs again, and a smile tugs at the corners of my lips.

I close my eyes and lean against the wall to listen to the bewitching sound. I can spot Lucinda's voice from anywhere.

"So, Dylan, did you have as much fun as Mia and Gavin?" Lucinda asks with another magical giggle.

"No," Dylan says. "Someone had to clean up the mess you left behind."

My wolf doesn't like the tone of Dylan's voice. I peak around the corner and glare in Dylan's direction. It takes all my power to stand still, but I'm able to control myself, this time.

Lucinda jumps from her seat on the couch and her voice peaks in a high-pitched tone. "Excuse me? Mess? What mess?"

"Going all wolf on that kid," Dylan says.

"Yeah, the kid that was rushing at Caiden with a knife. What was I supposed to do?"

"You don't get it, do you?" Dylan steps into her, their noses almost touching and he growls. "That kid wouldn't have landed a finger on Caiden. Caiden would've taken him down with a single move and restored confidence. You ruined everything! You've probably caused more damage than good."

"What the hell? I protect the Alpha, and you're pissed at me?" Lucinda pushes against Dylan's chest with her hands.

A spicy mint scent tickles my nose as it drifts through the air. My heart pounds again. *Oh, Lucinda, if only you knew what you did to me.*

Lucinda growls. "Why do you do that?"

"Do what?" Dylan turns away from Lucinda, brushing her off.

"One minute we're all having a good laugh and then the next you manage to make me so angry that I'm about to go all wolf on you." Lucinda sighs.

Gavin's deep voice cuts through the tension in the air. "I bet he does it on purpose."

"Yeah, to make my life a living hell," Lucinda slinks back and melts into her seat on the couch again.

"It probably makes it easier. You smell funny when you're mad," Gavin says.

Mia's hand flies through the air and smack Gavin on the arm. I stifle a laugh.

"Ouch! What was that for?" Gavin rubs his arm.

It falls quiet in the next room, so I decide this is as good a time as any. Turning the corner, I put on my game face and stroll into the room with purpose.

Determination guides my actions, and I want answers. "Tell me about the night you were announced the next Alpha."

Four sets of eyes turn to stare at me, but I hold the one set that's locked on mine—Dylan's.

Mia attempts to talk through the mindlink, but I block her. Everyone needs to hear these answers.

"Tell me about the gypsy," I demand.

Dylan casts his eyes to the ground, not able to meet my stare.

"Did she offer you a gift?" I ask in a calm tone.

Dylan's shoulders tense and his body freezes. His eyes slowly rise to meet mine.

I whisper, "A soothsayer came to me on my twelfth birthday. She wanted to give me a gift, but since I wouldn't choose, she chose for me. She gave me the gift of strength that is equal to no other. As with most gifts, there is a price to be paid—one equal to the gift itself. Because of this gift, I can't control my anger, lose control, and go off for days at a time. She called it a payment, but I call it a curse."

A warm hand rubs my back, my shoulder, and finally down my arm where it squeezes my hand. I know who it is before I see her, her sweet scent of mint and honey calming my nerves, giving me renewed strength.

"So, I ask you again," I say, returning my focus to Dylan. "Tell me about the gypsy."

Dylan looks between Lucinda and me and then down at our hands.

"Fine." He heads toward the couch to sit down.

Lucinda tugs me over, and we sit on the couch next to him. Mia and Gavin share a recliner on the other side.

"The night I was announced as the successor Alpha, I went out to celebrate," Dylan says in a dry tone and licks his lips. "I ran into the gypsy that had been performing tarot card and palm readings all day. She said she had a special gift for me—a gift for the next Alpha. I was young and stupid. At the age of twelve, you don't think too much about the future, so I took her gift, then paid the price. You're right, her payment is a curse."

"What was the gift?" Lucinda asks.

Dylan flares his nostrils and his eyes finally lift from the floor to lock with Lucinda.

"I can't speak of it. It's part of the curse."

"Does it have something to do with me?" Lucinda asks.

Dylan nods.

"It makes sense now," Lucinda says. "When Felix had me in the holding cell, there was an elderly woman there too. She said something that made no sense to me at the time. Something like, *'You've been touched by me child, and yet I don't know you.'* I thought her a kooky old lady, but I guess maybe it was the same gypsy that cursed you."

Lucinda smiles, and a warmth rushes through my veins. I want to push her down and smother her with kisses. I shake my head to gain control again. My wolf is not playing nice tonight.

"Oh! Felix was searching for a witch!" Lucinda's eyes lift to mine as she realizes what I did earlier. "Is Dylan's gypsy and Felix's witch one and the same?"

"Yes, there will be time for that, but I'm still curious about the Dylan's curse," I say, squeezing her hand. "Dylan, about your mother."

I watch his head fall forward and hear a sniffle.

In a calm tone I say, "There is no judgment here. We've all had horrible things happen to us because of this soothsayer, gypsy, or witch—whatever you'd like to call her. Please, just tell us what happened."

"My mother," Dylan stutters.

Lucinda lets go of my hand and goes to kneel in front of Dylan. She grabs his trembling hands with both of hers.

A fire burns in my soul, but I refuse to allow it to overtake me. *I have no claim on her.*

"My mother…" Dylan allows a small chuckle and starts again. "She followed me that night and overheard the gypsy's gift. She ran inside the tent just in time for me to receive the payment. But my mother was a clever woman—more clever than the gypsy gave her credit. She asked the gypsy for a gift for herself, and the gypsy agreed. Little did the gypsy know what gift my mother would ask for."

"What was her gift?" Lucinda asks.

"It was a smart and heartfelt gift," Dylan whispers. "She asked for her gift to be the ability of my gift to be reversible."

My heart pounds so hard that I am sure everyone in the room can hear it. "Wait. Your curse can be broken?"

"Yes, the gift can be undone, but not the payment," he says, lifting his head to look at Lucinda. "She was angered by this, so she cursed me to never speak of it. I'm unable to tell you the gift and how it can be undone."

Gavin asks, "What happened to your mother?"

Dylan adjusts his weight. "Her payment was her life."

Lucinda stiffens and then slides across the floor back over near me.

I cannot help myself, I reach out and stroke her back,

making small doodles with my fingertips between her shoulder blades.

Mia breaks the silence. "So, what about Felix? How does he fit into this?"

Lucinda tells them the same story she told me earlier. I do not listen. Instead, my mind races in all directions. I try to think of what we can do about Felix, but Lucinda easily distracts me. Each time she raises an arm or waves her hand, her scent floats in the air, tingling my nerves.

Once she finishes her story, and before others can speculate further, I ask, "Felix has the witch, right?"

"He *had* the witch, but there was no one left in the house when we tracked Cinda," Gavin says.

Dylan mumbles, "Our leverage is the witch. If we have the witch, then we control Felix. We can make a peace deal with him."

"Sounds like a plan to me," Mia and Gavin say in unison.

Lucinda's shoulders roll forward and she drops her head. She doesn't voice it, but watching her, I know she doesn't agree. I am not sure I do either, but I need to leave the room. I need to get away from her; she is too close.

"It's settled then, we'll discuss more in the morning." I stand and head into the kitchen. *I need food to calm my rattling urges.*

Later, as I am heading to my room, my wolf keeps pulling me to Lucinda's door. My hand is on her doorknob, and I fight with all my control to stop. But my wolf whimpers and the all too familiar cloudy veil covers my eyes.

Shit.

Lucinda wakes up, and I'm surprised she is not agitated to find me in her room, sitting in a chair a few feet from her bed.

"Is everything okay?" she asks.

I am concentrating so hard on staying in control that I don't respond.

She gets out of bed and walks toward me, wearing a tank top and underwear. My wolf whimpers and I growl.

She kneels in front of me, placing her hands on my knees. "Caiden, what's wrong?"

"We need to talk," I manage to say.

She bites her lip. "Okay, about what?"

"Earlier." I run my hands through my hair. "That shouldn't have happened."

"Stop." Lucinda holds up her hand. "I get it. I have a mate, and you think I should be with him. But the thing is, he doesn't want me. I'm over it."

The authority in her voice catches me off guard. I try to talk, but she shushes me. "If you're worried about what others may think, don't. No one knows about Dylan and me."

"I'll know," I say under my breath.

"He doesn't want me." She throws her hands up in the air.

"He's trying to protect you from the curse that horrid witch cast!" I pound my fist on my knee, clenching my jaw. "And his curse can be broken."

Sighing, I lean my head forward into my hands.

"Even if the curse is reversible, think about how he's acted the past ten years—how he's treated me and all that he's done." Lucinda grabs my hands, moving them from my head, forcing me to look at her. "How could I ever forgive him?"

"That's the thing about mates, you don't get a choice. Your souls are drawn together like magnets—an invisible string pulling your fates together to be forever bound." Reaching up to Lucinda's face, I touch a loose strand of her hair that has fallen forward. I slide my fingers down the silky lock and tuck it behind her ear.

Lucinda rests her cheek in the palm of my hand.

"That pull is what led me here, but I haven't felt it since I arrived," Lucinda whispers. "Being here, it's easier to be around Dylan. My wolf tolerates him well."

If my tail were out, it would be wagging.

"Stay with me tonight?" Lucinda crawls back into bed, lying on her left side.

"Lucinda," I say in a deep voice. "We can't."

"Just as friends."

Defeated.

I crawl into the other side of the bed, scooting close behind her so my chest is against her warm back, and drape my right arm around her midsection. She grabs my hand, twisting my arm so it lies between her breasts and cuddles with my forearm.

We're holding hands under her chin, and the light rumble of her wolf vibrates against my chest; my wolf responds with vibrations of his own.

This is just a friendly gesture. I'm an Alpha providing protection. This means nothing, I chant in my head until I fall asleep.

CHAPTER 27

LUCINDA

IN THE MORNING, I wake up with a lingering dream playing at the back of my memory. As I smile, I inhale Caiden's scent, and my thoughts of the dream fade away. I reach for him, wanting his touch.

Instead, my hand brushes against a cold sheet.

Turning over, I stare at the place he slept not too long ago, and my heart sinks.

Caiden is gone. *Was he even here at all, or was it only a dream?*

Reluctantly, I crawl out of bed and get dressed. On my way to the door, I stop and take a long look in the mirror. *Why would Caiden leave me in the middle of the night?*

When I reach the middle of the stairs, I smell Dylan, but before I can run back upstairs, he sees me from his perch on the couch.

"Hey, Lux."

"Hey," I say, walking toward him.

"You okay?"

"Yeah, why?" I crinkle my forehead.

"You're fiddling with your shirt hem. You always did that when you were nervous or anxious."

Looking down, I lower my hands to my side, then sit on the couch next to him. "Yeah, I guess some habits are hard to break."

"So what's up?" he asks.

"Have you seen Caiden?"

"No, why?"

I shrug and look anywhere but at him, finding an interesting little spot on the carpet. A bloodstain?

"You two have become close," Dylan says, drawing my attention back to him. He watches me with curious eyes.

"Yeah." I flash a small grin and reach for the hem of my shirt again.

"I'm…I'm happy for you." He squeezes my knee, giving it a little shake. He'd do the same thing when we were kids and he teased me about a boy I was crushing on.

I glance up at him and our eyes meet. Locked in a stare, I'm unable to look away.

My pulse quickens and fire explodes within my body. Every part of my skin burns like someone's pouring hot lava onto my head and it's slowly dripping down, covering my entire body.

Tears form at the rims of my eyes, threatening to fall.

Dylan's pupils dilate, and his eyes finally break from mine as he leans in, narrowing in on my neck.

My lip throbs with searing pain from where I bite through it, then a warm liquid runs down my chin. He peers up at me and does a slight shake of his head. Reaching up, he wipes the blood from my chin, then he stares at his other hand on my knee.

He stands abruptly and backs away from me. "I'm going to get some breakfast."

He storms into the kitchen, and I melt back into the over-sized cushions on the couch. *What the fuck just happened?*

I lick my lips. There isn't much blood left, but the throbbing pain remains. *Stupid nervous habit.*

Grabbing the nearest pillow, I cover my face and growl. I use it to wipe away the tears that found their way to my cheeks, then pull my knees onto the couch to hug them and lay my head on top.

Caiden, where are you?

I wipe the corners of my mouth and slowly open my eyes, letting them adjust to the light. I'm still on the couch; I must've fallen asleep. And I can't clear the eerie feeling that lingers from the dream I just had.

The room is empty and I shake my head to wake up. I stand and stretch, a small pop and crack coming from my back and neck.

My ears prick up at the hushed voices in the kitchen.

I yawn as I walk through the doorway. "Hey."

"Hey, sleepyhead," Gavin says with a wink. "Didn't get much sleep last night?"

I smack the back of his head as I walk past him to the sink.

"Are you feeling okay?" Mia asks.

"Me? Yeah, why?"

"You look a little off." Mia shrugs and takes a sip of her drink.

"Oh, I have a horrible headache, I think." I rub my temples.

"You think?" Dylan says in a dry tone.

Mia hands me a glass from the cupboard and I fill it with water from the sink.

"It's not a regular headache. I'm foggy and there's a slight throbbing." I gulp down a glass of water, then reach for more. "Is Caiden back yet?"

Mia takes a seat at the table. "I haven't seen him."

Dylan spins a coin on the table. "He's probably still in the woods on one of his runs."

I look at the clock; it's lunchtime. "Shouldn't he be back by now?"

"He goes off a lot. Hard to tell when he'll be back," Gavin says with a mouth full of food.

Mia props up her elbow on the table and rests her head. "Did you two have a fight last night? He usually runs off when he's upset because it helps him cool down."

"I don't think so." I push aside the uneasy feeling I still have and remember back to last night. *We talked. We didn't argue. He stayed with me. Maybe he's thinking about...*

"Do you hear that?" I knit my eyebrows tight together and concentrate on the low hum.

"Hear what?" Gavin asks.

"Shh!" I snap, glaring at him.

Dylan walks towards me. "Lux, why don't you lie down?"

"No, wait." I hold up my hand. I whine as my eyes widen in alarm. "Cody?"

I hate this mindlink I still have with Felix's pack. But today, at this moment, I am grateful beyond words.

"Felix has Caiden!" I run to the back door and jump off the porch, shifting before my feet hit the grass. I take off running into the woods. Through the mindlink, I holler, "Cody, tell me everything!"

"Where've you been?" Cody yells back. "I've been trying to reach you all morning!"

"I was sleeping!"

Branches snap behind me, and I glance over my right shoulder. Dylan's wolf is charging up behind me.

Cody says, "Felix made his move. We hit the border just before sunrise. We encountered a border guard, and he must've alerted your Alpha because he arrived within a few minutes."

I dodging a fallen tree that blocked my path. "What happened to the guard?"

"What do you think?"

Drool seeps from my lips as I snarl.

I have always appreciated Cody's laid-back and easy-going attitude, though it took a while for his dry sense of humor to grow on me. He is like a big brother to me—always watching out for my well-being. He is the one that helped me escape the first time I ran from Felix.

Something isn't right. My hackles rise and the scent of leather drifts in the air. I slow my pace, Dylan follows my lead and stops within a few feet of me. Felix steps out from behind a tree in human form. I let loose a lone howl into the sky, and soon, more howls join.

Behind me, wolves approach, flanking us. Dylan must have alerted the pack.

Why didn't Caiden mindlink anyone?

Felix says, "Ah, Lucinda dear. How nice of you to join us. I was just having the most wonderful conversation with the Alpha of this pack."

Unblocking him from the mindlink, I ask, "Where is Caiden?"

"He's fine," Felix says out loud. Through the mindlink, he adds, "For now."

I snarl with bared teeth.

"Your Alpha is a very caring man. He puts his pack before his own life," Felix says to the mob of angry wolves. "We came to an agreement. He comes with me, and we won't kill everyone in your pack."

A choir of growls echoes through the forest.

"I want to see him," I demand through the mindlink. Felix waves his hand to his left, and Cody brings Caiden into our view.

Upon seeing Caiden, my ears lay flat against my head, and I bare my sharp canines. I crouch low to the ground, ready to pounce if needed. The fur on my back stands erect, and saliva drips from my mouth as I deepen my growl.

Caiden shuffles with short steps. Chains bind his ankles and wrists, and they connect to another around his neck.

The chains must be coated in silver because deep red welts peek out from where they make contact with his skin. It's more than just chaffing. Caiden winces with each step.

Silver. A cruel form of punishment. The metal burns the skin on contact. And now I know why he didn't mindlink Dylan—silver blocks the mindlink ability.

"Stand down," Caiden says. His face is calm as he addresses the pack of angry wolves before him. "This man, Alpha Felix, is correct. We made a deal, and I trust him to honor his part of the bargain."

Felix places his palms together at mid-chest and does a slight bow with his shoulders and head.

Another growl slips from my teeth. He'll never hold true to his word.

"Dylan is a good Alpha," Caiden continues. "He's been there for you when I haven't. Give him your respect and your allegiance."

Whines and whimpers fill the silence.

"Dylan, take care of them. All of them." Caiden looks at me. His blue eyes burn deep into my soul.

I tuck my tail between my hind legs as I let loose a series of small barks.

Caiden jerks his head forward, motioning to Felix. And then he lowers his gaze to the ground.

"I'll watch out for him," Cody says through the mindlink.

I stand frozen, watching Caiden shuffle away with Felix and his men, wondering if any of them will survive this.

CHAPTER 28

LUCINDA

DYLAN NUDGES me with his muzzle. My eyes focus on the black strip of silky fur that covers his back, mixing into his tan and cream coat. A small whine escapes him, and I whimper in response. He nuzzles my neck, and I allow him to lead me back to the Pack House.

We walk through the woods, careful to make no sound beneath our heavy paws. Felix isn't to be trusted. Dylan stays alert and cautious of all movement in the forest.

Every so often, I glance behind us, hoping to see a beautiful white wolf charging through the woods. I sniff the air; I crave a rush of the tantalizing bergamot, but it's faded away on the light breeze.

This is all my fault. I caused this. If I never came here, Felix and Caiden wouldn't have crossed paths.

We stop just outside the back door of the Pack House to collect my composure.

How am I going to tell Mia?

Dylan leaves me and walks inside.

After a few minutes, I enter the back door, shift, and grab a spare robe from the hook to cover my bare skin. Turning the corner into the living room, I see Gavin kneeling over Mia, who's lying on the floor.

"What happened?" I ask, rushing to her side.

"I don't know." Gavin scratches his head.

"What do you mean you don't know?" I listen for a pulse.

"We heard the news about Caiden." Gavin's eyes flash up to mine.

"How?"

"It came through the mindlink. Everyone knows." Gavin directs his gaze back to Mia. "She said she didn't feel well, so I told her to sit down while I went to get her a glass of water. When I came back, she was on the floor."

"Okay, let's move her to her bed," I say, sitting back on my heels. "We'll put an ice pack on the back of her neck, and hopefully, she'll wake up soon."

Gavin picks her up as if she were a rag doll and starts upstairs. I head into the kitchen to grab an ice pack.

"Hey, Lucinda." Sammy's voice startles me. "Who's the ice for?"

"Mia. I think she fainted." I brush past him and head up to her room.

"Is she okay?" Sammy asks, following me.

"I hope so. I guess we'll see." I stop in front of her door and give Sammy a weak smile.

Sammy opens his arms for a hug, and I collapse into his chest. Willing myself to stay strong and to not shed a tear, I let him pull me close and hold me in a tight, comforting embrace. The warmth this small gesture brings is exactly what I need to settle my racing nerves.

"Caiden will be fine. He can take care of himself," Sammy coos in my ear.

Someone clears their throat behind us.

"Am I interrupting something?" Dylan asks.

Sammy releases me, and I step away, squaring my shoulders to face Dylan. "Mia's unconscious. I think she fainted."

I enter Mia's room without waiting for a response.

Gavin sits next to her on the bed, holding her hand. Dampness on the back of her hand glistens in the afternoon sunlight.

Gavin wipes his eyes and asks Dylan, "What are we going to do?"

"We can call the pack doctor if you think she's sick or injured," Dylan offers.

"No. What are we going to do about Caiden?"

After several beats of awkward silence, Dylan says, "Nothing."

I blink back the tears that threaten to fall and bite my lip, tasting metal. I walk across the room, place the ice pack under Mia's neck, and squeeze her hand before turning to walk out the door.

"Lux," Dylan whispers as I walk past. He reaches for my hand, brushing my palm with his fingertips. He follows me into the hall. "Lux, stop."

I keep going, striding into my bedroom.

"Lux! Will you look at me?" Dylan demands as he walks into my room.

I pull my tote bag from the closet and toss it on the bed. Folding my arms over my chest, I stand to face him.

"What are you doing?" Dylan asks, eyeing the tote bag.

"I'm going after Caiden," I say, point-blank, staring him in the eye, challenging him.

"No, you're not."

"Says who? You?"

His fists flex into tight balls, and he broadens his shoulders. "YES!"

I flinch at the surge of power he ripples through the room.

"Then it's a good thing I never joined this pack, Alpha." I turn and begin to fill the tote bag with spare clothes.

Gavin and Sammy walk into the room behind Dylan.

Dylan's shoulders relax, and he says, "Lux, please don't do this."

"Do what?" Gavin asks.

"I'm going to get him." I throw my tote bag over my shoulder.

"Lux, let's talk about this." Dylan steps closer, and his eye soften as he tucks a wisp of hair behind my ear.

"You don't understand," I whisper. "There isn't much time."

"Dylan?" Sabrina's silky voice calls from downstairs.

Dylan rolls his eyes, and I cover the grin that's on my face. We all walk downstairs.

"The entire pack got the message, Alpha," Sabrina says as she drapes her arms around Dylan in a one-sided embrace. She points to a group of men lounging in the living room. The group from the cookout who'd been shouting into the crowd. "You remember my cousins."

The kid that charged Caiden.

A growl escapes me.

"Oh, I didn't see you there. What's your name again?" Sabrina says to me with a smirk, then dismisses me with a wave of her hand. "Oh, it doesn't matter. As I was saying, now that you're Alpha, you'll need a strong and reliable Beta."

Sammy steps forward. "That can wait. He doesn't need to decide anything right now."

Sabrina motions to her cousins. "Oh, we disagree."

Gavin returns from the kitchen and slips power bars into my tote bag.

"Are you leaving us?" Sabrina asks with a devilish grin.

Gavin answers, "We're going to get Caiden."

"No." I motion between us. "*We* are not. *I* am."

"What? You can't!" Sabrina says with wide eyes, batting her long lashes at Dylan.

One of her cousins says, "If you break the peace treaty, they'll attack!"

"Whoever said anything about a peace treaty? Felix doesn't know what the word peace means. He's going to attack regardless."

Sabrina stomps her foot on the ground and charges to me with her finger raised. "How do you know that?"

"I know Felix, and he's not a man of his word."

The cousin that charged Caiden at the cookout asks, "Then what does he want Caiden for?"

"Torture," I say. "He'll restrain Caiden and make him witness the slaughter of his pack before being killed himself."

Dylan tenses at my words.

"You lie." Sabrina points her finger at my face.

I turn and walk to Dylan. Looking down at his hands, I grab one with both of mine and rub my thumbs across his rough skin. "Dylan, you need to prepare to defend this pack. I fear it'll be bloodier than the fate of our parents."

A fire burns behind his eyes. His pupils dilate, retract to a pinpoint, and return to normal.

"What do you have in mind?" he asks.

"Do you have a map of the territory?" I ask.

Sammy motions us to the Alpha's office. "Yup, in here."

Gavin, Dylan, and I follow Sammy into the room. Sabrina and her cousins also follow us, and I growl at their presence.

"Easy now," Dylan says. "We may need their help."

Sammy rolls out an old map on the desk. The edges are torn, and the paper has faded over the years, but the territory markings are still visible.

"We're here." He points to our location on the map.

It's the first time I've seen a map of Caiden's territory, and it's massive. Biting my lip, I run my fingertips over the map, hoping it will talk to me. Instead, a light scent of bergamot swirls in the air, and my heart skips a beat.

"You need to draw your battle line," I say. "This territory is too large to defend the entire border."

Dylan nods, his eyes focused on the map.

"Felix will probably come from here." I point to the northwest area where we met them earlier.

"Here." Dylan runs his finger across the map, just below the forest. "This is the battle line."

"That will be good. Keep the fight in the woods," I say. "It will give plenty of cover and obstacles."

"If there IS a fight, wouldn't it be easier on the clear plain?" Sabrina asks.

"Normally, yes," I say.

"If you have the advantage," Dylan adds.

We both studied battle tactics and defending strategies under my father. He was a mastermind in the art of war.

"But Felix has the upper hand," I say. "So, we need to use anything to our advantage. In this case, the land."

"We know the forest, and they don't," Sammy says.

I flash a wicked grin. "Exactly."

One of the cousin's sway on his feet and asks, "So now what? You've made a battle line, but what's that mean?"

Dylan and I exchange a knowing look.

I say, "You need to get all of the elderly, young, and anyone that can't physically fight below the battle line."

Dylan nods in agreement.

"Set your top guards at the line here." I point to the midsection. "And have them begin to curve north to the Pack House."

Pointing to the map, Dylan traces his fingers along a line and then marks a circle. "Keeping them to the northwest corner of the territory."

Sabrina rolls her eyes. "And then what? We just wait to be attacked? Great plan."

Dylan pounds his fist on the table and snarls. "No, that is our defense. The rest of us will attack."

I clear my throat. Even though I wouldn't shed a tear if Sabrina was injured or worse, it's in the best interest of this Pack's survival to share my knowledge.

"Felix's men will scatter, running rampant throughout the land," I say. "They'll be looking for weak targets and individuals they can quickly kill. This pack needs to stay together and show their strength."

Dylan nods and then points to the middle of the forest. "We can cluster in the center."

I study the location. It is halfway between the battle line and the northwest area. It's also halfway from the Pack House and the western border.

"Don't forget to use the forest to your advantage," I say, adjusting my tote bag on my shoulder.

"Here's a cluster of boulders. We can use them and keep the element of surprise," Dylan says.

I nod. "Okay, you know what you need to do. Now I need to get going."

"I still want to come," Gavin says.

"No, you and Sammy are strong and loyal. Dylan needs you here." I give Gavin and Sammy a hug, then offer Dylan my hand. "Good luck."

He extends his hand into a forearm handshake. My skin burns as it makes contact with his, but his eyes are clear and golden brown. He wraps his arms around me, pulling me into an embrace.

"Be safe," he whispers into my ear.

We both know that's a promise I can't make.

TURNING my back and walking away—away from her—was the hardest part of this deal. The whimpers and barks that escaped her wolf were almost my undoing; if I saw her face, that would've been the end of me.

Why does she have such an effect on me?

Felix leads us a few miles west through the thickest part of the forest until it opens into a field. I despise this field. This is where Elizabeth and I were held. The last time I was here, the grass bled red at my own hands.

Crossing the field of death, my head twitches, and I shake that memory from my thoughts.

Nothing dares to grow here after the brutal events Mother Earth witnessed. This once beautiful field is now nothing more than a barren wasteland.

I watch my feet as I walk, not wanting to look at the view any longer.

My heart skips a beat, and I'm brought to my knees. There's a little green speck in the dry dirt. It's a small rosette of soft, fuzzy leaves.

Before I can take another look, the chain around my neck tightens, pulling me off balance.

"Hurry up," the man called Cody says.

Standing, I glance at the small plant growing near my feet once more. Mullein. A small herb. How did it start growing here?

Lucinda's face explodes into my thoughts as I climb the small rocky hill that lies beyond the field. Her plump ruby lips and charming smile haunt me.

At the top of the hill, a single tree stands tall, looking down over the valley below. It's in full bloom with small white flowers, and as we walk near, I recognize it as a Bradford Pear.

Cody chains my back against the wide trunk with my arms behind me and walks away, leaving me alone to be consumed in my thoughts once more.

I can't stop thinking of that little mullein plant growing in the dusty soil. Beautiful things can grow from hardened and damaged goods.

The odor of dead fish fills the air as a light breeze blows the blossoms of the tree.

What is the horrific smell?

Twisting my torso, I strain to peer over my shoulder at the valley below. My stomach churns and my nostrils flare. Felix has no intention of leaving. His entire pack is below in the valley, and by the looks of it, they have been here a while. My lips twist into a silent snarl.

The morning sun crosses high into the sky before Cody comes to unchain my leash from the tree.

"Why do you support Felix?" I ask.

He pauses for a moment and then turns to me. "Things are happening in this world that you don't know about. And right now, Felix is the only one cleaning up the mess."

With that, he leads me down the hillside to enter their camp.

I'm surprised to see such a diverse group: young children, elderly men and women, and the strong warrior men and women. Walking between their tents, the smell of rotten carcasses and salty death fills the air.

I wonder how many before me have made this same walk.

People exit their tents and stand from their log seats at the fireside to watch me pass. The men, women, and children at the camp are dirty, and covered in grime from head to toe.

I guess hygiene isn't at the top of their priority list.

As we near the center of the camp, the putrid stench fades away and is replaced with a new sweet and savory, mouth-watering smell. And my stomach reminds me I haven't eaten anything all day.

Smoke rises from the iron pot that hangs over a campfire where two burly men stand. The scars on their faces and arms tell me they're warriors of this pack.

"Hungry?" Cody asks.

I look up to him, keeping my head bent down. "No."

He continues walking.

Would he have given me food if I'd said yes? It doesn't matter. I don't want anything from these people. I will be in no one's debt.

We stop, and he chains me to a pole near the outskirts of the camp.

"Be a good lad and maybe we'll throw you a bone," a young, cocky warrior bellows, and loud grunts and laughter fill the air.

Sitting down, I lean against the wooden pole. I haven't seen Felix since we arrived. How long will he drag this out?

Hopefully, my pack will obey my orders and be done with it. But my gut tells me Lucinda won't leave it be, so I need this business to be done before she does something stupid.

I wish I could've spoken to her one last time or told Dylan my plan. But if they didn't provide a true reaction, Felix would've noticed and suspected something.

I mentally kick myself. I should've taken Felix and his men on the field; I had been on the verge of losing control when the flood of memories came. *Why didn't I do it then? If I had, they'd be dead and I'd be free.* But this camp, the children... I can't have their death on my hands.

Tilting my head back against the pole, I close my eyes. My inner wolf is snickering. *Good job, Caiden. You've backed yourself into a corner. Now, what are you going to do?*

"Hey." A heavy boot kicks my thigh, and a rough voice says, "Stand up."

Opening my eyes, a dark figure stands above me.

"Hurry up. Alpha Felix doesn't wait for anyone," he says. His breath reeks of ale.

I stand and take a moment to stretch my back. The stocky guard grunts, and in a fluid motion, his cold palm slaps me across the cheekbone.

Pain throbs across my skin, but I will not give him the satisfaction. Resisting the urge to touch my face, I look the man square in the eye and smirk.

"Lead the way," I say.

The man's eyes narrow and turn the color of coal while his eyebrows knit together. His fangs extend past his lips, and he clenches his jaw.

"We wouldn't want to make Felix wait, now, would we?" I say.

With another grunt, he walks forward, leading me to Felix.

As we approach a large tent, my lips curl, and I try to spit out the bitter taste in my mouth. *How can Felix have a tent that would house a dozen families when I passed more than a dozen families that had no shelter at all?*

The man opens the canvas door, and a billow of smoke is released into the cool night air. When I step into the tent, I'm transported to another place at another time.

Incense hang heavy in the air, Persian rugs cover the ground—along with floor pillows of every shape and size—and decorative oil lamps scattered throughout the large tent provide the only lighting. There are three poles near the center of the tent, and I mistakenly think they're part of the tent construction.

However, as I stand in the doorway awaiting Felix, a woman takes to the pole, wrapping her legs around it and swinging her body as if the pole were part of her.

My throat burns as I force another swallow. *How can he live so lavishly, compared to the families I saw earlier?*

Felix sits upon a throne of lavish pillows near the center of the room. He motions me forward with his hands. I carefully shuffle past the girl without interrupting her dance. My chains clang with every step.

"Sit," Felix says.

I reluctantly sit down facing Felix. A small table divides us, full of platters of food and bottles of red wine.

"Hungry?" he asks.

"No, but thank you."

"Come on, eat. I don't want to kill you." Felix takes a swig of wine.

"Then what do you want with me?"

He licks his fingers and puts cheese, olives, and meat on his plate. "I've seen you before, several years ago back on that field we crossed."

I blink once, and my lips pull into a tight line.

"I watched the whole thing. A real shame what they did to that poor girl. Who was she—your mate, right?"

My nostrils flare, and I clench my jaw, but I remain silent.

"But the real beauty is what happened after. I almost

missed it. The encore—what your wolf did—was a master-piece," Felix says, placing his fingertips to his lips and kissing the air. "So tell me about your wolf."

"My wolf?"

"Yes. That rugged beast that knows no bounds." He leans forward, closer to me, and his eyes light up. "Is that beast always your wolf? How do you control it?"

"No. And there is no controlling it." I pick a cheese cube from his plate.

"No controlling it? Interesting." He hands me his plate of food. "Then how are you not that beast right now?"

I shove my mouth full of food in order to gain more time to think. How much do I share with him? He's cursed by the witch too. If he thinks he can use the beast, then he's wrong. I will not let him use me in that manner. I will kill myself before I let that happen.

"Well?" Felix asks.

"I'm in control right now." I swallow the rest of the food.

"That must be painstaking—to be in constant battle with yourself," he says. "So what happens when you lose control?"

"I leave."

"How often does your beast come out to play?"

"He doesn't come out to play," I say under my breath.

"You've piqued my curiosity, Caiden, and that doesn't happen often." Felix takes another sip of wine. Several beats of silence pass before he speaks again. "Do you see friend or foe as the beast? Do you recognize your friends?"

I give my attention to the dancer, allowing my silence to speak for me.

"I see," Felix says. "So how is it that you haven't hurt anyone in your pack on the rare occasions the beast has been let loose?"

Again, I let my silence answer for me.

"That must be a terrible burden. What would Lucinda ever think?" he says.

I turn back to him and stare into his dark eyes, refusing to be the first to look away. Finally, he looks to the woman still dancing behind me.

"Thank you for the food. Are we done now?" I ask.

"For now." He waves his hand for me to leave.

I stand and cross the room to exit. A hard object hits my head, and shadows hover above me as I lie on the ground.

When my eyes open, it takes a minute for them to adjust to the darkness. Though it won't be dark for long—dawn is on the horizon.

My hands and feet are no longer bound by silver chains. Instead, they've been replaced by a bamboo cage. I reach up to massage my neck and release a hiss. Blisters have formed from the heavy silver necklace that rubbed my skin raw. Wincing, I brush against the weeping scabs. It'll take longer for the damage made by silver to heal.

A quick glance around, I'm back on the open field, and my heart aches just being in this place.

Two figures approach from the tree line: Felix and Cody.

"You're finally awake. Now the fun can begin!" Felix clasps his hands together, looking like a pup on his first hunt. "Cody, go and ensure no one is hurt. We're just cattle drivers today, bringing them into a central location for the big event."

"What big event?" I ask through my teeth.

"Oh, don't worry yourself over the details. You'll find out soon enough." Felix strums his fingers in front of his face. "Our little chat last night inspired me. I need Lucinda, and I can't wait any longer. I've dreamt of marking her, claiming her as mine, forever—the moment my sharp canines pierce her soft flesh, tasting her metallic blood, feeling its warmth running down my chin and intertwining our souls for a lifetime."

I search the field; it's only him and me. If I'm going to release the beast, I need to do it now so I can be long gone before anyone else arrives. If I don't figure out a way to handle this myself, it will only lead to more deaths in my pack.

Heat rises to my head as my body begins to transform, and a growl escapes as my wolf is overcome by the beast. The last thing I see is the gray veil that covers my eyes, pushing me into unconsciousness while the beast comes out to play.

I hope I don't cross paths with any friends tonight because the beast will kill them all, friend or foe.

CHAPTER 30

LUCINDA

A DAMN BAT FLIES OVERHEAD, and an owl perched near me takes flight with a loud flap of his wings.

Why won't the creepy bat leave me the hell alone?

The very presence of that leathery creature of the night sends chills racing up my spine. I will kill that flying beast one of these days.

Sitting on a nearby rock, I swear under my breath. I may be good at climbing, fighting, and planning both offensive and defensive battle strategies, but tracking is not my strong point, especially in the dark.

Before sunset, I returned to the last place I saw Caiden's blue eyes and smelled his scent. But in the darkness of night, and in a part of the forest I've never traveled, making progress has proven to be a challenge. Their scent has faded, and I can't see their track marks. I've caught myself more than once walking in circles.

I slide off the rock to lie on the damp forest floor and gaze upon the cool mist beginning to form.

"Caiden, I'm so sorry I've failed you," I whisper to the

stars, and a small tear runs down my cheek. Closing my eyes, I let the tendrils of the mist cover my body.

"Lucinda?" a voice whispers, waking me as the first ray of sun lights up the night sky. "Lucinda are you near?"

"Cody?" I ask.

The voice is fading in and out. He must be too far away for the mindlink.

"Lucinda, where are you?" he asks.

"I'm in the forest. Where are you?" I sit up and shake my legs against the forest floor. A spark of hope flashes through my chest, causing my heart to flutter.

"In the forest too."

"Is Caiden with you? Is he alright?"

"Lucinda, you need to hurry!" The urgency in his voice surprises me, and I jump to my feet. "It's started."

"What do you mean? What's started?" My heart pounds against my chest.

"The attack—"

"Where's Caiden?" I start running, unsure where to go. "Cody?"

"Still here." His voice is stronger; he must be getting closer.

"Where's Caiden?"

"Felix has him in the field. You need to hurry. Set him free if you can—just get him away from the field before we return."

"Before who returns?"

"The battle. Go!"

"Got it," I say. "One question, where is the field?"

"West, go west, and hurry."

I stop and strip off my clothes, stuff them into my tote bag, and waste no time shifting into my wolf. Grabbing the tote with my teeth, I look to the sky and take off running away from the rising sun.

Ahead, the forest thins. This must be the field Cody spoke of.

I slow my pace and creep up to the forest edge, staying well hidden by the large ferns covering the forest floor.

In the center of the field, Caiden's large white wolf towers over Felix, and seeing him alive causes my heart to flutter.

Though something is wrong.

This wolf is playing with Felix, taunting him as a cat would a mouse. He lets Felix run away, only to be batted down again with one swoop. Then he picks Felix up in his mouth, his sharp canines drawing fresh blood as he tosses Felix in the air. Felix lands in a crumpled mess on the cold, damp ground.

I gasp. This isn't Caiden; it's his cursed wolf. My pulse quickens, and my paws tremble.

Growls and barks break the silence in the forest. With each yelp and snarl, the battle gets closer and closer.

Caiden watches the edge of the forest where I hear the oncoming wolves. He leaves Felix and prowls toward the battle sounds.

I need to stop him. He'll never forgive himself if he harms one of his pack members.

Before I realize what I'm doing, I leap into view on the open field.

My quick movement catches his attention, and he turns to face me. We're several yards apart, but there's no mistaking his crimson eyes and blood-soaked muzzle.

I plant myself firmly on all four of my strong legs. I hold my tail straight out in line with my back, and my ears stand tall.

Caiden snarls, his fur bristles, and his lips curl, showing his sharp incisors. He stalks toward me as if I were his prey.

With one flip of my tail, the dirt beneath me stirs, and I stride toward him.

His pace quickens.

Good. I need to lead him away before the others arrive. Isn't that what Cody said?

I turn on my heels and charge toward the hill in the opposite direction of the forest, hoping he'll follow. When I look back, I tumble to the ground, rolling three times before I stop. I underestimated Caiden's speed.

His crimson eyes glare at me from above, demanding my submission. He stands tall on strong, stiff legs, towering over me. His ears prick, and his hackles rise as he snarls.

In the corner of my eye, the other wolves reach the open field. I leap at Caiden, knocking him off balance, and jump over him. He catches my hind leg with his razor-sharp claws, and an involuntary yelp escapes me.

His claw runs through me like a zipper, cutting my hind leg open. But, I'm able to kick away and limp up the hill. But sharp teeth slice into my back and my legs collapse under the weight.

Twisting my body, we roll and tumble down the hill. I manage to free myself from Caiden's strong jaw, but not without damage.

My only hope is he understands the sign of submission.

I look up to him from my position on the ground and expose my throat and belly, letting loose a series of short whimpers.

He crouches low and closes in on my crumpled body. His lips curl, drool dripping from his teeth, and his hairs stand erect, displaying his dominance.

My heartbeat races.

He continues his slow prowl toward me. And then Dylan's wolf pummels Caiden, knocking them both to the ground. More wolves come to Dylan's aid, facing off against Caiden.

Do they know it's Caiden?

If only I could speak to them!

I howl and whimper.

Lifting myself off the ground, my front legs wobble, and as my back raises off the ground my back legs fold under me.

One wolf is thrown over my head, and another is tossed in the opposite direction. They both whine as their bodies slam into the hard ground.

Dylan still faces off with Caiden. They're doing the wolf battle dance, circling each other, baring their teeth, and growling.

I run to them just as Caiden goes in for the kill, aiming for Dylan's throat. Seeing it before Dylan, I force my weakened body to leap between them, blocking the fatal bite.

Caiden's teeth cut into my flesh, piercing my shoulder and ripping through skin and muscle. My body hits the ground with such force, I shift back into my human form. I yearn to smell his signature scent one last time, but the bergamot has been replaced with a musky smell, and my nose twitches.

The last thing I see is Caiden's crimson eyes fading to blue before I slip away into darkness.

Opening my eyes, I look around. I'm in my room back at the Pack House, lying in my bed. My body aches, and my head throbs; my head, shoulders, and midsection are covered in bandages.

My door is cracked open and low voices come from the hall. I perk up my ears and recognize Dylan and Caiden.

"You need to mark her," Caiden says.

"No," Dylan replies.

"Are you just going to leave her for Felix to claim?"

Caiden keeps his voice to a whisper, but I hear the demanding tone.

"I can't."

"Although, I have a feeling that still wouldn't stop Felix from taking her. But it would at least make her stronger. You need to mark her," Caiden says.

"You should," Dylan says.

"Should what?"

"You should mark her—claim her as your own," Dylan whispers.

A few moments of silence pass, then Caiden responds. "No. I won't."

CHAPTER 31

CAIDEN

DYLAN IS SO STUBBORN. He is testing my authority and my patience.

Pacing back and forth in my room, I try to calm down. Lucinda needs to be marked or else Felix will claim her as his own.

Dylan is her Fated Mate and the person that should mark her—the right choice—but he won't.

Sitting on the edge of my bed and pulling at my hair in frustration, I sigh. I know Dylan thinks he is doing what's right by trying to protect her from his curse, but there must be another way.

As the Alpha, I approve or disapprove of a pairing, but forcing someone to mark another...I can't do that. I won't do that. Other Alphas may, but I will never force a pairing. However, if Lucinda goes unclaimed, what will happen to her? Felix will always pursue her—I saw the desire in his eyes as he spoke of her.

I jump to my feet and with a growl, I twist and punch the wall. The plasterboard cracks around my fist, leaving a hole when I pull my hand back. I pant heavily and lean my forehead against the wall. I can't mark her, not after what I just did to her. I almost killed her.

A few minutes tick by before I take a step back, rub my right hand over the fresh hole in the wall, then examine the bloody cuts on my knuckles that have already started to heal.

Heading to the kitchen to clean up my hand, I hear voices from inside Lucinda's cracked door. I stand against the wall next to her door, carefully peering through the opening, and listen.

"You're stupid, you know that?" Dylan says and runs his hand through his hair.

Lucinda flops onto her bed. "Why?"

"You could've gotten yourself killed jumping in front of Caiden like that. What were you thinking?" Dylan paces in front of the bed.

Lucinda rolls over onto her back and stares at the ceiling. "Why are you complaining? I saved your life."

Dylan sits on the bed next to her. "You shouldn't have."

"You're welcome," she says dryly. "But what happened anyway?" She flips over on her stomach, and gazes at Dylan.

Dylan rubs her back. "Caiden calmed down and shifted back to his human form as soon as he saw you shift."

That is true—well, for the most part. It's what I told him.

The truth is that when I saw her lying on the ground with blood coming from her head, something inside me snapped. I recognized her, and at that moment, I took control of the beast; I saw Lucinda through his eyes and could control his actions.

I fear my wolf and the wild beast have intertwined. The sensation I experienced was the strangest thing, and I haven't been able to completely free myself of that feeling.

Lucinda's voice brings me from my internal thoughts.

"How did I get back here?" she asks.

"Caiden insisted on carrying you," Dylan says. "He was different—possessive."

My nostrils flare and my jaw clenches. I didn't realize anyone noticed the change in my behavior. I'll have to be more careful.

"And Felix?" she asks.

Dylan plays with Lucinda's hair. "We presume he's still alive. After you hit your head on the stone in the field and Caiden shifted back, all of Felix's men fled. We searched the bodies for Felix, but he wasn't found."

Lucinda jumps from the bed. "I have to go. We have to find him."

My heart aches. If only she knew.

"Lux, sit back down." Dylan pats to the bed next to him.

"Dylan, you don't understand. He'll come as soon as he's able," Lucinda says in a panicked voice.

Before I'm able to interrupt them, Dylan says, "He's already come."

My fingers curl into tight balls, my nails digging into the soft flesh of my palm. I didn't want to tell her yet. It all happened so fast. Felix was at the Pack House waiting for us when we arrived.

"What?" Lucinda says. "Tell me, tell me everything."

"He came with a peace treaty—"

"He can't be trusted."

"We know, but this one is different. This is peace in exchange for you."

My legs give out on me, and I slide down the wall to sit on the floor. *Now she knows, and I still don't know what to do. I wish we had more time to figure it out.*

"Oh," she says after a moment of silence.

"Lux, you don't have to," Dylan whispers.

"Answer me one thing. Have you ever loved me?"

"Yes," Dylan says. "But we'll never be anything more than friends."

Numbness spreads through my body as I stand. It's replaced with a surge of heat as I peek through the crack in the door again. Dylan sits on the bed next to her, caressing her cheek with his hand, leaning in as if he may kiss her. My heart explodes with a rage that I can't control.

Clearing my throat, I knock on the door and push it open.

"Caiden," Lucinda says.

My eyes soften when she leans away from Dylan as I enter.

"We'll talk later, okay?" Dylan says to her and walks past me. Stopping at the door, he adds, "I told her about Felix, so you two have things to discuss."

He closes the door behind him.

"How are you feeling?" I close the distance between us.

"Fine," she says without attempting a smile. Her shoulders round forward so she's slouching on the bed, and she won't meet my gaze.

She's upset, and I don't blame her. I did try to kill her, and now we're asking to trade her to Felix.

My heart sinks. I want to scoop her up in my arms and tell her everything will be okay, but I can't, so I remain silent.

"And how are you?" she asks, standing from her spot on the bed and finally looking at me.

I have no answer. My soul is split in two—both mentally and emotionally. The beast now shares a permanent place in my mind. I don't want to give her to Felix, but unless she joins my pack, I can't protect her.

No, I can't tell her that. Instead, I stare into her deep hazel eyes that twinkle with specks of gold.

"Dylan told me about Felix's peace treaty," she says.

"You don't have to go."

"Yes, I do."

"Stay." My voice croaks, and I reach for her hand, brushing her knuckles softly with my thumb.

"Why?"

A lump forms in my throat as I think of all the selfish reasons for her to stay.

"Stay for Dylan," I say.

"Nope, not good enough." Her eyes harden and she looks away.

"If you won't stay for your mate, then at least stay for your friends. Stay for Mia and Gavin."

"It's because of my friends that I have to leave."

"Your friends don't want to see you with Felix," I say through a clenched jaw. I don't want to be upset with her, but she's not making it easy.

"Maybe not, but he's apparently the only one that wants me." She gives a loud sigh, pulls her hand from mine, and sits on the bed. "I'm tired of running, always looking over my shoulder, wondering who I'll meet next—friend or foe. I just want a place to settle down and call home. No more running."

"You have friends here—people that care about you. This can be your home if you'll only accept the pack."

"It could've been in a different life, but not now," she says. "Not with Felix alive."

"We'll find him."

"You can't jeopardize your entire pack like that." She tosses her hands into the air. "You have injuries and casualties from this one battle. You don't want an ongoing feud."

I stand, thinking of exactly what to say. She thinks like an Alpha, always looking after her friends as if they were her own pack and putting the people of a pack before her own life.

"You're right. A feud isn't desirable. But if it'll keep you safe—"

"No. I will not let your pack destroy themselves to protect me. If I leave and go to Felix, I can at least ensure the safety of this pack."

"Lucinda!" I say in a low but firm tone and I kneel in front of her. "Think of your friends."

"I AM thinking of my friends!" She stands with such force I fall backward.

I stand to face her and reach for one of her hands. "Lucinda, you don't have to leave."

"Why should I stay? I'll only endanger my friends and your pack by staying."

I stare into her eyes and clench my jaw.

"Tell me, is there another reason I should stay?" she asks.

"Your friends care about you."

A cold shadow covers her eyes. It's not what she wanted to hear, but it's all I can offer.

She makes a slight nod as she steps closer to me. Leaning in, she kisses my cheek and whispers in my ear, "Thank you for your hospitality during my visit. I hope to see you again, but it's probably in our best interest that our paths don't cross in the future."

With that, she walks out of the room and out of my life.

Tiny needles stab my body, and shards of glass slice my heart in half. In a cloudy daze, I stand frozen in place, unable to move.

Tremors roll through my body, and I begin shaking with rage. A dark veil creeps into the shadows of my eyesight, threatening to overtake me. I can't control the beast this time.

I run out of the room and fly down the stairs. Glancing over my shoulder as I open the front door, I see Lucinda in the living room. She is sitting on the couch talking with Mia and Gavin. Dylan stands off to the side, staring at the ground.

"Caiden," Mia says. "You startled me. Is everything okay?"

Lucinda refuses to look at me.

I crinkle my nose and curl my hands into tight fists. *Why am I so angry with her?*

"Dude, you okay?" Gavin asks.

My eyes stay glued to the back of Lucinda's head, and a deep growl vibrates from low in my throat.

"Run it off," Dylan says through the mindlink.

I turn and walk out the front door, slamming it behind me. Leaping off the porch, I shift in midair, and my wolf charges into the forest.

For the sake of the beast within me, I hope Lucinda has left by the time I get home.

Or do I?

CHAPTER 32

LUCINDA

Caiden's big blue eyes shine with intensity, a deep hue of sapphire under a bright sunny day. He caresses my cheek with his hand; it's a bit rough and calloused, but his touch is soft and gentle. His hands move down to my neck, and his thumb crosses my lips as he steps closer, closing the distance between us.

With my chest pressed against his, his heart beats against my breasts. Lowering his head, he leans into me, and I am ready for his plump lips to meet mine…

I wake wide-eyed, grabbing at my face and chest as I try to slow my breathing. I had drifted off to sleep. *Damn it.*

One last rest in the safety and comfort of the Pack House. I gaze at the clear night sky through the window above my bed. The moon is almost full, and it lights up the sky to make the earth glow a beautiful silver.

I know he is there before he knocks. The scent of bergamot seeps through the door, causing my heart to flutter.

Three small knocks tap on the door. As I stand, a warmth rushes to my cheeks, and as I cross the room to the door and reach for the lock, I think of my dream. My wolf stirs, giddy with excitement. She's become anxious around Caiden the past few days.

"Lucinda, please open the door," Caiden whispers.

Leaning my head against the door, I move my hand from the lock. No. I can't let him in. I can't see or talk to him tonight. If I do, I may lose my nerve; I know what needs to be done.

With what small strength I can find, I take a deep breath and move away from the door.

I'll be leaving tonight. If I don't, I fear I will never leave.

I wait until I hear Caiden's bedroom door shut, then I peek into the hall. It's clear, so I hurry down the stairs, but a noise distracts me. Peering over the railing and down the hall, a light comes from Caiden's office. Again, I hear the shuffling of papers.

On tiptoe, I creep to the front door and slip through. The cool night air calms my nerves, and when I lift my face to the moon, strength surges through my soul. Is this boost real or just my imagination? It doesn't matter; it's exactly what I need.

I step off the porch and head into the forest.

A slow burn begins in the pit of my stomach—my wolf begs me to turn back—but no, I push forward.

Unsure of my exact destination, I head down the same path I took when I was looking for Caiden and Felix. Dylan told me Felix's camp is set up on the other side of that hill.

Walking through the forest, I can't help but daydream, and questions with no answers run through my mind. *What am I doing? If I hadn't overheard Dylan and Caiden talking, would I still be going to Felix? If Caiden would mark me, would that change things? Do I want Caiden to mark me? What does Caiden think of me?*

Lost in my own little world, I cross the field and climb the hill, still worrying about what Caiden will think of me after tonight. I stand at the top of the hill and look down at the tents and small campfires of my new home.

Not ready to give up thoughts of Caiden just yet, I spot a tree a few feet from me and sit down to lean against it. A faint scent of bergamot lingers among the bark of the trunk and my wolf whimpers.

Really, Lucinda? What were you thinking coming to Caiden's pack? What did we truly want? What did we expect from him? Did we just think the Alpha would take us in and protect us from Felix? No, silly girl, we knew better.

My wolf inside me stirs.

And after we saw Dylan, we knew we could never stay. We were planning to leave anyway, so why does this feel all wrong? Why does leaving the Blood Moone pack hurt so bad?

Every other time Dylan would turn his back and leave me or I would leave him, it always hurt—but never this bad. *Why now? What changed? Why is this pain so different?*

Taking a deep breath, I stand up and clench my jaw.

If I want the cover of darkness, then it's time to do this.

I head down the hill to face my new pack.

Since I prefer to be seen when I want to be seen and not before, I stay in the shadows, move between tents while placing each step carefully, and stay away from the light cast by the fires.

Felix taught me well; I would make a good rogue—a warrior—amongst his pack. Stealth, even in my human form, has become second nature to me, and with a little more practice I could be one hell of an assassin. But I will be the Luna of this pack—the Alpha's mate.

Chills ripple up my spine, causing goosebumps to prickle my arms at the thought of being Felix's mate.

Reaching my destination, I slip into Felix's tent, careful to stay in the shadows. I knew it was his as soon as I saw it; his tent is the most lavish in the pack.

"You're out of practice, my dear," Felix says with a sly grin.

Spinning, I spot him lying on a bed of furs near the rear of the tent.

"Felix." I step out from the shadows.

He turns up the small flame of an oil lamp to cast more light into the tent. "Finally, you've come to me. I was starting to think the Alpha—what's his name, Caiden—wasn't going to give you up."

His name pains my soul. Two large rocks pound together, smashing the shattered pieces of my broken heart. I blink back tears that threaten to escape and quiet the howls of my wolf inside.

"Sit, please sit." Felix motions to the large silk pillows that adorn the floor near his bed.

My eyes narrow as I glare at him and cross my arms over my chest.

"Fine, fine. Have it your way. We'll talk in the morning," he mumbles and lies back down in his bed.

I palm the hidden dagger that's tucked into my waist.

"Come on, he's not worth it," a male voice says behind me.

I flash a wicked grin. "Hey, Cody, miss me?"

"Welcome back." He pulls me in for a hug.

"I wish I could say I was glad to be back, but I'm not."

"Why are you back?" Cody asks. Pulling from our embrace, he looks deep into my eyes. "You shouldn't have come."

Felix stirs in his sleep. Cody raises his index finger to his lips as he grabs my hand and pulls me out of the tent.

We enter a smaller tent not too far from Felix's, and Cody motions for me to sit. There isn't much in this tent: a footlocker that I sit on, a stool, a candle, a cot, and a pile of furs.

"Here you go," he says, handing me a fur blanket.

"Thanks." I wrap the fur around me because the night air has become chilly.

"I'll make you a place to sleep. I'm not sure how long we'll stay camped here, but you can stay with me, or we can set up your own tent tomorrow."

"I'm not sure Felix would like it if I stayed with you," I say with a giggle. "So, let's plan on it."

"You're going to make his life pure hell, aren't you?" Cody asks.

I pucker my lips in a failed attempt to hide my mischievous grin.

"So why did you come back? You left here to get away from Felix, remember?"

Images of Caiden flash through my mind, and I grab my chest to stop my heart from aching.

"To kill Felix," I say.

Cody's smile wavers, and he studies me with a harsh grimace. "You may think you will, and you may want to, but you won't."

"Watch me." I twist in my seat.

"Do you want to tell me what really happened?"

I stare at the ground and shrug. "They don't want me."

Cody looks at me with an intense stare and then his lips pull into a devilish grin.

"What's so funny?" I ask, raising my eyebrows.

"Oh please, spare me the *'they don't want me'* bit," he says, using air quotes and mimicking my voice. "You have that Alpha's head spinning. I'm surprised he let you leave."

"Can't I ever have a pity party for myself? I should leave." I cross my arms over my chest. *It does sound like a lame excuse.*

"Stay. At least tonight?" Cody asks.

I reach out to Cody and squeeze his hand.

"I'll help you figure everything out tomorrow, okay?" Cody stands and throws a blanket on the floor.

I nod and lie down in the cot while Cody settles on the ground.

"Get some sleep," he says. "Tomorrow your new life in hell will begin."

Closing my eyes, I try to clear my mind, but Cody's right. Starting tomorrow, my life will be hell. If I run, Felix will follow. I'll forever be running.

But if I stay, my life will become a cruel and unusual punishment.

CHAPTER 33

CAIDEN

As soon as the sun begins to peek over the forest, I cross the hall and knock on Lucinda's door.

"Lucinda," I whisper through the door.

No response.

Leaning my ear against the door, I listen for movement and sniff for the scent my wolf yearns to smell. What I smell is an old lingering scent, nothing fresh.

I grab the doorknob, open the door, and step in. The room is empty.

"Where is she?" I ask Dylan through the mindlink.

"Who?" he says in a groggy voice.

"Lucinda. She's not in her room."

As I walk past his room, his door opens. He follows me downstairs, and we look through the rest of the house.

"She must've left after we went to bed," Dylan says.

I manage to choke back the growl that hangs in my throat.

"I guess your talk didn't go well before bed?" Dylan asks.

"No," I say through clenched teeth. "She wouldn't open the door."

Dylan leans against the living room wall, resting his head back and looking to the ceiling. "It's better this way."

"Better for who? You or Lucinda?" My lips curl as I speak her name.

"Both."

"I see how it's more convenient for you, but how is it better for Lucinda?" I dig my nails into the palms of my hands.

He sighs. "At least now someone that truly loves her will mark her and be her mate."

"That's not love. And she doesn't love him."

"Does any of that matter? If she stayed here, who would love her?" Dylan raises an eyebrow at me.

I haven't had a chance to think about my feelings for her. Is it love? I don't know. I do care for her, a lot. But I can't mark her. Knowing what it's like to lose a mate, I can't—I won't—claim anyone again.

I sit on the couch, rest my head on my hands, and look down. "Felix doesn't deserve her. He isn't capable of love."

"Then I guess you should've marked her," he says.

"Marked her and then what? Shipped her off to be Felix's mate?" I say. "No, I couldn't have done that."

"You could've marked her and had her stay."

"Condemning the pack to a life of war," I say under my breath.

I glare at him and watch his chest move in and out, taking slow, calculated breaths. A calming technique I know well.

Dylan crosses the room and picks up a glass figurine sitting on the mantle. "Do you believe in fate?" he asks.

"Fate?" Walking over to the window, I stare out into the forest and watch the fog rise off the cool ground as the sun rises to warm the morning mist. "Our mates are fated to us."

"What if being with Felix is Lucinda's fate?" Dylan asks.

"No, she had a choice. She didn't have to leave. As her mate, you are her fate," I growl.

Dylan joins me at the window. "The gypsy stole her fate years ago."

"And now she's carving her own destiny."

"She's a remarkable woman. Her fate was sealed by the gypsy witch, and the bravest of men would've been weakened by it, but not Lux. Oh no, not her. Rejection made her stronger," Dylan says.

I ball my hands into tight fists. They turn white at the knuckles, and I begin to shake. *Calm down, beast.*

"It may be her destiny to bring justice to that band of rogues and to what's left of Felix's Crescent Noir pack, but Felix is not her fate." I pound my fist into the palm of my other hand. An intense pressure bursts in my chest, and my lungs expand for fresh, cool air.

"I did some reading last night about Felix Noir and his pack from your father's notebooks," Dylan says. "They were once a real pack with land and territory. But over the years, their leadership stumbled and they became nothing more than a band of rogues wandering the forest."

My eyes sting, my lips itch, and my head burns. *What is happening?*

"She'll be good for them. She's a strong Alpha, so she'll be good for the weak people. Maybe it will even rise to be a real pack again."

A seething pain erupts inside my chest, and the sensation spreads through my veins, igniting every inch of my body until darkness consumes me.

Mia's voice rings through my head, pulling me from the darkness. "She left, didn't she?"

"Yes," Dylan says.

Flicking my fingers, I clench and unclench my fists, fighting for control.

"I love Lucinda and all, but it's best this way," Gavin says.

I turn from the window and glare at him. A smirk forms when Mia elbows Gavin in the stomach.

"Ouch! What was that for?" he says. "All I mean is calm down and stop thinking about it. We know how her mind works. Her first priority is to protect others. Her second priority is to protect herself. You know as well as I that she left to protect this pack."

"Where are you going with this?" Dylan asks.

"She must have a plan."

"A plan for what?" Mia asks.

"A plan to protect herself. I bet as we speak she's cooking up a scheme to kill Felix."

I hadn't thought of this before. That was my plan, but I failed miserably. I hope she knows what she's doing.

Turning to me, Gavin says, "And dude, you've gotta get yourself under control. You're starting to freak me out."

"Caiden?" Mia says, but her voice sounds off in the distance. "Caiden, are you okay?"

A jumble of voices rings out in my head, then a strong hand crosses my face, leaving a searing pain along my cheekbone and jawline.

Looking around, Mia, Gavin, Dylan, and Sammy are all standing in front of me, gaping and staring.

"Sammy! What the hell man?" I say, cupping my cheek.

"You'll thank me later."

"When did you get here?" I ask.

"Dude, you've been totally zoned out for like ever," Gavin says.

"It hasn't been forever—about ten minutes or so," Dylan corrects, then goes back to his lounging position against the wall.

"I walked in at the tail end of Gavin and Mia's little spat," Sammy says.

"Where were you, Caiden? What happened?" Mia kneels in front of me, placing her hands on my knees.

"I was thinking of Lucinda," I say. But where was I for real? *Am I losing my hold over the beast?*

"You wanna know what I've noticed?" Gavin backs away from Mia's reach.

"It's getting easier for Dylan but harder for you."

"What are you talking about?" Dylan asks from across the room.

"You know, the whole '*mate*' thing," Gavin says while using air quotes.

"What mate thing?" Sammy asks, looking around the room.

"Dylan is Lucinda's mate, but he rejected her," Gavin says.

Dylan growls and glares at Gavin.

"Gavin!" Mia yells. "That was a secret."

"I thought everyone here already knew," Gavin grumbles and turns to walk into the kitchen.

"Hello. Can someone please fill me in?" Sammy asks.

"There isn't much more to it," Dylan says under his breath.

"Okay, then let's start with why you rejected her."

"Because of the curse," Mia blurts.

Sammy rubs his chin. "Curse?"

"It's a long story," Gavin says, entering the room again eating a bagel. "Short story is that Caiden, Dylan, and Felix were all given gifts by a witch when they were named their Pack's next Alpha, but the gifts turned out to be curses."

"Right," Sammy says. "And where does Lucinda fit into all this, besides being Dylan's mate?"

Standing up I stomp across the room to look out the window at my sanctuary—the forest—again.

"I don't know," I say after a moment.

But Gavin is right. I've noticed my pull to Lucinda getting stronger and my wolf's protectiveness over her growing—even becoming possessive. What's going on?

Sammy's voice breaks the silence. "So, what are we going to do?"

CHAPTER 34

LUCINDA

IN THE MORNING, Cody is gone, and Felix is not around either, so I head to the closest fire pit, sit on a log, and watch the wild boar that's roasting on a stick just above the glowing embers.

"Get your own," says a man with a short and well-kept beard.

"I'm not hungry."

"Oh no? So whatcha want?" another man asks. He has a deep scar starting in the middle of his forehead and continuing at a diagonal through his eye, down his cheek.

I try to remember these two men, but I don't. And taking a quick look around the campsite, I realize I don't recognize many of the other warriors either.

"You a mute now, or just playin' hard to get?" The man with the scar winks.

"I don't want anything," I snap. These are the type of men that get my wolf anxious, and she's starting to stir inside me, causing the hair on my arms to stand on end.

"Oh, no?" the man with the scar says. "Do you hear that, Gregory? She doesn't want anything."

Both men begin to laugh, and I focus on steadying my breathing, calming my inner wolf.

"Haven't seen you around before," the man with the beard, Gregory, says.

"You haven't been with Felix very long, have you?" I ask.

"What's it to a little girl like you?" the man with the scar says.

"Leave her alone, Brutus," Gregory warns.

"I'm not bothering her, am I, kitten?" Brutus kneels in front of me and flashes a cruel smile.

"Maybe I do want something after all," I say.

"And what is that, sweet thing?"

I stand, walk over to the roasting boar, and tear off a chunk of meat.

"Breakfast, thanks!" I glare and sit back down.

"Sassy little thing, aren't you?" Brutus rubs his grubby hand on my shoulder.

"Don't touch me," I growl.

"No? Women like it when I touch them. You," he shouts at a woman walking by carrying two buckets of water. She puts down the buckets and cowers in front of him. He grabs the woman's breast and licks her cheek. "See, kitten. Women like my touch."

"Leave her alone." I deepen my voice and straighten my posture.

"Why? Are you jealous?" He continues to roam his hands over the woman's body.

"STOP!" I stare into his eyes as I pull the woman away from him.

Anger builds up within me, and I fight for control of my wolf—she wants to tear into Brutus's neck. I push out a wave of power, exerting my Alpha dominance over him like a flood of rushing water on a mountain stream.

Brutus mentally fights the urge to submit; the vein across

his forehead throbs and swells, but eventually he gives in, bowing his head and kneeling at my feet.

"Don't ever touch her again." I point to the woman behind me. A growl slips through my lips. "Or anyone else in this camp. Do you understand me?"

"Hello, darling," Felix says, walking up behind me. "I see you're reacquainting yourself with our pack members." He places his hand on the small of my back and adds through the mindlink, "If you ever display dominance over my warriors again, you'll be punished."

Slowly twisting my head over my shoulder to glare at Felix, the intensity of my hard eyes and tight lips cause him to lose his fake smile.

"I will not stand by and allow your so-called warriors to do what they wish to other members against their will," I say to Felix through the mindlink.

"You'll be beaten and whipped for disobedience," Felix threatens.

I raise my eyebrows. "You'd do that?"

"As my mate, you'll do my bidding," he says out loud in a stern but low voice. "And I'll do what needs to be done."

"You may claim me, marking me as your own, but I'll never be your mate."

Felix's lips curl into a devilish grin. "You aren't the scared little girl that ran away."

"No, I'm not." A snarl escapes and my nostrils flare.

Silence weighs heavily on us. A hush spreads over the camp, and everyone freezes in place, witnessing our exchange. I can only imagine they've never seen anyone talk to Felix in this manner and live.

"I will enjoy this more than I thought," Felix taps his fingertips together in front of his face.

My lips curve up into a lopsided smirk. "I won't, but you better keep your promise—"

"What promise is that? I make so many."

"The peace treaty with the Blood Moone pack. I'm here, so—"

"Oh, right, right…" He dismisses me and the conversation with a flick of his wrist and turns to leave.

"Felix, do I have your word?" I ask.

"Of course, of course. Our ceremony will be at dawn, so enjoy the rest of your last day and night as an unmarked female," he says from a distance as he continues to walk away, leaving me standing in the same spot with everyone's eyes watching my next move.

"Hey, Cody," I say, finding his familiar face among the bystanders.

"Ballsy, Cinda. When did you grow a pair?" Cody teases as he ambles over.

"Someone needs them."

"Come on, let's go talk." He pulls my arm to follow him. Once we've passed the outskirts of the camp, he asks, "What are you doing?"

"What do you mean?" My thoughts drift to Caiden and Dylan as I look over the grassy nook. It's so peaceful; the sun is shining and the birds are singing. *I wonder what they're doing right now, at this moment.*

A nudge to my shoulder knocks me slightly off balance and brings me back to reality. Cody stands next to me.

"Cinda, why are you here? The truth this time," he asks.

"Hm. What am I doing here? I'm here because I don't want to see the Blood Moone pack attacked—"

"No, seriously. If that were the case, why not kill Felix in his sleep?" Cody spins to face me and we make eye contact.

"Maybe I will." I look away to the forest in the distance.

"You're not a bloody killer. So honestly, what is it you want?"

Sitting down in the middle of the field, I play with the long grass.

"Life with Felix won't be easy," Cody says.

"I know. I don't expect it to be. And I don't plan to make it easy for him either." I flash a smile, but it doesn't reach my eyes. "I think I can help these people."

He sits next to me. "And what about yourself? Who's going to help you?"

"That's what I have you for, right?" I bump him with my shoulder.

"If this is what you really want—"

"I'll have a mate who wants me more than life itself, a pack to call my own, and a place to call home. What more could I ask for?" Any attempt at enthusiasm fades with each breath. "It's all I've ever wanted."

"If you think being mated to a psychotic Alpha is the only chance you'll have at happiness, damn it, who am I to stand in your way?" Cody laughs, and the sound is contagious. I laugh along with him so hard that tears stain my cheeks.

But as our laughter dies down, I stand up and gaze out into the forest, allowing myself one last thought of all the friends I left behind.

"Come on, we should be getting back," Cody says.

"Yes, I'm eager to be bonded for eternity to the dark and sinister Alpha." I roll my eyes and growl.

Arriving back at camp, we walk past Felix's tent, and hushed voices come from inside. Standing on the outside of the tent, I listen.

"Yes, tonight," Felix says. "I want it done by the time the ceremony is over."

"We'll head out at dusk," another man says.

"Oh, and Brutus," Felix says, "bring me the Alpha's head on a stake. I want to present it to Lucinda as a gift to commemorate our union."

Fighting against my wolf's urges to shift, I move to stand in the doorway and ensure my presence is known. The grin on Felix's face tells me that he knew I was listening before he made his last comment. My stomach turns to acid and threatens to spill up my throat.

"Lucinda, darling, how nice to see you," Felix says.

"And what Alpha do you plan to present to me during our Mating Ceremony?" I ask through a clenched jaw.

Excitement flashes in Brutus' eyes. "The beast."

CHAPTER 35

LUCINDA

"FELIX." My voice is low and strained. I crack my knuckles as I rein in my wolf, and I lick my lips as my cool, moist fangs protrude out of my mouth.

"Oh no, my dear, you misunderstand," Felix says in his silky voice as he walks over to me.

"I should've known better," I growl. "Why did I think this time would be any different?"

"Blinded by love, or is it heartbreak? Either way, darling, you really should calm down." Felix's pupils dilate and we lock eyes.

"I came to you of my own free will. How can you do this?"

"And exactly what is it that you think I'm doing?"

"You're breaking your promise to the Blood Moone pack."

Felix examines a walking stick in his hand. "No, dear, I assure you I am not."

Tilting my head, I arch my eyebrows, but I hold my stare. I will not be the first to look away. I will not submit to Felix.

"You see, my dear, this is all a misunderstanding," he coos.

"So, explain it to me."

He leans against the stick, supporting his weight. "My

promise was that no harm would come to the Blood Moone pack. And I don't intend to harm the pack—"

"Just the Alpha," Brutus says, his eyes wide with excitement and his lips curling into an arrogant smirk to match his enthusiasm.

"Why?" I ask. "He's no threat to you."

"A threat? That's yet to be determined. But that's not why I want his head. You misunderstand me again," Felix says in his silky voice and waves his walking stick in the air.

"Don't be coy with me." I choke back a growl.

"Darling, he's competition. That's all, plain and simple. You have feelings for him, and if you're to be mine after tonight, then he can't live." Giving up his dominating tactics, he looks away.

"I will be yours. That's why I'm here." The pit of my stomach ignites into an unquenchable burning sensation. And, I fight back my wolf's urges to shift and attack.

"But for how long? I need reassurance. In the little amount of time I spent with that Alpha, I could tell he had feelings for you too."

"You're going to kill him because you're jealous?" I say under my breath.

"I can assure you I've done much worse."

"I won't let you do this." Anger boils in my stomach, moving down to my legs and up into my arms. My hands shake with rage.

"Of course not, my dear, so please forgive me for this." Once again, Felix examines the handle of his walking stick and then motions in the air with it and two guards approach me from behind. "Tie her up and chain her to the pole."

Four strong hands grab my shoulders, pulling me back.

"What? No!" I yell.

I kick my legs as I'm pulled backward, punching my arms in the air as I struggle to break free. Just as I'm about to shift into my wolf, a chain tightens around my neck, making it impossible for me to fully shift.

Looking over my shoulder, I see Cody holding the other end of the chain.

Pieces of my already shattered heart fall again, breaking into more fragmented pieces that will never again be fully whole.

"Lucinda," Cody whispers, "don't fight it. You'll only make it worse."

"You're worried about this situation getting worse?" I ask.

"Yes, it could be much worse."

A low, wicked laugh escapes through my lips.

"Is something funny, my dear?" Felix asks.

"Oh no, nothing at all," I say, flashing a sweet and innocent smile.

"Take her away then, and Brutus, get your men ready to go." He waves his hand in the air to dismiss us all.

"Damn straight it could get worse," I say to Cody through the mindlink. "Just wait until I get free."

Cody ties me to the pole but leaves the ropes around my wrists and ankles loose and the chain around my neck unlocked.

"These should hold you," he says with a wink, then he walks back into Felix's tent.

Brutus struts across the campsite and talks to a small group of men that sit around sloshing mugs of ale.

Being tied to the pole isn't as bad as I thought it would be. Yes, everyone stares as they walk by or watches me from where they sit from afar, but from my seat, I can see everything and everyone in the camp.

A group of young warriors plead with Brutus to tag along on his mission tonight. Other men take their leave of the mission, wanting nothing to do with the beast. And women throw themselves at the brave warriors that have accepted the mission.

I roll my eyes in disgust.

Shrills of laughter catch my attention, and I turn toward the back of the camp where the non-warriors live. For a moment, I smile, watching a group of kids run around chasing each other with a ball. They laugh as they tumble on the ground when the ball hits them.

A young warrior—one Brutus denied earlier—takes the children's ball between his hands and flattens it. A snarl replaces my smile as the warrior returns to his group of friends and deep bellows of laughter fill the air. Several rounds of hoots, hollers, and pats on the back follow.

I spit in the dirt next to me. They make my stomach ill.

Leaning my head back against the pole, I close my eyes to think.

———

A kick to my thigh wakes me from my thoughts.

"You got a message you want to be delivered? Any last words for the beast?" Brutus asks.

I snarl. "I'll tell him myself next time I see him."

"You do realize it'll only be a head on a stake that I bring back, right?"

Shifting my weight, I stare up at Brutus. "You sure about that?"

Brutus growls and storms away.

Cody sits on the ground next to me. "What was that about?"

"Just a few words of encouragement." I shrug.

Cody eyes me carefully and shakes his head while Brutus and his small group of men get ready to leave on their suicide mission. They down a few more pints of ale, sharpen their teeth and claws on a sharpening stone and do one last hurrah around the campfire.

Such arrogant SOBs heading into their hunt for Caiden's head. I pity them.

Instead of focusing on Caiden and the impending attack, I focus on Felix. He steps out of his tent, takes a long glance in my direction, and gives one last order to Brutus through the mindlink for all to hear.

"The Alpha will be brought back to me alive. I want his death to be part of the mating ceremony with my new mate."

How romantic. A nauseous sensation stirs in my stomach, and a fire rages deep inside my soul.

"Oh Kitty, you and I will kill him together, sealing our fate to one another for all of time."

Vomit threatens to coat my throat, but I choke it down.

As soon as Brutus and his pack of wild dogs run off, I stand from my seated position and lean against the pole.

I yell across the campsite. "Felix!"

"Ah, my dear," he strolls over to me with his arms open, reaching for an embrace. "I trust they've been taking good care of you."

"I will kill you before this night is through," I whisper, dropping the ropes and chain that bound me. Leaping through the air, I shift into my wolf and pin Felix onto his back with an audible thud.

"Oh, so is that how you like foreplay?" Felix grins.

I snarl with bared teeth, and drool drips onto his face.

Men run to form a circle around us. A few of them have spears pointed at me, trying to poke and prod my wolf.

I bite and snap my heavy jaw at the spear tips that come close.

"Is it a good idea to agitate an already agitated wolf?" I ask them through the mindlink.

A few falter in their stance while others continue to step closer.

"Stand down," Cody says to the men. "She's challenged the Alpha, and she deserves a fair fight."

I look to Cody and nod—a small sign of appreciation. Felix uses this small distraction to push me from his chest. I roll onto my back and quickly get back on my feet as he shifts into his wolf.

Felix and I face off, circling each other, and my canines slip past my lower lip and a deep growl vibrates up my throat. I bared teeth as any aggressive predator would do. My heart beats at a rapid pace, and I need to steady it. *He can't know I'm nervous or he'll use it against me.*

My tail thrashes, and Felix leaps for me, all four paws leaving the ground.

I see my opening.

Twisting my body at the last moment, I dodge his attack and sink my teeth into his hind leg before it touches the ground.

A yelp escapes him. He turns to look at me; his eyes are fully dilated and turning jet black, and his razor-sharp canines drip with saliva.

The crowd surrounding us has grown considerably. It seems the entire camp has formed a large circle around us, watching as spectators would watch gladiators fight in an arena.

My heart pounds and Felix rushes toward me, only this time I'm not quick enough to dodge him. His teeth find my shoulder, sinking through my fur, and pierce my skin. He clamps down hard and gives a slight jerk of his head, successfully tearing more skin before I'm able to throw him off me.

Limping around to face him again, I flash my incisors and growl.

He charges me. I leap, meeting him in midair.

We're dancing, both standing on our hind legs and trying for a bite.

Felix raises a paw and knocks me to the ground. Before I can roll out of the way, he's on top of me, sharp fangs in my face.

He's trying to have me submit to him. Funny. He's worried about dominance, and I'm trying to kill him.

Struggling against his strong grip, I knock him onto his side and roll with him, sinking my teeth into his neck, just under his muzzle.

Whispers travel through the crowd of spectators, and they begin to take steps forward, making our circle even smaller.

I bite harder, sinking my canines even deeper into Felix's soft flesh, and then the wind is knocked out of me as I'm pummeled to the ground. I roll a couple of times before stopping, and I look up to see the face of a young warrior standing over me. He's holding a wooden baseball bat, and five more warriors soon accompany him, all carrying similar bats.

"Lucinda, get out of there," Cody sends through the mindlink.

I search for Cody in the crowd, finding him being pinned down by several other men.

The warriors in human form circle me, taunting me with smiles, whistles, and laughter.

Saliva drips from my muzzle as I growl. The first one to swing a bat at me gets a face full of teeth. I lunge forward and sink my teeth deep into the soft tissue of his neck. His warm blood drips from my mouth as he tries to scream.

In my peripheral, I catch a glimpse of a baseball bat, but too late to move, the hard wood smashes into my back, and I crash to the ground.

The remaining four warriors hover over me, swinging their bats, ensuring each swing finds a spot somewhere on my body.

I attempt to roll over onto my paws—my only chance of survival is to stand—but the onslaught of attacks keeps me pinned to the ground. Crawling as close to the ground as I would if I were stalking prey, my back takes the brunt of the blows.

Cody still struggles against his captives, and Felix remains on the ground in the same spot I left him. No help is coming.

I lift my head and let a deep howl vibrate up my chest, but a wooden bat strikes me hard across the face, extinguishing the sound.

The last thing I hear before darkness takes me is a lone howl in the distance.

CHAPTER 36

LUCINDA

A WARM BREATH blows on my neck, and I whimper. A moist muzzle brushes against my fur, nuzzling just under my ear, making me twitch.

"Leave her alone!" a woman's voice says. "Shoo, shoo."

The cool, damp earth brushes against my cheek. I flex my palms, my fingertips scratching the surface of the ground. My eyes flutter open and my vision is blurry as I try to adjust to the darkness and the scene unfolding.

There's movement in the shadows and shivers snake up my spine.

Something large jumps through the air over top of me and lands a few yards away. A wolf pounces on the campfire, kicking up the fiery coals, sending flaming pieces of wood in every direction.

A misguided flame finds the tent holding Felix's stash of expensive liquor. And just like that, the once small and manageable fire begins to rage out of control, traveling through the campsite and burning everything and anyone in its path.

Squinting against the bright flames, I pull myself into a

sitting position, and lower my chin to my chest with a wince. A groan slips through my lips, and I roll my eyes.

I've shifted.

A soft blanket is draped over my shoulders, and I peer up to see the young woman that Brutus molested earlier.

"Come on, my lady. We need to go," she whispers.

I try to stand, but my legs buckle and I fall. Landing on the hard ground, I wince and grab my pounding head.

"Now, my lady," she says. "Before he returns."

Searing pain shoots through all parts of my body. I struggle to heave myself off the ground. The woman reaches to help me.

"Before who returns?" I cling to the woman and stand on shaky legs.

She looks over her shoulder and leans into my ear. "The white wolf."

I start to fall back to the ground but catch myself on my knees just as two of Felix's men take notice and charge toward us.

On wobbly legs, I take one last look at the shadows. The white wolf jumps through the fire, landing on the two men, ripping a chunk out of each of their necks, and spitting the flesh to the ground.

Caiden! My heart flutters.

"We need to go," the woman says, tugging at my arm.

Reaching my right arm out to Caiden, I take a step toward him but fall to my knees. He stands, his paws cemented in place as he watches me struggle to walk.

Another wolf jumps through the fire that blazes behind Caiden to flank him—Dylan.

He shifts from his wolf form as he runs up to me. "Lux, are you okay?"

"I'm fine. What are you doing here?" My feet wobble and

give out on me once more as I try to stand, but Dylan catches me. I flash a small smile. "Thanks."

"Are you sure you're okay?" His strong arms steady me, tightening their grip around my waist.

"Yes, I'll be fine. I just need time to recover. I guess I took more of a beating than I thought."

Warmth rushes through my body as little sparks ignite on my skin. And then I smell it—the strong scent of bergamot. My breath catches in my throat.

Caiden has shifted from his wolf form and storms closer to where we stand, eyeing me up and down. Streaks of black snake through his eyes, and he scowls.

Stopping a few feet from us, he stares deep into my eyes, which burns a fire in my soul. My lips begin to throb, and all I want is to run to him and to be secure in his embrace.

Looking away, he speaks to Dylan. "You should get her back."

My heart sinks as he turns to leave.

"Caiden," I call after him.

He does not face me. Instead, he angles his head to the side just enough for me to know he is listening.

"Where's Felix?" My gaze flitters over to the last place I saw him, but his body is gone.

"I don't know," Caiden says with a low growl.

"Have you seen my friend Cody?" I ask.

"No." He once again turns to leave.

"What will happen to the non-warriors? You won't kill them, will you?" I call after him, my shaky voice betraying my emotions.

"No."

"He's granted them a temporary pack membership to try it out and see how they like the pack," Dylan adds. "Those who don't want to take the offer are free to go elsewhere."

A smile finds its way to my lips, and Caiden returns a

small grin before leaping into the air and shifting without looking back.

"Come on, let's get going," Dylan says.

I take a few steps and collapse, even with his support.

"She's too injured to walk," the woman says. I blush because I forgot she was still there.

"I'm sorry, we haven't actually been introduced. I'm Lucinda and this is Dylan," I say reaching out my hand. "And you are?"

"Grace." She gives me a shy smile, but it fades the second she peers at Dylan, and her gaze quickly finds the ground.

"You don't have to be afraid of him. He won't hurt you."

She nods but still will not look at him.

I take in Dylan's naked body and whisper, "Maybe you should cover up?"

Dylan and I were naked together for much of our childhood as we were first discovering our wolf forms, but not everyone feels the same way.

"With what?" he asks, laughing.

Grace pulls a robe from her bag and tosses it to him.

"Thank you," he says, and she nods.

"I...don't think I can walk," I whisper.

Dylan's expression changes from his prior lighthearted exchange over nakedness. He takes a step back and gives me a once over. Pulling the blanket away to fully examine my body. "I suppose not. I didn't want to say it, but you look awful. Someone did a number on you."

"Gee thanks."

Dylan wraps his strong arms around me and picks me up with little effort. "Come on, let's get you home."

My heart warms at the word *home*. I didn't realize how much I missed the feeling of having one.

I turn to Grace, and she backs away, shaking her head.

"Grace, it's okay. You can come with us—you'll be safe," I say.

"Safe? That's what Felix said when I joined this pack," she says.

"Yeah, well, Caiden isn't Felix, and his pack isn't this group of idiots. Come with us and you'll see."

"You'll be fine," Dylan says. "No one will harm you, and if they try, they'll have to answer to me."

She nods and takes a slow step forward.

While carrying me, Dylan guides Grace through the darkness that's befallen the area and away from the burning campsite. I take one last look back and watch Caiden still fighting the last of Felix's men that haven't turned to run away. Sammy is there too, leading a group of non-warriors away from the campsite.

A warmth spreads through my heart to see such a large group of people willing to trust Caiden and his offer for temporary pack membership.

"What are you smiling about?" Dylan asks.

"Nothing."

Dylan follows my gaze. "Whatever."

I find Caiden again, and our eyes lock for a split second before he turns away. My heart twists, and I blink back tears.

Dylan, Grace, and I travel in silence across the blood-stained field on the other side of the hill.

"Let's hold up just a minute," Dylan says. "Sammy sent word through the mindlink, let's wait."

"What for what?" I ask.

Dylan places me on the ground, but still offers his arm for support.

"The fighting has stopped. Caiden has joined Sammy and the group of survivors." Dylan peers behind us toward the hillside.

I follow his gaze. And then Sammy and Caiden in their

human form appear. They're both wearing a robe similar to the one given to Dylan. I cover my mouth to hide a grin.

As they approach, I watch Caiden but he doesn't look my way. As he draws closer his expression grows more grim— his forehead pulled tight with a deep scowl.

I lean into Dylan and whisper, "Is Caiden okay?"

Dylan looks between Caiden and I. "He'll be fine."

"He looks like he's in pain." I wrap my arms around Dylan's elbow.

He looks down at my touch and covers my hands with one of his own. "He has a lot going on right now, but he'll get through it."

"I've only been gone a couple of days. What did I miss?"

Dylan pats my hands. "Nothing really. Don't worry about it."

The group begins to trudge forward, and Dylan picks me up again.

"Just tell me." My protest loses strength since I'm being carried, and I curse myself.

But then, Dylan casts a curious glance and me and sighs. "Fine. Sabrina waltzed into the Pack House with her cousins again. Only this time, they threatened to challenge Caiden for the title of Alpha."

"What?"

"She claimed if he went after you, then he wasn't putting the safety of his pack first and he should forfeit his claim of Alpha. If he didn't forfeit then they would formally challenge him in front of the pack."

The movement of my chest stops, all of the air in my lungs freezing.

He came after me.

"What has he done?" I whisper in a strained voice.

"Well, we didn't exactly decide to come after you. Caiden knew he couldn't rescue you and still keep the pack's approval, but the longer you were gone...I could tell..."

"Tell what?" I ask.

"Caiden needs you. Something has happened with his curse because ever since the beast struck you..." Dylan stumbles over his words. "He's bonded with the beast."

I slide down from Dylan's arms. "What? Really?"

"Yeah, it's weird. But he's fighting through it." Dylan shrugs.

Dylan helps me climb over a fallen tree in our path and then he follows.

"But Sabrina, damn it! What has he done? I left so nothing would happen to his pack, and he's just gone and—"

"No. He told Sabrina we weren't going after you. That you made your decision and we would honor it," Dylan says.

"Oh." My chest tightens and nausea swirls in my stomach. "So how did you three end up here?"

Dylan opens his arms again and I climb up into his sturdy embrace. I rest my head on his shoulder for support.

"We were at the Pack House still arguing with Sabrina when the first message of the attack came through the mindlink. There was a border breach," Dylan adjusts his grip. "We easily took the small group down and followed one back here."

Caiden wasn't coming to my rescue.

Dark fuzzy clouds form at the edges of my vision, so I close my eyes until the feeling passes.

"We caught up with him on the hill," Dylan says. "That was an easy kill, and that's when we saw you fighting Felix."

"How long did you watch?" I'm curious because they didn't arrive until well after my fight with Felix was over, and the hill isn't that far away. Were they just sitting up there watching the entire time?

"Right, about that..." Dylan says. "We watched awhile just

to make sure you were okay. You held your own against him —we were so proud. We were getting ready to leave when the other members ganged up on you with the bats. That's when we charged down the hill."

"My heroes." I snuggle closer to Dylan. "Thank you."

"Close your eyes and get a little rest. Mia won't let you sleep at all once we get back," Dylan says with a laugh.

Taking another look over Dylan's shoulder, Caiden walks alone with a dark expression. My heart aches, and a tear rolls down my cheek remembering our prior conversation. I lay my head on Dylan's shoulder and close my eyes, but all I see are visions of Caiden.

Two ruby-red eyes stare at me through the surrounding darkness. The intensity is too much—too powerful—and I bow my head in submission.

A gut-wrenching snarl, followed by an eerie howl, causes the hair on the back of my neck to stand on end, and shivers run rampant through my body. A light touch brushes my chin.

I lift my face to look into the eyes of the man-beast standing inches from me. Only this time, the eyes are sparkling blue, and Caiden's face appears as the darkness washes away.

"AH!" I shout out.

Opening my eyes, I frantically look around and pat my face. I'm back at the Pack House and lying on the couch. I was dreaming. A flush covers my cheeks as Caiden walks into the room.

"Are you okay?" Caiden asks, keeping his distance.

"Yes, thank you." I prop myself up to sit on the couch.

"CINDA!" Mia rushes into the room and covers me in her warm embrace.

My lips quiver, and I whimper under the weight of Mia's small frame.

"Mia, off. You're hurting her," Dylan says, pulling Mia to a standing position.

She looks at me, and tears flood her eyes. "Oh Cinda, what did they do to you? We'll fix you up, okay?"

Kneeling on the floor, she takes my hand and leans her cheek into it. She sniffles, blinking back more tears.

I look around the room. Caiden leans against the doorway of the next room, just as he did the very first time I saw him. My heart flutters and my lips throb. *I yearn to be wrapped in his strong arms—for him to tell me everything will be okay.*

Our eyes lock and heat spreads through my body, only to be doused when he turns to leave.

Mia squeezes my hand, pulling my attention from Caiden's back to her warm and wondering eyes. She motions with her head to the spot where Caiden was standing just moments ago. "Let's get you fixed up first, and we'll worry about that later, okay?"

I nod and force myself to swallow. "Do you know why he's giving me the cold shoulder?"

"No."

"The pack doctor is here." Sammy's voice carries from the other room, and the doctor walks into view, followed by Sammy.

His gaze darts around the room, and his arms tense. When his eyes fix on Grace, her eyes grow round.

"Um, Sammy, this is Grace," I say, but I don't think either is listening.

He walks across the room and introduces himself, and her blush and small giggle light up the room.

"My mate," Sammy says.

A loud cheer floods through the house. Mia squeals in delight, and Gavin runs in from the other room to congratulate them. Dylan slaps Sammy on the back and shakes his hand. I offer my congratulations with a smile and wink from my seat on the couch.

Sammy picks up Grace, holding her at the waist, and spins her around. Their laughter warms my heart.

At least one good thing came out of this. I guess things do happen for a reason.

Glancing behind me, Caiden stands in the doorway again. For a second, a small smile crosses his face, then his eyes move in my direction and the smile fades.

He promptly turns and retreats down the dark hallway once again.

The pack doctor begins to examine my wounds. "Now, let's see what we have here."

Time to find out if I'll ever be able to shift again.

CHAPTER 37

LUCINDA

RECOVERY IS A LONG, boring, and lonely process. After the doctor looked me over, she found fractures and broken bones that had already started to heal incorrectly. This then led her to re-break my bones in order to set them so they could properly heal, and I was ordered to stay in bed until further notice.

Normally, I wouldn't obey a doctor's orders. However, she warned me that even if I follow her instructions, I still may never be able to shift again.

Dylan stopped by once to check on me, but he's been busy keeping the peace between the rogues that left Felix's camp and the regular pack members. Some of the pack members aren't happy that Caiden brought on this number of potential new members without holding a meeting.

I'm sure Sabrina's been busy twisting the events of that night too. That's why Dylan's working hard to talk with everyone individually to explain everything.

Sammy and Grace visited once too. Sammy is busy finding homes for the new temporary pack members and getting them set up in town. And I'm sure his free time is spent getting to know Grace.

Mia visits the most, but still not often enough. She's taken a liking to Grace, and they are planning Sammy and Grace's Mating Ceremony. I haven't seen Gavin, but Mia says Caiden sent him on an errand. I can only imagine what that is.

And Caiden, I haven't seen him since the night of my rescue, which has been almost a week. But often, after I wake, I smell his lingering scent and wonder if he's been here.

While being left to myself for several days to recoup, I think about Felix: where he is, what happened, and what he'll do next.

In my solitude, dark thoughts surface.

Is the Blood Moone pack really my home?

It doesn't feel right, not anymore. I'm surrounded by so many people, and yet I still feel so empty inside—I'm alone among many.

A smile hasn't surfaced on my face since the announcement of Sammy and Grace's ceremony. Every hour of each day passes by in a blur, and a hazy fog covers my thoughts and dampens my mood. Mia says it's the pain medicine the doctor gave me, but I know better—I don't belong here anymore. It's time to move on.

Will they let me leave?

Let's be honest, they can't stop me. But where will I go? I need to find Felix and kill him once and for all, then I'll find Cody—he's the closest thing I have to family, after Dylan and Mia.

The doctor's cool fingers jabbing my side jolt me from my musings. She pokes and prods my stomach, chest, and back in various places. And then examines my arms, shoulders, and spends a great deal of time scrutinizing my legs.

"Well, doc?" I ask.

She takes a couple steps away from me and clasps her hands together. "You are a very strong, yet extremely lucky, wolf. You have healed exquisitely well."

Relief washes over me and the tension in my back melts.

Sitting up in bed, I swing my legs over the edge. "I can shift again?"

A smile lights up the doctor's face. "Yes, you'll be able to shift again, but let's start with smaller movements, such as stretching and walking."

I slide off the edge of the bed and stretch my arms high over my head. A small moan escapes.

The doctor scribbles something on a sheet of paper and hands it to me. "You are officially released from my care. Take it easy and rest often until you regain your entire strength."

Once I take the sheet of paper in my hands, the doctor turns and exits my room.

A good long stretch is just what I need, and it feels good. I reach up again and give a good squirm to pop my back. A smile plays on my lips. Maybe it was just the pain medicine darkening my mood.

I toss the doctor's note on the nightstand and quickly change into new clothing. My hand shakes as I reach to open the door to my room. But then laughter travels up the stairs and helps to ease my nerves.

Naturally, I follow the sounds of joy to the kitchen.

I stand in the doorway, and my gaze flutters around the room, taking in the scene. Mia and Grace sit at the table with magazine clippings surrounding them while Dylan and Sammy stand at the counter, looking at a map of the territory, deep in discussion.

Caiden catches my attention, leaning with his back

against the sink, listening to Dylan and Sammy talk. He is the only one who notices my presence, and from his grim expression and the dark circles under his eyes, he's not happy about it.

He balls his hands into tight fists to control his shaking arms.

Is that because of me?

Sabrina walks into the kitchen through the back door and winks at me as she walks over to Caiden and drapes her arms around him. An uneasiness rises in the pit of my stomach, and waves of nausea swirl through my chest.

I pivot of my heels and run back upstairs. My body aches from the sudden movement, but I need to get away.

A loud commotion echoes from downstairs in the kitchen, but I don't care. I can't take the outpouring of hatred from Caiden anymore.

Continuing into my room, I shut the door behind me and lean against it. I slide down and sit, resting my head against the wooden door. Unshed tears that I've held back since the night of my rescue stream down my face, and I wipe them away with the back of my hand.

I refuse to cry for another man. I spent my tears on Dylan. I will not shed tears for another. I will not stay where I'm not wanted another night.

Wiping the last of the tears away, I regain composure and stand. After finding my balance, I walk across the room and pull out the small bag Mia gave me with spare clothes and toiletries, then I begin to pack what few belongings I have.

Caiden bursts into my room and slams the door behind him.

"What are you doing?" he asks as his eyes bore deep into my soul, causing my hands to shake and my throat quivers as I swallow.

I can't stay here, not like this—alone in a pack of thousands. If I'm going to be alone, I'd rather be alone in the wild.

My fists curl into tight balls, and my nails dig into my flesh. I close my eyes and slow my breathing.

"I'm leaving." I send a force of power vibrating off my body, channeling it directly at Caiden.

His eyes pull tight, creating a crease in his forehead, and he flinches when the power surge hits him.

"Why?" he asks in a low voice that's void of all emotion.

I whip around and study him; his body stiffens and his shoulder muscles tense as our eyes meet.

"Seriously?" I ask, watching his Adam's apple move up and down as he swallows. "Whatever. It doesn't matter. I just am."

"It does matter, and no, you're not."

"Caiden, I'm leaving," I say again, this time with more force in my voice.

"No, you're not." He steps closer to me, meeting me in the middle of the room, and we face off, looking each other square in the eye.

"Oh really? Says who?" I ask.

"Me." He growls.

"You forget you're not my Alpha." I turn my back to him and stroll to the bed where I left my bag.

"No, not yet," he says.

"Caiden, you can't force me to stay and join the pack." I turn to look at him, and his eyes are as black as coal.

"I didn't realize I had to force you. Why are you running away?"

"I'm not running away," I say under my breath as I play with the hem of my shirt.

He closes the space between us and takes my hands into his. Looking at our entwined hands, his face softens. "Then stay."

"No," I whisper.

Another growl escapes his lips, but this time, I return the growl with one of my own.

"I won't let you leave," he says. "Not again."

"Oh really?" My eyebrows raise in question.

"Yes, really."

"And how do you plan to keep me here against my will?"

Stepping closer, he cups my cheeks with his hands and looks into my eyes. "Do I really need to force you to stay?"

"There's nothing for me here."

"Your friends are here."

"Right. I'm not sure Dylan is in the friend category yet, Mia has Grace, and you, well you have Sabrina—"

"Sabrina?" His brow line furrows, creating several ripples in his smooth skin.

"I saw you two in the kitchen a few minutes ago."

"No. You saw Sabrina doing what she does best—being a bitch," he says.

I tilt my chin, silently asking him to elaborate.

"I've opened a case against her with the Pack Elders for plotting against the Alpha," he says. "They'll decide her fate. She thought she could talk me out of it."

"Opening a case is good, I think," I say. "But it still doesn't change my mind."

"Lucinda…" he sighs and runs his right hand through his hair.

"Caiden, is there a reason I should stay?" My pulse quickens. *Déjà vu.*

He licks his lips and swallows. "Felix is still out there."

My heart skips a beat.

"Right, then there's more reason I should leave," I say with bitterness.

"Stay for me," he whispers.

My heart flutters as the words leave his mouth.

Caiden leans in close and whispers in my ear, "Please don't leave me."

"Caiden—" My body gives up. My shoulders slump forward, and my head falls against Caiden's chin.

His arms instinctively open, wrapping me in his warm embrace. He pulls me closer, resting his cheek on the top of my head. "I can't lose you again."

I push away from his secure embrace. "Why have you been so distant? You've been an ass since I got back."

"I'm sorry," he says, as if that were enough to explain everything.

"Yeah, and?"

"And what?"

"What's been going on?"

Caiden shrugs.

"That isn't good enough." I cross my arms in front of my chest.

Taking a deep breath, he leans against the edge of the bed and looks to the floor. "It's my wolf. He's fused with the beast, and it's hard to control his urges and actions."

"Dylan mentioned that, but what does it have to do with me?" I ask.

"He—" Caiden pauses. "The beast is very powerful, and he wants what he wants when he wants it. And he wants you—all the time."

Heat rises to my cheeks.

"I see." A smile plays at the edges of my mouth, and I bite my bottom lip. "So, you've been giving me the cold shoulder and being an ass because you like me?"

"No, well yes, but…" Caiden reaches out and tucks a loose strand of hair behind my ear. "I was keeping my distance because every time I catch your scent, my wolf wants to jump you and claim you as his own."

My eyes grow wide as realization hits.

"What about Dylan?" I ask.

After a short pause, he shrugs his shoulders. "Dylan had his chance, and he gave you up."

"And that's okay with the honorable Caiden, Alpha of the Blood Moone pack?" I bite my bottom lip again.

"Dylan's already given me his blessing." Caiden grins.

"Really?"

"Yes. I want you to be mine—I want to claim you."

"You want me to reject my mate and take another? I thought you didn't approve of that."

"That was before." His eyes soften and return to their beautiful ocean blue.

"Before what?" I ask.

His lips turn up into a boyish grin. "Before I fell in love with you."

I smell fear and sense his uneasiness as I gaze into his questioning eyes. He reaches up and tucks a piece of hair that's fallen loose behind my ear.

The touch of his fingertips as they brush my cheek sends a rush of heat radiating through my body. I crush my lips into his and wrap my arms around his neck.

He instantly engulfs me in his embrace. Our kiss starts slow and passionate but quickly becomes needy. The connection I feel with Caiden is like no other I've felt, not even the bond with Dylan.

My feet leave the floor and my legs wrap around his waist as he lays me down on the bed.

"Does this mean you'll be mine?" he asks, his voice deep and husky as he nibbles my ear.

"Yes." I moan.

Lifting my chin and exposing my neck, I let him trail kisses down to the sweet spot. My wolf stirs inside me.

His fangs graze my bare skin, and I arch up with anticipation.

He bites down, his sharp teeth penetrating deep into my delicate skin. The initial puncture is painful, sending a burning sensation through my body, but I don't flinch. Soon I'm rewarded with a sweet tingle throughout my body.

My head swirls as if I were on laughing gas, my lips turn into a mischievous grin, and I claw at his back, tearing his T-shirt into pieces. I'm eager to have his bare chest against mine.

Sparks rush through my body as I touch his skin, and my stomach twists with desire. He releases my neck and cools the fiery wounds with the dampness of his tongue.

My wolf churns inside me, fighting for control.

Caiden sits up with a satisfied smirk, straddling me and eyeing me with desire. Sitting me up, he pulls my shirt over my head and his pulse throbs in his neck.

I clamp down hard, and my fangs slice through his skin. He trembles, I've taken him by surprise. A rush of excitement extends throughout my limbs, and he pulls me closer, holding me tight. A burning fit of passion threatens to engulf my heart.

"You bit me." He smirks as I lick his matching wounds closed.

Resting my forehead against his, I smile. "No, I marked you."

His face lights up with amusement. "Well, aren't you the little Alpha."

"I'm *your* little Alpha."

"You're my Luna." He nuzzles the marking he left on my neck, then kisses me softly.

"I love you," I whisper against his lips as he lays me down.

His fingers gently touch my bare stomach before firmly grabbing my hips. Our kiss deepens and our movements turn heady just as the door bursts open, flying off the hinges and landing on the ground a few feet away from where we lie on the bed.

Caiden spins around, covering me with his body.

"Dylan?" I whisper. *Shit.*

CHAPTER 38

LUCINDA

Dylan stands in the doorway, pupils fully dilated and jet black, his fists balled tightly with white knuckles, and his arms trembling. His eyes roam my body, and he looks between Caiden and me. His brows furrow, and his eyes squint into narrow almonds.

Caiden stands, facing Dylan, ready to fight if needed.

"Dylan, are you okay?" Caiden asks in his assertive but cautious Alpha tone.

Dylan's eyes lock on mine. He ambles closer, never breaking our eye contact.

Caiden stands in front of me, and I search around the bed for my shirt, then hastily put it on. Stepping around Caiden, I give his arm a gentle squeeze as I pass and stand face-to-face with Dylan.

"What's going on?" Dylan asks, ignoring Caiden's warning growl.

I bite my lip, unsure what to say.

"I felt the bond break, and I thought something happened to you," he says with a strained voice.

Walking closer to him, I reach for his hands and hold them in my own. "I'm sorry for making you worry. I'm okay."

He brushes my long hair over my shoulder, revealing my fresh marking. "So you finally did it."

"Did what?"

"You accepted rejection," he says in a low voice.

"You're free now." I reach up and touch his cheek. His eyes meet mine, their beautiful green color shining through. I wipe away a lone tear that runs down his cheek, and he wraps his arms around me, pulling me close.

"I'm sorry," he whispers in my ear. "I failed you."

"No. We just…" I don't know how to word my feelings. I thought he'd be happy—relieved—that the bond is broken.

"Forgive me," he whispers.

"There's nothing to forgive." I tilt my head in question. "Friends?"

"Always." His signature smile creeps to his face—the one that sets my heart on fire—and he extends a hand to Caiden. They embrace each other in the traditional one-arm man hug. "Congratulations."

Running his hand through his shaggy hair, Dylan looks between Caiden and me with a boyish grin.

"What?" I ask.

"Our bond isn't the only thing that broke with your marking," he says.

"What do you mean?" Caiden asks.

"The payment for the gypsy's gift broke too."

"How?" I ask, raising my eyebrows.

"Now that it's broken, I can tell you what my gift was." A reddish blush rises to his cheeks.

"Only if you want to. You don't have to," I say.

"I need to. You should know the truth. But you may want to sit down."

Caiden and I sit on the edge of the bed, and Dylan paces in front of us.

"Lux, I've always loved you, and that was the problem. The night the gypsy offered me a gift, the gift she offered was you," he says, looking away as soon as my eyes meet his.

"What do you mean?" I ask.

"You were always promised to me by our fathers' arrangement, but I worried you'd find your Fated Mate and leave. The gypsy offered me the gift of choice so that my heart would cheat fate. Whoever my heart most desired would become my Fated Mate. I thought the gypsy was a fake, so I accepted the gift, and then she issued the payment.

"The payment for this gift was that my bite would be the mark of death. When I claimed my mate, my mark would be poison and kill her. I still didn't believe her, until—"

"Dylan, are you okay?" I cross the room to hold his hands. Squeezing me back, he gives a small smile.

"Remember what I said about my mother?" Dylan asks, and Caiden and I both nod. "When the gypsy cast payment for my mother's gift and struck her dead, I started believing. So when you were my mate, I had to believe the payment was real too. Lux, Caiden is your true mate—your mate destined by fate and cheated by my greedy heart."

"I'm confused." I rub my temples to try and make sense of everything.

"My mom asked that when you found your Fated Mate, your bond would be more powerful than our faux bond and the marking from your Fated Mate would have the ability to break the curse," Dylan says.

Caiden and I look at each other, then back to Dylan.

"What about Elizabeth?" Caiden's voice cracks as her name leaves his lips.

Dylan shrugs. "Maybe she was my mate? I'm not sure."

"It felt so real," Caiden says, more to the ground than to anyone else.

"How does it compare with the bond you feel with Lux?" Dylan asks. "When you think about everything, all the clues support you two being Fated Mates. Caiden, you said yourself that it was eerie the way you felt so comfortable around Lux from the moment you met her, despite the fact she was a rogue. And Lux, the sense of comfort and security you feel around him—"

"How?" Caiden and I both say in unison.

"I'm more observant than you two give me credit for."

"Hey, guys," Mia's voice rings out from the hall.

"In here," I call, and she enters the room, looking at the broken hinges and the door lying on the ground.

She flashes her lopsided grin. "What type of party did I miss?"

"We'll talk about it later," Caiden says before anyone else speaks.

"Promise?" Mia says.

Caiden glares at his little sister. And then Mia turns her dagger eyes toward me.

"Pinky promise," I say with a wink, and she nods.

However, this reminds me, although Caiden marked me, I still have not formally accepted his pack. I will have to do that tonight so I can talk to Mia through the mindlink.

"Caiden, Gavin's back," Mia says.

Caiden grabs my hand and motions for Dylan to follow. We all head downstairs and find Gavin waiting in the Alpha's office.

"What did you find?" Caiden asks.

"Felix is still alive," Gavin says.

I march toward Gavin. "You found him and let him live?"

Gavin stands from his seat. "He's in no shape to battle, and I wasn't about to kill him in cold blood."

"I will!" I say. "We have—"

"Don't get your panties all in a bunch. Just because I didn't kill him, doesn't mean—"

Caiden growls. "Where is he?"

"I chained him up in the cellar," Gavin says. "Sammy and a few others are standing guard."

Caiden nods.

"Did you see Cody?" I ask.

Gavin's gaze falls to the ground as he shakes his head.

My throat tightens, and it becomes hard to swallow as I think about Cody's fate.

Mia steps next to me and squeezes my hand. "I'm sure Cody is fine."

I give her a small nod and try to smile.

"Is Felix chained in silver?" Dylan asks, breaking the awkward silence.

Please tell me he hasn't escaped.

"Of course. What do you take me for?" Gavin rolls his eyes.

Turning toward Caiden, I ask, "What are you going to do with him?"

Caiden shrugs. "He can stay there until I am ready to deal with him. We have more important things to focus on right now."

His eyes dance with fire as he brushes the hair off my shoulder to expose my new marks. Mia's squeal of excitement is the only thing that keeps my focus while Caiden's soft kisses send tiny jolts of electricity coursing through my body.

"Yes, we do have more pressing matters at hand." I giggle.

"No way! Dude, when did that happen?" Gavin asks. "Get over here and give me a hug."

Gavin pulls me into one of his giant bear hugs, and Mia

runs over, squashing me in the middle. I cannot remember the last time I was so happy.

With Caiden and I bonded, it only makes us stronger—a real force to be reckoned with. I just hope our strength doesn't paint a target on our back for Felix's enemies.

And I hope our uniting of the Dark Ravens and the Blood Moones don't welcome the devilish witches to conjure more sinister plots. Only time will tell.

THE END...Continue with Lucinda and Caiden's journey in The Alpha's Secret, Book 2 in The Raven Chronicles.

ABOUT THE AUTHOR

USA Today Bestselling Author Missy De Graff writes Urban Fantasy, Fantasy, and Paranormal Romance. Drawing inspiration from her vast array of interests, she weaves together worlds of romance and intrigue, mixed with supernatural elements, suspenseful storylines, and addicting characters.

When she isn't writing about sassy heroines, forbidden romances, and enemies to lovers; she enjoys fresh air, sunshine, hiking, and river time. A dedicated lover of sweet treats, a collector of antiques, and fascinated by all things mystical.

Missy resides in Virginia at the foothills of the Appalachian Mountains with her husband and son. She can often be found wandering through their Southern Heirloom Apple Orchard with their mountain cur dog and barns cats close on her heels. She is a bohemian by nature and a Gemini by birth.

Stay up to date on all the latest scoop from book releases to exclusive reader content subscribe to Missy's monthly newsletter today! linktr.ee/authormissydegraff

Fire Glass (Realm of the Fire Fae)

Crimson Legacies

Printed in Great Britain
by Amazon